In the Midst of It All

A Novel

TIFFANY L. WARREN

GRAND CENTRAL
PUBLISHING

NEW YORK   BOSTON

Grand Central Publishing
Hachette Book Group
237 Park Avenue
New York, NY 10017

www.HachetteBookGroup.com

Printed in the United States of America

First Edition: February 2010
10 9 8 7 6 5 4 3 2 1

Grand Central Publishing is a division of Hachette Book Group, Inc.
The Grand Central Publishing name and logo is a trademark of Hachette Book Group, Inc.

Library of Congress Cataloging-in-Publication Data

Warren, Tiffany L.
    In the midst of it all / Tiffany L. Warren. —1st ed.
        p. cm.
    Summary: "A tale about a woman who struggles with her own beliefs and those of her mentally ill mother"—
    Provided by publisher.
    ISBN 978-0-446-19516-4
    1. Mothers and daughters—Fiction.   2. Children of schizophrenics—Fiction.
    3. Life change events—Fiction.   I. Title.
    PS3623.A866I52 2010
    813'.6—dc22   2009024272

To my people still in the struggle... there is life after the borg! Stay encouraged...

Acknowledgments

Okay, so these are really, really hard to write—harder to write than the stories, I think, because I always feel like I sound so repetitious. But there are so many people I need to thank over and over again, because they help me continue this dream.

I thank God because He is awesome beyond measure! I don't have words for the appreciation I feel for the doors He continues to open.

My husband, Brent, and my five little chickadees are the best! I get to go on the road and they have pancake suppers without a complaint. This is such a blessing.

To the book clubs and women's ministries who continue to support me by buying my books (and not sharing them ☺), thank you for all you do. I appreciate you.

The team at Grand Central Publishing is priceless— Karen, LaToya, Linda, and Samantha! Thank you for your continued support!

Afrika, Shawana, Tiffany T., Robin, Myesha, Kym, and Leslie—who could ask for a better crew of friends and prayer partners? Thank y'all!

Pattie Steele Perkins is the best agent! Thank you for listening and for your wisdom on publishing.

To the circle of authors who support me with sage wisdom, reviews, quotes, friendship and more: ReShonda, Rhonda, Sherri, Victoria, Dwan, Yolonda, Dee, and Bonnie! God bless you with more book sales than you could ever dream of counting!

In the Midst of It All

Prologue

"Zee, are you going to get that?"

Zenovia blinked a few times, glanced at the clock, and shook her head. "Three a.m. It's not good news."

She closed her eyes and buried her head under the covers, trying to escape the ringing telephone. Her husband reached over her and took matters into his own hands. Zenovia was grateful that he was home. This kind of news didn't need to be left on an answering machine.

Audrey lay in a pool of her own diluted blood, but the room was permeated with the scent of lavender. Pink bubbles floated on top of the pool. Scented by lavender; stained by blood.

Zenovia's husband talked for a few moments then pressed the "end" button on the cordless telephone. He touched Zenovia on the shoulder. She jumped. She was expecting him to wake her, to be the town crier of her misery, but she was startled nonetheless.

"That was your stepfather. Your mother has passed away."

"How did she die?"

"He says in her sleep."

Zenovia rolled her eyes. "He's a liar."

"Did you see it?"

She nodded. "But not in enough time to stop her."

Zenovia turned away from her husband and buried her head into the pillow. A salty river trickled down her face, but Zenovia was not ready to share her tears with her mate. She wanted two minutes of private grief.

She heard him pressing buttons on the telephone.

"Who are you calling?" she asked.

"Bishop. You can't preach in the morning."

"I'm preaching."

"It's okay, Zee. He'll find someone else. You need to handle your mother's affairs."

"That can wait. I've got a word from the Lord that cannot."

Part One

Chapter One

Zenovia heard knocks on the door.

They were not the soft knocks of the children in the apartment next door. There were two of them—a boy and a girl. Always dirty, with unwashed faces and mismatched socks, if any. Their mama was on crack, like so many of the mothers in King Kennedy, one of Cleveland's most notorious housing projects.

The two children visited Zenovia and Audrey every morning looking for breakfast. But it was ten a.m. and they were probably plopped in front of their television, watching the Saturday morning cartoons.

Zenovia waited for the knock again. This time it came with a voice. "Hello? Is anyone home? We'd like to share the Gospel with you today."

Zenovia laughed. She had been thinking that the person behind the door was a drug boy running from the police or a crackhead hustling some stolen property. But it was a lady, and she wanted to share the Gospel. No harm there.

Still, she didn't answer the door.

Audrey rushed from the bedroom of the one-bedroom apartment. She was wearing a ratty yet colorful house-coat. Wild red hair framed her face like a flame, perfectly complementing her freckles and green eyes.

"Why don't you get the door?" she asked.

She didn't wait for a response, but went to the door herself. She swung it open wide and smiled at the two ladies who stood before her.

"Good morning!" Audrey sang.

"Well, good morning to you, too!" said the lady.

Audrey asked, "Did I hear y'all say, y'all was talking about the Gospel this morning?"

"Yes, you did. The Gospel of our Lord and Savior Jesus Christ."

"Well, come on in and keep talking! Zenovia, some-thing told me we were going to have good news today."

Zenovia felt a smile tickle the sides of her lips. That *something* was a vision. Audrey had been having them since she was a little girl, and Zenovia had started having them when she'd turned twelve. They were haphazard messages, sometimes future, sometimes past. Usually there wasn't enough information contained in the visions to do anything useful. Most times, Zenovia was annoyed by the visions; treated them like unannounced visitors. Just like the two Bible ladies.

Both of the ladies stepped gingerly into the spotless apartment. Their eyes darted back and forth; inspect-ing. Their nostrils flared; inhaling the scent of the ocean breeze candles that Zenovia had lit. Zenovia watched their facial expressions change from cautious to pleasant surprise.

Zenovia narrowed her eyes. "You can sit down. Although I'm sure you saw roaches in the hallway, none of them have taken up residence here."

The ladies smiled nervously as they took their seats on the worn, but clean sofa. Audrey sat across from them in her leather recliner.

"My name is Charlotte Batiste," said the lady who'd knocked.

Audrey's smile beamed. "Charlotte. Like the little pig in that book."

"Actually, the pig's name was Wilbur," Zenovia corrected. "You're talking about the spider."

For a fleeting instant, Audrey looked irritated, but it quickly faded. "Well, that doesn't matter. My name is Audrey and the smarty pants is Zenovia."

Both ladies looked from Audrey to Zenovia with tight yet friendly smiles on their faces. The second lady, not Charlotte, actually wasn't a *lady* at all. She was a girl, no older than Zenovia, but she was dressed in a much older woman's apparel— a long corduroy skirt and sweater with a turtleneck. At their feet were little bags stuffed to the hilt with tracts and pamphlets.

"Well, it's nice to meet you both. This is my daughter Alyssa," declared Charlotte with yet another smile.

She never seemed to run out of smiles. Zenovia wondered if her face was sore.

Charlotte continued. "I am here this morning to share a wonderful thought from the Bible. Do you have a Bible?"

"Of course!" replied Audrey.

Audrey reached into a side compartment on her recliner and pulled out a huge white leather Bible. The kind grandmothers pass down to their grandchildren with the family tree on the inside cover and the picture of Jesus in the center. There was no family tree in the front of Audrey's Bible; only her name, in big block print.

"I'm going to read you some verses in the Book of Revelation Chapter Twenty-one. It's the last book of the Bible."

"Oh, I know where Revelations is," Audrey said.

Zenovia cringed. She wanted to say, *It's Revelation not Revelations*, but since she had already been labeled as a smarty pants, the critique went unspoken.

Charlotte read: "And I heard a great voice out of heaven saying, Behold, the tabernacle of God is with men, and He will dwell with them, and they shall be His people, and God Himself shall be with them, and be their God. And God shall wipe away all tears from their eyes; and there shall be no more death, neither sorrow, nor crying, neither shall there be any more pain: for the former things are passed away."

Zenovia liked that scripture. No tears and no sorrow sounded like just what she needed. Apparently, Audrey liked it, too, because there was a tear in the corner of her right eye.

"Well, I can't wait to go to heaven and see Jesus. He's going to take away all sadness and death. I believe that," Audrey stated with conviction.

"What if I told you that this scripture was talking about a paradise here on earth?" Charlotte asked.

Zenovia almost slipped from her usual academic self and said *What you talkin' about, Charlotte?* like Arnold querying Willis on *Diff'rent Strokes*, but she held her tongue. She wanted to see Audrey's response.

Audrey asked, "This scripture ain't about heaven?"

Charlotte went on to explain how God was going to make the earth over into a big park and that believers were going to live there in a utopian nirvana. She said that children would have lions and bears for playmates and go unharmed. Zenovia was a little skeptical, but Charlotte flipped through her little orange Bible with such skill that she had to be telling the truth.

After she was done, Charlotte let out a loud sigh. "Now, Audrey, don't you think God wants you and your sister to live in paradise and not squalor?"

Audrey looked confused, but Zenovia laughed. It was not the first time that she and her mother had been mistaken for sisters. Audrey was a young-looking thirty-two, and Zenovia was a mature-looking seventeen.

"She is my mother, not my sister," Zenovia said.

"Oh," Charlotte replied, and then...with recognition, "*Oh!*"

Audrey dropped her head. "Had her when I was fifteen."

"Well, that's all right," Charlotte said. "That doesn't matter once you give your life to God and get baptized."

"I've been baptized," Audrey replied.

"Oh, but not like this. When you get baptized as one of the Brethren of the Sacrifice, your life will surely be changed."

Zenovia cleared her throat. "I've never heard of the Brethren of the Sacrifice. What denomination are you?"

"We're not a denomination at all. We are *true* Christians, teaching *true* Christianity." She said this with such conviction that Zenovia wanted to pump her fist, yell *power to the people*, and hand her an afro pick.

Charlotte turned her attention back to Audrey. "Would you like to come to one of our services?"

"I'd like that," Audrey responded eagerly.

Zenovia rarely saw her mother get excited about anything, so again she held her tongue. She wanted to object, and tell Charlotte that she and Audrey had a church home. First Gethsemane Baptist Church, up the street, was where they had fellowshipped for the past two years.

But maybe it was time for a change. Audrey had gotten into a particularly embarrassing scuffle with one of the usher board members. The usher, Sister Brown, had told Audrey that she couldn't sit on the Mother's row. Audrey had responded by accusing Sister Brown of being jealous because Audrey was pretty and Sister Brown was "black and greasy."

After the altercation, Zenovia had done what she always did. She apologized to First Lady Benson and Sister Brown. She'd explained that Audrey had just been prescribed new medication for her schizophrenia and that it had not yet taken effect.

That all happened a month ago, and they hadn't been to church since. Zenovia liked to let things die down before they returned to worship. Admittedly, though, she missed the anointed singing of the choir and the spirited preaching.

Audrey looked over at her daughter. "What do you say, Zee? You want to join a new church?"

Zenovia shrugged and answered her mother's question with a question. "Why not?"

Chapter Two

"Zee, hurry up! They're going to be here any minute."

Zenovia rolled her eyes. Charlotte and her husband, Thomas, were coming to pick them up for their first visit to the Northeast Devotion Center. Charlotte had said that they would be there at six thirty and it was only six o'clock.

Zenovia thought that Audrey's excitement at visiting this church or "devotion center" was bizarre and unnecessary. They had worshipped all over the city and to Zenovia, it was all the same. A rose by any other name is still sweet and a church called a devotion center is still church. Zenovia knew churches and she knew evil church folk.

Audrey's father was the pastor at a Holiness church. She was raised singing in the choir and going to Sunday school. When she became pregnant at fifteen, her father had put her out and told her to never return.

Audrey had packed her bags that day. She'd had a vision that she would be married, so she wasn't worried at all. Audrey had never looked back and Zenovia was deprived of the father, grandparents, or any other family members she might have had.

"Are you ready yet?" Audrey pestered.

A scowling Zenovia responded, "As ready as I'm going to be."

Zenovia turned her frown to the mirror. She was not satisfied with her reflection. She had curled and recurled her short, relaxed hairstyle with a curling iron, but a little bit of frizz remained. Her outfit was a plain black wool skirt and a sweater.

"You look fine!" Audrey encouraged as she stood in the doorway wearing an alluring hunter green, form-fitting sweater dress and knee-high leather boots.

"Yeah, right."

Zenovia wished that she had been blessed with her mother's silky red hair. Audrey had flat ironed her tresses and they hung in layers, softly brushing her shoulders. The differences in their appearance always made Zenovia wonder what her father looked like, because she had to be his spitting image.

"Your hair would grow if you'd stop putting all that mess in it. Go natural."

Zenovia's response was a hearty laugh. She thought that her hair was *too natural* to go natural. "My hair is too nappy for that."

"Your hair is curly, rugs and sweaters are nappy."

A honking horn ended their conversation. Zenovia watched her mother's eyes light up as she raced to grab her purse and the orange Bible that Charlotte had given her.

Charlotte was grinning and waving as Zenovia trudged

and Audrey bounced to the silver minivan. Alyssa slid the back door open, and the two of them got into the vehicle.

Audrey sat in the second row of seats, next to Alyssa and directly behind Charlotte. Zenovia sat in the last row next to the most beautiful boy she'd ever laid eyes on. She wanted to kick herself for not running over those curls one more time.

He stuck out his hand. "Hi. I'm Tristan and you're Zaviera?"

"It's Zenovia." She shook the outstretched hand without making eye contact.

"Can I just call you Zee?"

Zenovia nodded, but she wanted to say something like, *You can call me any letter of the alphabet . . . just call me.*

Tristan had smooth caramel-colored skin—straight-from-the-Mother-Land dark with a little bit of cream. His eyes were big and dreamy, framed by dark eyelashes that looked like they belonged on a girl. His large nose and deeply waved hair gave away some obvious Indian commingling with his African ancestors. He even had the audacity to smell good, too, like drier sheets and Nautica cologne.

For the majority of the car ride, Audrey chatted and gushed about how sweet Charlotte was being. Zenovia wanted her to be quiet, but she left well enough alone. Better to endure some chatter than to see the *other* side of Audrey—the out-of-control schizophrenic side that could curse a grown man out in three languages and make him wish he'd never met her.

They pulled up to a small brick building and Charlotte exclaimed, "We're here!"

The Northeast Devotion Center was nothing special from what Zenovia could see. There were no lines drawn on the ground for parking, no steeple, cross, or stained-glass windows. Actually, there weren't any windows. Zenovia thought that they could really use a building fund.

As if reading her thoughts, Charlotte's husband, Thomas, said, "It might not look like much now, but in about six months we're doing a weekend build."

Audrey asked, "What is a weekend build?"

"It's when we give the center a complete overhaul all over a three-day weekend. Everybody gets to help," Tristan answered.

The prospect of seeing Tristan in jeans and work boots was enough to convince Zenovia. "Sounds like fun," she said.

Audrey and Zenovia walked into the Devotion Center arm in arm. Mother's contagious enthusiasm had infected daughter. Both had smiles plastered on their faces.

Zenovia expected to go in, sit down, and fade into the background. Fading was something that she was exceptionally good at. It was a skill learned from many years of guarding Audrey. Watching for signs that she was going to have an episode. Lately they had been far and few between, but medication or no medication, there was always a risk.

Mother and daughter took a seat on the second to last row. Zenovia's eyes followed Tristan as he went and talked to a group of young people. Envy threatened to turn her ebony skin green when Tristan hugged a stylishly dressed Latina. She felt her body tense as they walked in her direction.

"What time does this thing start?" Zenovia asked Audrey. She didn't want to meet Tristan's girlfriend. She was still reminiscing about his drier sheet aroma.

Audrey looked at her watch. "In about fifteen minutes, if they start on time. But most churches don't start on time."

Tristan and the Latina sat down on the row in front of Zenovia and turned around in their seats. He said, "Zee, this is my friend Mia. Mia, meet Zenovia."

On closer inspection, Mia wasn't a Latina at all. She was a black girl; another somebody with "Indian in her blood." Zenovia bit her lip as Mia tossed her hair over her shoulder.

Mia said, "It's nice to meet you, Zenovia. Do you go to Carver?"

Zenovia stifled a chuckle. "Um, no. I'm at West Marshall. Class of 1995!"

"Oh," Mia said. She sounded so dejected, in fact, that Zenovia waited to hear her condolences.

Tristan offered, "You know, Zee, there is a vocational exchange program from West Marshall to Carver. You can transfer and take dental assisting or secretarial careers."

"I'm in college prep classes," shot Zenovia with pride.

"Seriously?" Mia asked.

Audrey boasted, "Yep, she's in IP-AB!"

Tristan and Mia looked confused so Zenovia explained, "International Baccalaureate, Advanced Placement. IB-AP, Mom, not IP-AB."

"You know what I meant."

Tristan said, "That might change if you hang around

us long enough. But right now, service is about to start and I'm on duty tonight."

Mia hurried off to her seat next to Alyssa and Tristan stood on the wall holding a microphone that was attached to a long pole. There were three other young men stationed around the room also holding microphones. Zenovia wanted to think of the room as a church sanctuary, but somehow that word just didn't seem to fit.

A gruff-looking older man took the podium. His beard and short afro were peppered with gray, and he wore small glasses that sat sternly on the bridge of his nose. He opened his mouth and led the congregation in a song that Zenovia had not ever heard before. There was no choir; everyone sang in unison.

Just as the Devotion Center didn't quite seem like a sanctuary, the song didn't quite feel right for a congregation full of black folk. There was none of the pain and hope that etched the Gospel hymns she'd heard her entire life. The songs that were reminiscent of old negro spirituals. The songs that promised joy in the morning after weeping all night long.

This Brethren of the Sacrifice song reminded Zenovia of one of the church scenes from *Little House on the Prairie*. Since she and Audrey didn't know the words to the song, a lady seated in their row handed them a yellow songbook. The lyrics were nice and the melody was pleasant, but Zenovia felt nothing to stir her emotions and make her want to say, "Thank you, Lord!" Which was a good thing because no one else was giving God the glory.

Not a Hallelujah. Not a glory. Not a thank you Jesus. Nothing.

After the song, the gruff-looking man said a prayer, then took his seat. Another middle-aged man stepped to the podium and started the Bible study. He read a selection from a pamphlet and then posed a question to the congregation. Zenovia assumed that it was rhetorical until hands shot up as if they were in a classroom.

The young men carrying microphones scurried around to the names that were called. Most of the responses were read word for word from the pamphlet, but a few attempted to put the answers in their own words. Zenovia noted that the latter responses came mostly from the older men.

After an hour of questions and answers, another older man took the podium and closed in prayer. There was no altar call and no one opened the doors of the church. It was just over.

Audrey leaned over to Zenovia and asked, "Is that it?"

"I guess so."

People had started mingling and having private conversations. Tristan and Alyssa came over to Zenovia. Tristan grabbed her hand and pulled her away from Audrey. Zenovia did not want to leave her mother alone, but found herself vulnerable to Tristan's charisma.

Zenovia asked, "Where are we going?"

"To meet the rest of the young people."

Zenovia stopped. "Oh. I'm good, Tristan."

"What do you mean, you're good? You don't want to make new friends?"

Zenovia didn't know how to explain the answer to that question. Making new friends was not part of her plan. She preferred to not connect with people. That way, when Audrey inevitably had an episode, they could leave and it wouldn't hurt too much.

She finally replied, "I'm a little shy, I guess."

"Don't worry. Tristan will do all of the talking." Alyssa laughed as she linked arms with Zenovia.

And Tristan *did* do all of the talking. "Hey, everybody. This is Zenovia. She and her mother are visiting with us."

Zenovia couldn't keep up with the flurry of hellos and introductions. She caught the name of Tristan's best friend, Kyle. When she and Kyle made eye contact, Zenovia was blindsided by a vision.

Kyle sits on the edge of his tiny twin-size bed. Tears streak his face, but he does not look sad. He's angry. Both his shirtsleeves are rolled up above his elbows and he bleeds from little cuts on his arms. Suddenly, in the midst of his tears, a smile spreads across his face.

Tristan asked, "Zee, are you okay? We lost you for a sec."

"I'm cool. Just tired."

It was very difficult for Zenovia to regain her composure after a vision. Because of her keen sense of empathy, she briefly experienced the emotions of the person in her vision. It always seemed so real.

On the way home, Zenovia was again seated next to Tristan. He asked, "So what did you think of service?"

"It was...different."

"Really? In what way?"

Zenovia chuckled. "Well, it's nothing like any of the churches I've ever attended."

"That's a good thing. It's supposed to be different."

Zenovia leaned in close and said quietly, "To be

honest, it was a little boring. I'm used to a lot of singing and a lot of dancing."

"We come to the Devotion Center to learn about God, not to get excited," Tristan replied in a hot whisper that threatened to intoxicate Zenovia with its cinnamon scent.

"You can't get excited about God?"

"I get excited about having accurate knowledge. You can't really know God anyway, but the Council of Brethren has painted us a wonderful picture of his character."

Zenovia was confused. "The Council of Brethren. What is that?"

"It's a group of anointed men who study the Bible all day long and then they write our Bible study lessons."

"Wow. I've never heard of such a thing."

Tristan touched Zenovia's hand. She felt herself shiver. "It's good to be different, Zee. The Brethren of the Sacrifice are on the narrow road."

"But what about other churches? Aren't they on the narrow road too?"

"Not if they aren't teaching the truth."

Chapter Three

It was Friday. Two days after Zenovia and Audrey's first visit to the Northeast Devotion Center and already they were invited to a party. Well, Charlotte had called it a gathering, but Zenovia wasn't sure of the difference.

Audrey poked her head into their shared bedroom and asked, "What are you going to wear?"

"With so many choices it's hard to decide," Zenovia replied.

Audrey chuckled and went back to her flat ironing, while Zenovia looked at her very limited clothing selections. A few pairs of jeans and some off-brand T-shirts were spread across the bed. Zenovia snatched up her favorite pair of jeans and a tiny red shirt.

She put on the outfit, looked in the mirror, and smiled. It may not have been a designer ensemble, but it definitely flattered her round behind and tiny waist. She had wrapped her short haircut and was wearing it plastered to her head.

"Here you go. I picked these up from the dollar store," Audrey said as she handed Zenovia a little bag.

She reached in and pulled out a pair of large hoop earrings. "Thanks, Mom."

Zenovia took the gold-colored earrings from their package and coated them with a layer of clear nail polish to keep the color from fading. While they were drying, she slicked Vaseline on her lips, eyeliner on her bottom eyelid, and mascara on her short lashes. The earrings topped off her whole look.

"You look good, Zee. Tristan is gonna do a triple take."

Zenovia pondered for a second. "I don't know if I care what he thinks."

"You should. He's cute, and nice too!"

"He's all right," Zenovia agreed.

There was a knock on their apartment door. Audrey brightened, "Speak of the devil—"

"Mom, you know I hate when you say that."

Audrey ignored Zenovia's objection and went to open the door. Zenovia heard her mother greeting Tristan while she selected a worn but comfortable corduroy jacket.

When Zenovia entered the room, Tristan looked her up and down. She smiled and said, "Are you done gawking?"

"You look nice." Tristan laughed.

"Thanks."

As they walked out of the apartment Audrey nudged Zenovia in the ribs and mouthed, "I told you."

Tristan was driving a little red Ford Escort that looked about ten years old. "Is that your ride?" Zenovia asked.

"Yes. You like it?"

Zenovia laughed, "It's no Impala, but it'll get us from point A to point B."

"Dag, you ranking my ride?"

"It's a cute car for a chick," Zenovia teased.

"What are you driving?"

Audrey burst into laughter. "He got you there, Zee. You know you be hoofin' it."

Zenovia joined her mother in laughing. She was shocked when Tristan opened the car doors for her and Audrey.

Audrey voiced Zenovia's thoughts. "You're a real Prince Charming, huh?"

Tristan smiled and a blush warmed his caramel cheeks.

"So what kind of party is this?" Zenovia asked when Tristan closed his door and pulled out from the parking spot.

"It's not a party really, just a get-together. Some of my parents' friends, Mia's folks, and a few other people."

Zenovia ventured, "Is Mia your girlfriend?"

"Mia? No. We're just friends. I'm not going to date anyone until I get ready for marriage. I'm too busy serving God to worry about girls."

Zenovia raised an eyebrow, but didn't respond. Tristan seemed so cool until he started talking about the Brethren of the Sacrifice. When he talked about his faith, he became serious and seemed much older than his seventeen years. His zeal impressed Zenovia, even if she wasn't sure about his beliefs.

Finally, they pulled up to Charlotte and Thomas's home. Zenovia gasped with a combination of awe and envy. It was a two-story colonial with beige vinyl siding. The lawn was meticulously landscaped and in addition to the silver minivan, the two-car garage boasted two luxury cars.

Zenovia looked back at Audrey whose face wore a similar expression to her own. Zenovia knew what her mother was thinking. It was the kind of home they could only dream about.

"Come on in!" Charlotte sang as they approached the house.

Charlotte hugged Audrey and Zenovia. Audrey said, "Thank you so much for inviting us."

"Oh, this is nothing! Tristan, take Zenovia downstairs."

Tristan led Zenovia to the finished basement rec room. "Zee's here, y'all."

Alyssa and Mia said, "Hi!"

Kyle looked up from his conversation with another young man that Zenovia did not know. "Hey, Zee."

The other young man stood up and shook Zenovia's hand. "I'm Tristan and Alyssa's older brother Justin."

"Um h-hi. I'm Zenovia," she stammered.

"I know."

Zenovia was caught off guard by his voice. He looked about nineteen or twenty, but his voice was deep and smooth. He pronounced each of his words slowly and deliberately. His chocolate-colored complexion and dark features made his presence overwhelming. Zenovia could hardly breathe from the overload of pheromones.

"You got here just in time," Mia said, "We were just about to start practicing salsa dancing."

"Salsa dancing." Zenovia's response was as much a

question as it was a statement. What black teenagers danced the salsa?

Tristan laughed. "She thinks we're strange y'all. Some Brethren from the Spanish-speaking congregation on the west side invited us to a wedding reception."

"I think I'll just watch," Zenovia said as she sat down on the plaid sofa next to Kyle.

Kyle said, "I don't blame you."

"Don't listen to him," Mia teased. "He's a square."

Tristan turned on the Spanish music and the four-some started dancing. The siblings were very good; swiveling their hips and stepping in time to the music. Mia was embarrassingly bad. She crushed Justin's toes, while Kyle and Zenovia laughed.

Justin grabbed Zenovia's hand. "You think you can do better?"

"I know I can," she replied with a gulp.

Justin and Zenovia danced together fluidly. So well, in fact, that everyone else stopped to watch them. Zenovia spied a momentary look of jealousy on Tristan's face, but then he was all smiles. When the song ended, Zenovia fell backward onto the couch, exhausted.

"I thought you couldn't dance," Tristan said.

Zenovia responded between gasps, "Didn't . . . say that. I didn't want . . . to show you guys up."

Everyone laughed at the joke. Zenovia felt herself getting comfortable with her new friends. She'd never belonged to a group of any kind, and it felt good.

Too good to be true.

Instinctively, she wanted to check on Audrey. She

wanted to make sure that her mother wasn't upstairs with the adults breaking down and ruining her chances at being a normal teenager.

"All that dancing has made me hungry. Is there anything to eat?" Zenovia asked.

Alyssa answered. "Of course. Come on, Mia, let's go get some food."

"Alyssa, can you fix my plate?" That was Justin, the Barry White sound-alike.

"Me, too," Tristan chirped.

Kyle added. "There's three women. How about each one fix a man a plate."

"Um, what?" Zenovia asked. "First of all, I only see one almost man. The other two are boys. Second of all, I'm not making anybody's plate unless they're my husband."

"Well, you go girl," Mia said with three snaps of her finger. "While you're being all liberated, Alyssa and I will fix their food."

"Speak for yourself. I'm with Zee," Alyssa chuckled.

Tristan stood up. "Zee's right. I don't need a girl to get my food. I'm a grown man."

"I think Zee said you were a boy, and perhaps I'm the almost man," Justin said.

Justin also stood to his feet and walked over to the girls. He tipped Zenovia's chin upward and said, "I like you. You're a little fireball."

Zenovia scrunched her nose, unsure if that was a compliment. "Thank you...I think."

Upstairs, the adults were already eating the hearty appetizers. The young people filled their plates with buffalo wings, meatballs, and shrimp dip with crackers. Tristan reached into a cooler and extended a can of pop to Zenovia.

"Will you accept a beverage from a man?" he asked.

Zenovia narrowed her eyes playfully. "Sure," she replied and then took the can of pop that Justin was holding.

"Oooh...little brother. She got you again," Justin laughed.

Tristan joined in the laughter. "Okay, Zee! I concede defeat."

Zenovia smiled and peeked into the living room where the adults were sitting. She let out a sigh of relief when she noticed that Audrey was having a good time. One of the men that Zenovia remembered from the Devotion Center was saying something that Audrey found quite amusing. She was giggling, tossing her hair, and touching the man's arm in a very flirtatious manner. He absolutely did not mind.

After a few hours of dancing and shooting pool, it had gotten late and Tristan still had to drive Zenovia and Audrey home. Justin offered to accompany them, but Tristan refused.

Almost as soon as Tristan started the car, Audrey dozed off. She'd been enjoying a glass of wine with her new friend, but alcohol plus her meds equaled sleep. Zenovia did not look forward to waking her after their half an hour drive back to the hood.

"I had a lot of fun tonight, Tristan. I'm glad I came."

"Did you think about not coming?"

Zenovia answered honestly. "Yes."

"Why? Don't you like us?"

"Of course. I was worried that I wouldn't fit in with you Carver kids."

Tristan asked, "Is that an insult?"

Zenovia looked away from Tristan's searching eyes. She blew breath on his window and then wrote her name in the frost. "No, Tristan. I just come from a different background."

"The only thing that's different about you is that you're going to college, and we're not."

Zenovia thought of a host of other differences. They had two parents, they lived in a neighborhood that didn't have a drive-by every day, and they didn't have to worry about how they were going to stretch their food stamps until the end of the month.

"If you're not going to college, then what are you going to do? You seem too intelligent to work at a fast-food restaurant."

"Zee, the apocalypse will be here soon. We might not even graduate from high school. I'm going to do all I can for God's kingdom while I'm young and don't have any responsibilities."

Zenovia objected, "Well, I think I can be a God-fearing computer programmer."

"Of course you can, but I just feel the need to tell as many people as I can about God. It's the only thing that matters." Tristan's words were filled with passion.

"So I'll be less of a Christian if I have a career?"

"No. I'm just saying that, well, some people want to wear the C for Christian on their chest like Superman wears his S."

"But not you?"

"No, Zee. I want to live this thing. God has blessed me so much, I just want to share his love with everybody."

Zenovia didn't object anymore. "I admire you, Tristan. I don't know any young men like you."

"You said I was a boy."

"I was wrong."

Chapter Four

The smell of blueberry pancakes woke Zenovia from a deep slumber. She remembered dreaming about dancing with Justin. The memory made her feel warm on the inside, but her conversation with Tristan made her feel even warmer.

Audrey had already made a huge stack of pancakes and was still flipping away. "Are we having company?" Zenovia asked.

"No. I just feel like making pancakes."

"I don't know who is going to eat all of those."

Audrey shrugged. "Whatever we don't eat, we'll throw away."

Zenovia took a plate from the cupboard and forked three pancakes. She smothered them with butter and syrup and plopped down at the kitchen table.

Audrey was humming to herself as she cooked. Zenovia remarked, "You're in a good mood."

"Do you want to know why?"

"Sure, Mom."

"I met my husband last night. Or the man that will be my husband."

"Unh-uh."

"Uh-huh! I saw Phillip in a vision fifteen years ago. He's the one."

"The vision you had when you left home, pregnant with me?"

Audrey nodded. "Yep."

"So what are you going to do about it?" Zenovia asked with genuine curiosity.

"Well, I'm going to join this church and get baptized. You too."

"Hold up, Mom! I don't know if I'm joining there. Did you know that their kids don't go to college?"

Audrey rolled her eyes. "That's nothing! You can do whatever you want when you turn eighteen."

"But you don't think that's strange?"

"I thank they have their reasons," Audrey said, slipping into her native Texas drawl. "Most folk just believe what they been taught."

"Well, I'm not going to believe something just because someone tells me it's the truth."

Audrey patted Zenovia on the cheek. "Everybody ain't like you, Zee."

Zenovia changed the subject. "So tell me about Phillip. He looks kinda young for you."

"What are you trying to say? I look old?"

Zenovia chuckled. "No. I'm not saying that at all."

"Well, Ms. Smarty Pants, he's *not* too young. He's thirty-four."

"Does he have any kids?"

Audrey replied, "No, he's been one of the Brethren his whole life."

"What does that have to do with anything?" Zenovia asked.

"They don't have kids out of wedlock, because they don't do it until they're married."

Zenovia sighed wearily. Sometimes Audrey communicated like a little girl. She talked in code anytime she had to mention sex to Zenovia. Needless to say, they'd never had the "talk."

"Anyway, me and Phillip, we're going on a date tonight."

"A date? Do I need to go with you as a chaperone?" Zenovia was only half joking.

"No. Charlotte and Thomas are going to join us."

"Are you going to tell him?"

"Am I going to tell him what? About the vision?"

"That, too. But I was talking about your illness."

Audrey's expression changed to an irritated frown. "You sure know how to kill a mood."

"Sorry."

"He doesn't need to know about that right now. I'll tell him after he's in love with me."

"Mom, do you think that's fair?"

"It doesn't matter. I had a vision."

Zenovia shook her head angrily. She never let the visions control her life like Audrey did. There had been men interested in Audrey at other churches, but she hadn't given them the time of day, all because she hadn't seen them in a vision.

Audrey answered a ringing telephone. "Hello...Zee, it's for you."

Zenovia took the phone. "Hello."

"Hey. It's me, Alyssa. Do you want to hang out with me and Mia today? We're going to the mall and then to the movies."

"Sure."

"Goodie! My brother is going to drive us. We'll be there to pick you up in an hour."

"Alrighty then."

Zenovia hung up the phone and felt herself spiraling into panic mode. She had no idea what it meant to hang out. She'd never hung out alone, nor been asked to hang out with anybody else. She thought about her stash of money from shoveling snow, raking leaves, and babysitting. She had close to four hundred dollars, but that was for emergencies only. Living with Audrey made an emergency fund imperative.

"Who was that?" Audrey asked.

"It was Alyssa. She and Mia want me to hang out with them."

Audrey beamed. "Is someone getting a social life?"

"I guess so."

"Well, have fun! You deserve it."

Zenovia got dressed in a similar outfit to what she'd worn the night before. She then went into her treasured stash of money and took out one hundred dollars. She hoped that she wouldn't have to spend that much.

When the horn sounded the arrival of her friends, Zenovia's heart started to race. Having girlfriends was brand-new territory for her and the idea of a boyfriend was as alien as Clark Kent and planet Krypton.

Zenovia skipped outside. A grin stretched across her Vaseline-covered lips when she saw Tristan's car. It quickly switched to a frown when she noticed Mia sitting her hair-flinging behind in the front seat.

Tristan got out and opened the back door for Zenovia. She noticed that he was wearing a suit and tie. "Hey, Zee," he said.

Zenovia mumbled a hello and plopped into the backseat. "Hey, Alyssa. Hey, Mia."

Tristan asked, "Alyssa, which mall are you guys going to?"

"Beachwood, of course."

"There is no movie theater at Beachwood."

Mia touched Tristan's arm and said, "That's why you and Kyle can pick us up when you're done with your Bible studies. Then we can all go."

"I don't have money for the movies," Tristan stated.

Zenovia relaxed a little. She didn't know how Tristan's family was rolling, and she so did not want to feel like the hood chick with the princesses of Bel Air.

Alyssa laughed. "Quit playing, Tristan. Daddy just gave you fifty dollars yesterday."

"And one of my Bible studies needed some new tennis shoes. That's what I used it for."

Mia said, "Oh, well. I guess you're just our chauffeur today, then."

"I got you, Tristan, if you want to go," Zenovia said, feeling totally impressed with this teenager who would spend his allowance buying somebody's kid some shoes.

Tristan smiled into the rearview mirror. "Thanks, Zee. I see I have one friend in this car."

"I'm your friend," Mia said, "but I don't pay for guys to get into the movies. That's one of my rules."

Alyssa chimed in, "Okay! It looks like we need to school Zenovia."

Zenovia grinned to herself. This was exactly the reason that she did not have any girlfriends. She never felt the need to play games and was up-front about her feelings, good or bad. Boys were so much easier. She could be straight with them and they didn't hold grudges.

Tristan dropped them off in front of the mall and Zenovia's nervousness returned. They were shopping at Beachwood, the upscale mall where all the "buppies" spent their credit card bucks. Zenovia had only seen the mall in passing. She doubted if they had any of her favorite stores like Rainbow, 3-5-7, or Fashion Cents.

The first store they went to was a high-end leather store where Mia bought a leather jacket and leather pants and Alyssa bought a purse. They whipped out their credit cards with a quickness, neither of them thinking to look at a price tag.

Their next stop was a shoe store. Alyssa bought a seventy-five-dollar pair of penny loafers and Mia bought some leather boots to go with her outfit. Zenovia didn't see anything she liked that was within her budget.

When the credit card queens decided to break for lunch, Zenovia was relieved. The food court was something that she could afford.

Mia started the conversation while munching a mouthful of fried rice. "Zenovia, are you going to buy anything? It's no fun just window-shopping."

Zenovia wiped the pizza grease off of her face before she replied. "I'm having a great time, but these stores are just too expensive for me."

"Where do you shop?" Alyssa asked.

"TJ Maxx, Marshall's, Fashion Cents..."

Zenovia burst into spontaneous laughter from the expressions on Mia and Alyssa's faces. It was as if Zenovia was speaking Swahili to French Canadians. *No es comprende.*

Alyssa replied, "My brothers shop at Marshall's and they get name brand stuff, but it's always, like, last season's stuff."

"What's wrong with that?" Zenovia asked.

Mia and Alyssa exchanged glances, and Mia replied, "Nothing, I guess."

Zenovia spent the rest of the day looking at her watch and counting the minutes until Tristan's return. When he finally came back to pick them up, Kyle was sitting in the front seat, so all of the girls piled in the back.

"It looks like you guys broke the bank," Kyle commented after Tristan put all of Alyssa and Mia's bags in the trunk.

"I didn't spend that much," Alyssa replied, "but Mia maxed-out her credit card."

"Must be nice," Kyle said.

Tristan got back into the car and he was singing and smiling, obviously in a great mood. Alyssa asked, "What are you singing about?"

"My Bible study is getting baptized at the next regional meeting."

"That's great!" Mia exclaimed.

"Zee, are you gonna get baptized too?" Kyle asked.

Zenovia replied honestly, "I've been considering it."

"You should. It's the best decision you could ever make." Tristan spoke with excited conviction.

Tristan's enthusiasm was contagious, and Zenovia was coming to enjoy her new life. Audrey had found her husband and Zenovia had friends and plans on a Saturday afternoon. If getting baptized and joining the Brethren of the Sacrifice was all she needed to do to keep Tristan in her world, she'd do it all a hundred times.

The teenagers walked into the movie theater all holding tickets for the new Tom Hanks movie *Forrest Gump*. Zenovia thought the whole idea of the movie was a little silly—a mentally challenged man going through life making history—but it was the only movie Tristan was willing to see. Everything else was rated R and the Brethren did not attend R-rated movies.

"I can't believe we're going to see this stupid movie, Tristan!" Alyssa fussed.

Tristan replied, "I can't believe you thought I was going to see some demonic horror movie."

"Yeah, you guys know better than that," Kyle added. "One of the Brethren might be here."

Zenovia rolled her eyes and shook her head. It always seemed like Kyle's major motivation for doing or not doing anything was who might see him.

"Well, God is here all of the time, Kyle. Even behind closed doors where the Brethren can't see," Zenovia said.

"Zee's right," Tristan said. "That's all the more reason why we're going to see *Forrest Gump*."

As they walked into the theater, Mia attempted to situate herself near Tristan. Zenovia was certain that Mia was trying to make sure that she sat next to Tristan during the movie. Zenovia was also certain that Tristan was purposely dodging Mia by holding a trivial conversation with her.

"So do you like these pants, Zee?" Tristan asked as he

walked around Mia to stand in front of Zenovia. "Alyssa says they're ugly."

"They are ugly," Alyssa said. "Zee, please tell me you agree."

Zenovia narrowed her eyes and bit her lip. Tristan was wearing a pair of black M C Hammer pants. It wasn't so much that the pants were ugly, it was how Tristan paired them up with a Nautica sweatshirt. The ensemble looked crazy, but Zenovia didn't dare say so.

"Do you like your pants, Tristan?" Zenovia asked.

Tristan laughed. "So you're going to answer my question with a question?"

"Um...I'm going to plead the fifth. That's what I'm going to do," Zenovia said.

Mia interjected, "Well, Tristan, I think they look good. They are in style right now."

Tristan ignored Mia's compliment and raced Kyle down the aisle to find a seat. Alyssa, Mia, and Zenovia took their time navigating the crowded theater.

Alyssa said, "Mia, you don't have to sweat Tristan like that. I mean, you guys are already friends, and he's not trying to have a girlfriend right now."

"Boys always say that they don't want a girlfriend, but deep down, they all do. Tristan will do like all of the other Brethren boys. He'll work at the headquarters and then he'll come home looking for a wife."

Zenovia asked, "And that would be you?"

"If I have my way!" Mia exclaimed. "And I always have my way. I guess I'm a little spoiled."

When the three girls finally got to the seats, Tristan and Kyle were already seated. Zenovia was the first down the aisle and she deliberately skipped the seats next to

Tristan and took the seat on the other side of Kyle.

"Is it okay if I sit next to you?" Zenovia asked.

Kyle replied, "Sure, as long as you keep your hands to yourself."

Zenovia twirled her index finger in the air and brought it down on Kyle's arm. "Do I have to keep my finger to myself, too?" she asked.

Kyle snatched his arm away as if Zenovia had hurt him. "Yes. Don't ever touch me like that."

Alyssa laughed as she sat down on the other side of Kyle. "Stop acting weird, Kyle. That's why we never take you out of the house."

Mia triumphantly plopped down in the seat next to Tristan. Even though there were three people between them, Zenovia could still inhale Tristan's scent. She looked at the movie screen, even though nothing was playing yet, not even those trivia questions that came on before the movie.

"So you really don't like my pants?" Tristan asked from down the row.

Alyssa threw a piece of popcorn at him. "Give it a rest, Tristan! Nobody cares about those clowny-looking pants!"

"I was talking to Zee," Tristan answered.

"Why do you care whether or not I like your pants? You're the one wearing them!"

"You tell him, Zee," said a voice from a row or two behind them.

Zenovia whipped her head around to see where the voice came from. It was Justin and a pretty brown-skinned girl that Zenovia supposed was his date.

Alyssa had also turned around at the sound of her

oldest brother's voice. "Justin! What are you doing here?" she asked.

"I'm not allowed to go to the movies?"

Kyle replied in a whisper, "Not without a chaperone."

There was no way that Justin could've heard Kyle's rebuke, but Zenovia was sure that Justin would not care. There was an edge to Justin that was exciting and frightening. Zenovia felt attracted to him, but she feared that it was for all the wrong reasons.

"Of course you can go to the movies, Justin. We're just offended that you didn't invite us," Zenovia replied.

Justin gazed intently at Zenovia, seeming not to care about his date's feelings. "I didn't think you'd say yes."

Zenovia felt herself blush and was thankful for the dimmed lights. She turned around in her seat, feeling a bit uncomfortable.

Tristan, who had watched the exchange between his brother and Zenovia with rapt attention, stepped over Mia, Alyssa, and Kyle and took the empty seat next to Zenovia. He leaned back and put his feet up on the seat in front of him.

"What are you doing?" Zenovia asked.

"I want to talk to you and Kyle during the movie. Is that cool?"

Zenovia playfully echoed Kyle's warning: "As long as you keep your hands to yourself."

"I'll be good, I promise," Tristan replied.

Zenovia glanced over her shoulder at Justin. He was now paying close attention to his date. He was telling her something, but Zenovia couldn't make out the words. Maybe Justin wasn't thinking about her at all. Maybe it was all in her imagination.

Chapter Five

What do you believe is God's view of capital punishment?"

Zenovia was unnerved by the question. It wasn't in any of the baptism study guides that Tristan had given her, but Brother Clark, the regional leader, was waiting patiently for a response.

She drew in a deep breath. "Well, I would think that since God is the creator of life . . . that He would be against needlessly taking anyone's life, even a murderer's."

Zenovia could tell by Brother Clark's deep frown and the shifting of his Coke-bottle eyeglasses that she had misspoken. Zenovia looked to Audrey for help, but she shrugged her shoulders cluelessly. Audrey's questions had been simple things like "What does it mean to be a Christian?" and "Who died for your sins?"

Brother Clark responded. "Turn your Bible to Exodus Chapter Twenty-one, and read Verses Twenty-four and Twenty-five."

Zenovia bit her lip and turned to the passage. She didn't see the whole point of interrogating people before they could give their lives to Christ, especially seeing that she and her mother were *already* Christians.

She read out loud, "Eye for eye, tooth for tooth, hand for hand, foot for foot, burning for burning, wound for wound, stripe for stripe."

"So you see," Brother Clark explained, "this scripture is expressing God's view on justice and retribution. A life for a life."

Zenovia searched her memory for a verse to counter this, but she could not find one. She asked timidly, "What about mercy?"

"Justice is one of God's four attributes. He cannot be unjust."

Zenovia nodded and wondered if her answer would keep her from baptism...and Tristan. But Brother Clark's face softened. He straightened his glasses with a crooked index finger and smiled at Zenovia.

"Don't worry, young lady. A lot of people get stumped on that one. As long as you understand."

"I do understand," Zenovia replied without missing a beat.

"So it looks like the two of you are going to officially be members of the Brethren of the Sacrifice after Saturday," declared Audrey's *friend* Brother Phillip Sullivan.

Audrey clapped her hands together. "I'm so excited! Aren't you Zee?"

Zenovia nodded although she was nowhere near as ecstatic as her mother. She *did*, however, have butterflies in her stomach at the thought of sharing her news

with Tristan. He would be beyond happy about her decision to join the Brethren.

Phillip commented, "Zee, you should be just fine as
long as you keep yourself chaste. Be careful with the
boys from now on. You're dedicated to God."

"Okay," Zenovia replied.

Zenovia was annoyed by the comment that came out
of nowhere. Had Phillip already formed an opinion of
her? And if he had, what was it based on?

The two men stood to leave the apartment, Brother
Phillip lingering a few moments behind the older
Brother Clark. When the senior man was safely in the
car, Brother Phillip gave Audrey an extra-friendly hug.

The unexpected showing of affection caused a satisfied grin to grace Zenovia's full lips. She enjoyed seeing
her mother have normal human interaction. It helped to
know that Audrey *could* be just like anyone else's mom.

Zenovia could see why Audrey was so taken with
Brother Phillip. He was totally her type; chocolate
brown and shiny. His eyes were tiny and slanted, almost
Asian-looking and the bulges of his bodybuilder's phy-
sique showed through his ill-fitted suit.

"On Saturday we're going to take you out to celebrate," Brother Phillip said.

Audrey smiled. "We who?"

"Me, Charlotte, and Thomas."

"Why can't it just be you and me?" Audrey asked, this
time coupling her smile with a few affectionate strokes
on Phillip's chest.

Phillip suddenly turned serious. "Because it wouldn't
be proper for us to be seen alone. I know I've explained
that to you before."

"Right, right. The chaperone thing. Well, whatever. I'll see you Saturday." Audrey's face was still smiling, but Zenovia knew her well enough to discern the irritation in her tone.

"Bye, Brother Phillip," Zenovia called as he walked out the door.

Audrey closed the door behind him and then sulked as she headed toward the bedroom they shared.

"He's a little different, Mom."

Zenovia couldn't pinpoint her feeling, but there was something not quite right about Phillip.

"Naw, he ain't. He's just fine."

"Well if he's fine, what's wrong with you?"

Audrey snapped. "Nothing! What makes you think something is wrong with me?"

"Because you're pouting."

"I ain't pouting. You don't know what you're talking about, but you think you know everything."

Zenovia did not respond. Audrey stood there, waiting for the retort, but Zenovia refused to oblige her.

After seventeen years of living with Audrey's illness, Zenovia knew when to leave well enough alone. The medication only subdued the inner demons; it did not eradicate them. They were alive and well, waiting to be unleashed on the unsuspecting.

Zenovia was not the unsuspecting, but Brother Phillip would be.

When it was clear that Zenovia was not up for battle, Audrey moved her sulking to the bedroom. She slammed the door and Zenovia could hear her push a wooden chair under the doorknob, barring her from entry.

Zenovia went into the kitchen, fixed herself a snack of

tortilla chips, salsa, and Pepsi, and got comfortable on the couch in front of the television. There would be no visiting with her pillow that night. Audrey would see to it.

She flipped through the channels until she found her favorite show, *Star Trek: The Next Generation*. It was a repeat, but she did not mind. Captain Picard was her hero and television crush, with his baldheaded self.

The telephone rang just as the captain was about to make his move on Dr. Crusher.

"Hello?" Zenovia said while keeping one ear to her program.

"Hey, Zee. It's me, Tristan."

One syllable of Tristan's almost baritone was enough to snatch Zenovia's attention away from Captain Picard. "Hey, Tristan."

"I heard you answered your questions with flying colors. Congratulations."

Zenovia asked, "How did you know?"

"Brother Phillip called my dad. He's really happy about your mother. I think he wants to marry her."

Zenovia sat straight up on the couch, clutching the phone for dear life. "Marry her? I thought he was just attracted to her. He's only known her for like five seconds, Tristan. He doesn't know her well enough to marry her."

"You sound like you don't want your mother to have a husband."

"I do. That's not it at all."

Tristan prodded, "Then what is it? Do you not want a stepfather? Because Brother Phillip is good people."

"Are you serious? Brother Phillip seems a little off to me."

Zenovia had lived around mental illness for long enough to know when someone was a bit touched. In her opinion, Phillip was a little fuzzy around the seams; maybe not as bad off as Audrey, but definitely not normal.

But Zenovia was skeptical of any man who was interested in Audrey. A man couldn't be in a relationship with Audrey for very long without noticing that something wasn't right about the woman. If a man continued to see Audrey after a few dates, Zenovia assumed he just wanted to sleep with her or that he was mentally ill himself.

"Zee, you don't have to worry about him. He's harmless. So how are we going to celebrate your big day?"

"My big day? Oh, you mean the baptism. I don't know. My mom is going out with Brother Phillip and your parents, so I guess I'm free."

"If they're going out, we can have a get-together over here."

"When you say 'we,' are you just talking about your brother, sister, and Mia?" Zenovia could not help but roll her eyes at the thought of Mia.

"Kyle will be there too."

"Oh. I forgot about Kyle."

"Don't forget about my boy!"

Zenovia was quiet and contemplative as she recalled the vision she'd had about Kyle. She couldn't forget about the vision even if she wanted to.

"Zee, you still there?" Tristan asked after the silence had carried on for too long.

"Yeah, I'm here. Can I ask you a question?"

"Absolutely."

"Is everything cool with Kyle? I mean at home and stuff. Is he okay?"

"I think so. What makes you ask that?"

Zenovia sighed. There was a hesitation in Tristan's tone that told her he was holding something back.

"Nothing," she replied, "just a feeling that I had."

"Oh. Well, he's cool. His dad isn't around, but other than that he's good."

Noises came from the bedroom causing Zenovia to sit up straight on the couch. She released another sigh, this one burdened down with weariness. Audrey was throwing something against the wall, taking her anger out on some innocent, inanimate object.

"Um, Tristan," she said, "I've got to call you back."

"You cool?"

For a fraction of a second, Zenovia considered sharing the facts about Audrey's illness with Tristan. The secret was too heavy a load for her to bear alone, and yet she had borne it for seventeen years. But the thought disintegrated as quickly as it had emerged. Tristan was not ready to be her confidante, and she was not ready to share.

"I'm fine, Tristan. I'll see you Saturday."

He chuckled. "Not if I see you first."

Chapter Six

The regional meeting of the Brethren of the Sacrifice was merely a supersize version of their regular meetings. Still no choir, still no "Hallelujahs" and still no giving God the praise. Zenovia had expected so much more.

About midway through the meeting, the people who were going to be baptized were called to stand on the stage. Several of the regional leaders prayed for them one at a time. When it was her turn, Zenovia trembled with fear as she listened to the words of the brief prayer. Then everyone in the room stood to their feet.

The brother who was leading the prayers said into a microphone, "Dear Brethren, these are the newest among us, babes in Christ and babes in their walk. Do you, congregation, accept your role in grooming, preparing, and chastening these newly won souls?"

Everyone responded in unison. "We do."

The brother turned his attention back to the baptism line. "We, as a joint congregation, accept you into our ranks. We will groom you to meet our savior on earth.

We will prepare you for service, and we will chasten you as the Holy Spirit deems necessary, in the name of Jesus."

"Amen," chanted the still-standing congregation.

Zenovia felt weak in the knees. What had he meant by "chasten"? She knew what the word meant; it was on her SAT vocabulary list. To punish by suffering.

To punish by suffering?

What place did punishment and suffering have in a baptism ceremony?

Everything in the room went blurry. Her instincts told her that she was making a grave error. Zenovia wanted to run off the stage and right out the door. She wanted to drag the beaming Audrey right along with her. But as she looked into the audience, she saw Tristan's lovely smile.

The giant red EXIT sign at the rear of the building beckoned to her, but Tristan's smile made her stay put.

She stayed put, even though the instincts that she'd always trusted told her to run.

Everyone applauded, but Tristan's seemed more spirited than anyone else's. The baptism line was then led away, back down a long tunnel. The men and women were separated, and they were given long white robes and white turbans for their heads.

When all of the women were dressed, they were led down another tunnel to an Olympic-size swimming pool. Right outside the pool was a spectator room for the friends and family of those being baptized. Brother Phillip was there, smiling and waving at Audrey. And all of Zenovia's new friends were there, too; even Alyssa and Mia were beaming with pride and joyousness. Zenovia guessed they all felt partly responsible for helping to shape her decision.

The men filed into the pool room from the other side and were dressed in similar outfits as the women, but without the turbans. Another prayer was said over the group and then each person was baptized one at a time. Zenovia had never heard so many "In the name of the Father, in the name of the Son, and in the name of the Holy Spirits" at one time.

Over two hundred people were baptized as Brethren that day. The sheer numbers eased some of Zenovia's fears. If nothing else, the Brethren of the Sacrifice were intent on spreading their message. And plenty of people liked what they were hearing.

After the baptism ceremony, Zenovia and the other newly christened Brethren were taken back to the changing room. Audrey's feet barely touched the ground as they walked. Zenovia watched her with interest and suspicion. She looked for all of the signs that the zone would metamorphose into an episode.

"What are you guys doing for lunch?" As if she sensed Zenovia's caution, Audrey asked this normal question.

"They're probably already off eating somewhere. I saw a Burger King across the street. Do you want me to pick you something up?"

She shook her head adamantly. "No. Phillip is waiting for me."

"That's nice."

Zenovia had been mistaken. When she emerged from the changing room, Tristan and Kyle were outside waiting for her. As promised, Brother Phillip was there, too, waiting to whisk her mother away.

"Congratulations!" Tristan exclaimed as Zenovia stepped into plain view.

Tristan grabbed Zenovia's arm and pulled her into an enthusiastic embrace. Even though he squeezed the breath from her lungs, he still managed to make the hug feel brotherly. That part was disappointing. Zenovia had expected the Red Sea to part the first time she was in his arms.

Kyle also hugged Zenovia, but his was much lower on the Richter scale. His arms barely brushed Zenovia's shoulders, almost as if he was only halfheartedly mimicking Tristan's sincere gesture.

"Where are Alyssa and Mia?" Zenovia asked, because she thought it was the polite thing to say, not because she cared.

"They're off chasing some boys," Kyle replied.

Zenovia grinned. Mia chasing boys was good news. It meant that she *wasn't* chasing Tristan. Not at that moment, anyway.

Tristan asked, "Are you hungry?"

"I suppose so," Zenovia answered with a shrug.

"Don't get *too* excited," Kyle said. "You might just faint dead away."

"Faint dead away?" Zenovia giggled. "Man, who talks like that?"

After Kyle was finished scowling and Zenovia and Tristan had composed themselves from their laughter, the three companions stepped out of the nondescript brick building. One whiff of the brisk October air was all Zenovia needed to know that another lovely Cleveland winter was on the way.

She rubbed her arms. "It's cold out here."

"Here, take my jacket," Tristan offered.

Kyle said, "Are you sure you want to do that, bro? Someone might make something of it."

Tristan had extended the arm that held his jacket, but on hearing Kyle's words had snapped it back like the neck of a jack-in-the-box. Zenovia didn't know who these *someones* were and she didn't care anything about their *somethings*. She did care that Kyle was quite earnestly putting figurative salt in her proverbial game.

"Do you want me to go inside and get your sweater?" Tristan asked. Obviously, *he* cared about the someones.

"No," Zenovia replied through tight lips. "I'm fine."

Kyle said, "Okay, then. Let's go."

The two boys started walking, but Zenovia stood, frozen in place. When he noticed that she wasn't with them Tristan asked, "Zee. You coming?"

"Nah. I'm not really hungry."

"Zee..."

She waved a dismissive hand at Tristan and Kyle. "Go! I'm cool. I'll see you guys at the end of the afternoon session."

Zenovia fumed her way through the entire afternoon session. She seriously considered firing Tristan, although he wasn't officially hired, not to mention she was starving! Zenovia's fury plus her hunger was a mixture that resulted in folded arms and a frown when everyone else in the room was applauding an inspirational message.

She tried to turn her attention to the speaker, but his words about "God's loving arrangement" just couldn't hold her interest. What did he mean by *arrangement* anyway? Was it a code word for blessing? Zenovia found herself to be a novice in Brethren vocabulary.

Audrey was eating it all up and clapping her heart out. If they were at a *real* church, Audrey would be standing from her seat with uplifted hands and shouting "Hallelujah" at the top of her lungs.

Zenovia recalled with fondness the Pentecostal churches where she'd first learned about God, and all of the Baptist, Holiness, and Methodist churches that she and Audrey had attended before the Brethren. These Brethren of the Sacrifice meetings didn't have anything on a Sunday-evening revival. The Brethren didn't even have testimony service. But what the Brethren lacked in religiosity, they made up for in kindness and orderliness.

And, of course, the Brethren had Tristan. The beautiful, inconsiderate, cowardly Tristan. Zenovia squinted over in his direction. She felt her solemn expression transform into a full-fledged glare when she noticed that Mia was seated between Tristan and Alyssa. Zenovia wondered what those *someones* would think of their seating arrangement.

Just as she got ready to roll her eyes at Tristan, Zenovia was thrust into an unexpected vision.

The young man waits impatiently in the rain. He stands in a dark alley, partially to shield him from the elements, but also to hide him from the passersby. His black trench coat renders him virtually invisible, and only the glint of his gold watch signals his presence.

He looks down at the expensive timepiece and sighs. Just as he seems ready to give up on his mission, a woman appears in the shadows. Her coat is red patent leather and clings to every voluptuous curve on her body. She, unlike her partner, is not trying to hide her existence from the world.

The young man smiles hungrily upon seeing his partner.

They grab and claw at one another in a desperate embrace. She smears her strawberry-red lipstick on his face with her messy kisses. Tears of joy form in both their eyes that commingle with the falling raindrops.

Just across the street, another kind of teardrops fall. A young woman clutches the wedding band on her finger as she watches the apparent lovers. With no alley to shield her from the rain, she just stands there—drenched. Not only by the thunderstorm, but by her own sorrowful tears.

Zenovia blinked rapidly, trying to hold back the tears that were threatening to rush down her face. The woman in her vision had been heartbroken or would be in the future; Zenovia wasn't sure which. She had no idea of the identities of either woman—neither the sobbing wife nor the sexy vixen.

She did, however, know the identity of the young man in her vision. He was standing in front of the Brethren, wrapping up his forty-five minute lecture about blessings.

Zenovia could almost see the streaks of lipstick on his face and neck. She felt a shiver rip through her body.

The always perceptive Audrey whispered, "You are going to have to learn how to play it off better than you do."

Even though Audrey had not been specific, Zenovia did not need clarification on the observation. Zenovia was always visibly rattled by her visions, but Audrey would go on as if life had not just skipped a beat and a half.

Though she was still feeling the forlorn misery of the wife in her vision, Zenovia refused to let a tear fall. Just in case Tristan was looking her way and just in case he thought she was sad due to his lack of courtesy.

After the regional meeting ended, everyone had their share of unnecessary chitchat. This included the young people, many of whom came up to Zenovia to offer congratulatory words of encouragement.

When she got tired of smiling and nodding, Zenovia pulled on her sweater and went outside to the parking lot. She trudged over to Tristan's car and waited for her friends to join her.

Justin was the first to appear. "Hey, Zee. Congratulations."

"Thanks." She punctuated her reply with a breathless sigh.

"What's wrong?"

"Nothing."

Justin leaned on the car next to Zenovia. "Well, clearly there is something wrong, and you telling me nothing is merely an invitation for me to figure out what it is."

"There were way too many words in that sentence." Zenovia ignored the sudden warmth from where Justin's arm brushed against her own. "I'm going to need you to rephrase that mess."

"Did Tristan do something wrong?"

Zenovia's response came after an obvious and transparent pause. "No. I'm cool."

"He *did* do something! It's always Tristan. What did Boy Wonder do this time?"

"It was nothing really. Now that I think about it, I probably overreacted."

Justin laughed. "Why don't you tell me what it was?"

"We were on our way to lunch, and Tristan offered me his jacket because I was cold. Kyle warned him that

someone might see, and then he took back his offer."
Zenovia gave the abbreviated version.

"He just let you be cold?"

"Um...no. I came back inside."

Justin's widened eyes locked with Zenovia's. "So you
didn't go to lunch?"

"No."

"Are you hungry?"

"Why," Zenovia asked with a smile, "do you have
food?"

Justin reached into his briefcase and pulled out a
slightly damaged apple Danish. Zenovia salivated as
Justin ripped open the paper, allowing the sweet aroma
to tease her nostrils.

He tore off a piece. "Open wide."

"I can feed myself," Zenovia objected.

"Do you want it?"

Zenovia nodded.

Justin bit his bottom lip and repeated slowly,
"Then...open wide."

Zenovia formed her lips into the shape of an O. Justin
placed the small piece of buttery Danish into her mouth.
She shivered as he grazed his thumb against her bottom
lip. Zenovia hoped that was an accident, because if it
wasn't, Justin was shamelessly moving in on his brother's
unclaimed territory.

"Want more?" he asked.

Zenovia quickly shook her head. The whole exchange was unsettling. It made her feel like she was not
being faithful. She prided herself on being faithful and
loyal.

Justin continued, "You full, Zee? From that one little bite?"

She did not get a chance to respond, because Tristan and Kyle approached the car. Tristan wore an apologetic smile on his face. As much as she wanted to roll her eyes, Zenovia could not help but smile back.

"Zee! I didn't know you were out here. We were inside, looking all over for you."

"I hope you didn't go to too much trouble," Zee replied with a gallon of sarcasm dripping from her tongue.

Tristan's gaze traveled to the point of intersection on Zenovia and Justin's bodies. His expression held questions that Zenovia had no intention of answering. Justin must have also discerned the unspoken clues because he stood from his post on Tristan's car and tossed Zenovia the rest of the pastry.

"Enjoy!" he said in a chipper tone, with none of his usual flirtatious undertones. He saved those for when no one was around.

Tristan asked his brother, "Are you coming back home? We're having a get-together to celebrate Zee's baptism."

"Maybe later. I have a date."

"With who?" asked Kyle.

"Shanna, and her parents."

Kyle high-fived Justin. "My man!"

"Shanna is the white girl?" asked Tristan.

Justin shook his head. "She's not white. She's Latina."

Zenovia shook her head and chuckled. Justin asked, "You got a problem with interracial dating, Zee?"

"No, dude. Whatever floats your boat."

Tristan opened the car door for Zenovia, and she climbed into the backseat. She pretended to check her hair and lip gloss in the rearview mirror, but she really wanted to watch Justin as he swaggered his way across the parking lot.

Without a doubt, his fineness was excessive.

Finally Tristan and Kyle jumped into the front seat of the car. Tristan asked, "Is pizza okay? That's what we ordered. And the girls went to get a cassata cake from Barcelli's Bakery."

"You didn't have to do all of this, Tristan." Zenovia felt guilty for lusting after Justin when Tristan was being so kind.

Tristan turned around in his seat. "Of course I did. You're my friend, and you just made the best decision of your life."

Chapter Seven

Although the party was no surprise to Zenovia, she did not anticipate the number of teenagers who would be crammed into Tristan's basement. As they descended the stairs, the loud music rattled the handrail as did the stomps of one hundred feet executing the Electric Slide.

At the center of the crowd were Alyssa and Mia. Alyssa spiced up the line dance with a few exotic hip gyrations while Mia could barely keep up with the basic steps. Zenovia wanted to join in, but she felt that dancing provocatively would be quite ironic since she'd just taken a dip in the baptism pool.

Zenovia said to Tristan, "I didn't know that this was going to be a house party."

"Well, you know how word of mouth is!" Tristan replied as he waved to some girls beckoning to him from across the room.

"I guess."

Tristan bobbed his head to the music and asked, "You wanna dance?"

"I'm good. I'm going for snacks."

Kyle cosigned, "Me, too. I saw some pizza upstairs."

"Lead the way, my brotha."

Zenovia followed Kyle to the kitchen and they both grabbed plates full of food. Then they moved to the living room couch to eat in a semi-quiet environment.

After practically swallowing a chicken wing whole, Kyle cleared his throat and said, "Sorry about earlier, Zee. It was nothing personal."

"*What* was nothing personal?" She assumed that he was referring to the whole lunch incident, but wanted to make sure.

"You know, when I told Tristan not to give you his jacket."

Zenovia nodded slowly. "Okay, apology accepted. But can I at least get an explanation?"

"Well, Tristan is planning to volunteer for mission work at the Brethren headquarters as soon as we graduate," Kyle explained. "And he has to stay chaste if he wants to do that."

"What exactly is not chaste about letting me borrow his jacket?"

"Nothing. But he doesn't want anyone to get the wrong idea. I mean, you're new to the faith. You haven't been raised in it, and there's a..." Kyle paused as if he was searching for a tactful way to say something ignorant.

Zenovia took it straight to the hood and gave Kyle a serious neck roll. "There's a what?"

"An adjustment period. I mean, it's unspoken, but the Holy Spirit has to purify you of any... improper lusts."

Zenovia nearly choked on her laugh. "Boy, quit playing. You can't be serious."

"If people had seen you wearing Tristan's jacket, some would've assumed that you were seducing him."

"Well, we wouldn't want anyone thinking that."

"Tristan's future depends on it."

Zenovia cocked her head to one side and digested Kyle's words. He seemed so concerned about Tristan's reputation and Tristan's future. She was starting to think that maybe Kyle was her competition and not Mia.

She asked, "And what about your future? What are you going to be doing when Tristan becomes a missionary?"

"I'll get a job, get married. The usual."

"Don't you want to be a missionary too?"

"Well, of course. But they'd never accept me. My family doesn't have enough clout."

Kyle quickly stood up and walked toward the kitchen, but not before Zenovia noticed the pain on his face. She understood his anger. She'd also been prejudged and excluded because of her young, husbandless, and schizophrenic mother.

"Kyle, not everyone has two parents, a nice house, and a family dog."

"You're right." Kyle smirked. "But wouldn't it be nice to be on the right side of the tracks?"

Zenovia did not reply, mostly because Kyle's dark expression made her think it was a rhetorical question. After a few moments, she went back downstairs to join the party. It did not take long to find Tristan in the crowd. He and Alyssa were dancing in the center of a huge circle of teenagers who were chanting, "Go, Tristan . . . go, Lyssa" to the beat of the loud rap music.

Zenovia marveled at how chaste he looked.

When the song was over, the crowd dispersed, and went back to one-on-one dancing. Tristan smiled at Zenovia and waved for her to come over. She declined with a tight head shake and found a seat close to the door—in case lightning decided to strike the holy Brethren partygoers.

Sitting back and observing from afar was more Zenovia's style anyway. She watched as Mia chatted with Tristan, her hands doing more talking than her lips. But Tristan seemed only partially engaged as he made brief eye contact with Mia before scanning the room for perhaps a more interesting conversant.

Zenovia's attention shifted toward Kyle as he attempted to learn a dance step from Alyssa. He was a pitiful dancer. So bad, in fact, that Zenovia placed a hand over her mouth to stifle her giggles.

"What are you laughing at?" Justin whispered. Zenovia had been so busy observing from afar, that she had not noticed him sit down behind her.

"Wouldn't you like to know. Where's your date?"

"Her parents wouldn't let her come to a party. They're really strict."

Zenovia gave a faux expression of sadness. "Oh, that's too bad."

"You're so phony." Justin chuckled.

"I am not," she said defensively. "I was so looking forward to meeting her."

Justin stood from his seat and extended his hand to Zenovia. "Dance with me."

"N-no. It's a slow song."

Justin took Zenovia's hand and gently pulled her from her seat. "So we'll slow dance."

Zenovia felt powerless to refuse. She wanted to protest, but her words turned into a gulp in her throat.

"Don't be nervous," he whispered. "I won't freak on you."

Zenovia swallowed her giggle and let Justin lead her to the dance floor. He took her right hand in his left and placed his right hand high on her back. A very modest pose from the immodest Justin. Zenovia completed the stance by placing her left hand on his shoulder.

"Ready?" Justin asked.

She nodded her response and Justin swayed them back and forth. He tried to maintain eye contact with Zenovia, but she quickly looked away from his demanding stare.

From out of nowhere, Tristan appeared. Well, it wasn't out of nowhere, but it seemed that way to Zenovia, because, in her mind, the entire room had disappeared when she and Justin had started dancing.

"Can I cut in, big bro?" Tristan asked.

Justin replied with a wicked grin. "That's up to the lady."

"Of course he can cut in," Zenovia hissed.

Defeated, Justin raised both hands and handed her over to Tristan. Tristan took Zenovia's hand exactly as Justin had, except that Tristan's palms were hot and moist. His forehead glistened with perspiration too; the result of his intense dancing.

Zenovia briefly glanced at Justin who was already engaged in another conversation. He saw her looking and slowly rubbed his thumb across his own bottom lip. Zenovia gave him the evil eye in response. He laughed.

"I thought you didn't want to dance," Tristan said.

"I didn't, but Justin is pretty relentless."

"And I'm not?"

Zenovia chose her words carefully. "I guess you are. In some things anyway...the good things."

"What does that mean?" Tristan asked. His voice defensively rose an octave and his handsome face tightened into a frown.

"I just mean that you're relentless when it comes to serving God, and being a good person."

Tristan's expression softened. "I'll take that as a compliment."

"Please do. It's how it was meant."

Tristan suddenly twirled Zenovia in a small circle. Before she could catch her breath, he twirled her again. She felt herself lose balance for a moment, but Tristan steadied her. Then they were back in their groove again, swaying to the music.

He whispered, "I'm sorry...about earlier."

"Not a problem."

"Seriously," he said, smiling, "you can wear my jacket anytime you want."

His apology was sweet, reassuring, and exactly what Zenovia needed to hear.

Chapter Eight

Zenovia peered down at her math test. Her geometric proof did not look quite right, but she was tired of thinking on it. She would come back to the problem when she was done with the rest of the test. Hopefully there would still be time to tweak her response.

She struggled through the rest of the exam because, unfortunately, she'd spent the entire weekend with the Brethren and hadn't gotten in much study time. Geometry was actually one of her best subjects, right behind English. Zenovia liked that the problems were more about logic than computation, because critical thinking was one of her strongest traits.

As she finished up the last problem, Zenovia found herself critically thinking about Justin and Tristan. Although she'd only known him a short time, Tristan was her friend. He cared about her soul's salvation and her general well-being as long as the *someones* were okay with it.

But with Justin, it was pure carnality. He made her heart race and it scared her. She was seventeen going on eighteen and no one had prepared her for sweaty palms and racing heartbeats.

Zenovia's teacher, Mr. Benjamin, walked up to her desk with a troubled expression on his face. "Your mother is in the main office," Mr. Benjamin said as he wrote her a hall pass.

A sense of dread filled Zenovia's body as she rushed to the main office. All thoughts of Tristan and Justin took a backseat to this new crisis. There was no telling what emergency had brought Audrey out of their apartment and up to the school.

To Zenovia's surprise, Audrey was standing in the office, animatedly chatting to the secretaries. She had apparently just said something funny, because everyone was laughing. Audrey waved her left hand in a sweeping fashion, emphasizing some point with her gesture, and nearly blinded Zenovia with the flash of what looked like a diamond ring.

"Mom," Zenovia said interrupting the conversation, "what's up?"

"Oh, hey, Zee! I'm signing you out early today. Phillip just asked me to marry him and we're going out to lunch to celebrate."

Zenovia's mind reeled. She and Audrey had been baptized as Brethren for only two days, and already Audrey was engaged. Things were moving much too quickly for Zenovia's liking and there seemed to be nothing she could do about it.

Zenovia sat silently in the car while Audrey and Phillip planned their wedding.

"I've always wanted a wedding, Phillip! And Zenovia can be my maid of honor."

"Mom, don't you think you're a little old for all that? Y'all just need to go downtown."

Or call the whole thing off, thought Zenovia.

Phillip smiled at Audrey and stroked her cheek. "If my bride wants a wedding, a wedding she'll get. I'm sure Charlotte and Thomas will let us have our reception in their basement."

Audrey turned around in her seat to face her scowling daughter. "Zee, aren't you happy for us?"

"If you like it, I love it," Zenovia replied as she turned to look out of the window.

Audrey sighed and seemed to abandon the notion of getting Zenovia to ride the happy train. She turned back to her man and beamed with excitement.

"So who's going to be your best man?" she asked.

Phillip responded without hesitation. "Oh, that's easy. My friend Bryce Goodman."

"Have I met him yet?"

"No, not yet, but he gave a sermon at the regional meeting. It was right after lunch. Young black guy..."

Audrey didn't seem to remember, but Zenovia's eyes opened wide. The cheater from her vision now had a name. Bryce Goodman. Her mother's fiancé had a cheater for a best friend. Wow.

Zenovia let it all sink in. She hoped that the two men weren't birds of a feather, because Phillip definitely did not want to rumble with Audrey.

Audrey cleared her throat and said in an almost whisper, "Honey, Phillip and I made another decision too."

"What? Don't tell me you two are planning on having children."

Phillip laughed. "We are living way too close to the apocalypse to be thinking of having children."

Zenovia rolled her eyes. "Okay, then what?"

"I'm not going to be taking my meds anymore," Audrey announced.

"Mom!"

"Wait, Zenovia," Audrey explained. "Don't flip out. We're going to do it gradually."

Her mother, without medication, was not a mother at all. She was a monster. Phillip had no idea what kind of Pandora's box he was ripping open.

Zenovia asked, "Phillip, was this your idea?"

"Yes. Well, it was a joint decision."

"Have you spoken with her doctor?"

"Zenovia..." Audrey tried to interject, but Zenovia glared angrily at her mother.

"Mother, I'm talking to Phillip."

Phillip responded to the question. "No, I have not talked to any doctors."

"I know you haven't, because if you had, you would know that my mother's schizophrenia is fully advanced. Without her meds, she is violent and delusional."

Phillip chuckled. "First of all, your mother and I do not answer to you. We're the parents. You're the child."

Zenovia seethed, but held her tongue. She stopped herself from spewing curses all up into the front seat because she wanted to hear what other foolishness Phillip had to offer.

Phillip continued, "Second, your mother's past illness is the work of the adversary. We have faith that she'll be healed. In fact, I believe she's already healed."

Zenovia shook her head. She had faith too, but hers

was based on a reality and childhood of living with a deranged mother.

"She's not the same person without her meds. You won't love the person she becomes," Zenovia said somberly.

"To the contrary," Phillip declared with confidence. "This medicated person is not your real mother. She can't begin to realize God's plan for her life until she accepts her healing."

Audrey pleaded with Zenovia. "Zee, don't you want to see me get better?"

Zenovia blinked back tears. She wanted nothing more than to see her mother get better. It had been her prayer ever since a zealous Sunday-school teacher had told her there was someone listening—and that He would answer her.

Leaving Audrey's question unanswered, Zenovia turned to stare out of the window. Phillip pulled into the parking lot for the Homestyle Buffet, a cheesy all-you-can-eat pseudo-soul food restaurant that Zenovia hated.

"You guys go ahead," she said, "I'm not hungry."

"You aren't coming? You gotta eat." Audrey asked, with audible concern in her tone.

"No, thanks. I've got a book I should be reading for an exam on Friday."

Zenovia watched as her mother and Phillip linked arms and lovingly strolled across the parking lot. She felt helpless to stop the impending disaster.

She cracked open her copy of *Manchild in the Promised Land* and thought about the A essay that she planned to write. No matter what foolishness Audrey decided, she was going to college and she was going to program computers like nobody's business.

Because she was fully engrossed in her novel, Zenovia jumped when she heard a loud tap on her window. Tristan and Kyle stood outside the car, both wearing trench coats—highly appropriate for the chilly October afternoon.

"Roll down the window!" Tristan's warm breath frosted the window.

Zenovia smiled slowly, and her troubled mood disappeared immediately. "No! It's cold out there and I've got the heat on in here."

"We're out here doing God's work, but we can't get in to warm up! You are cold, Zee."

Kyle saw an elderly couple crossing the parking lot and ran off to share the Brethren gospel with them, leaving Tristan standing alone, still looking cold.

Zenovia paused for a second and wondered what Phillip might think if he caught her snuggled up in the backseat with Tristan. Especially since he seemed to have adopted some strange "I'm the parent" complex. Then she decided that she didn't care and leaned forward to unlock the doors.

Tristan flashed his beautiful smile and jumped in the backseat. He breathed in his hands and rubbed them together. Zenovia inhaled as Tristan's drier-sheets scent filled the car. She pretended not to notice when he sat close enough for their thighs to touch, even though there was plenty of room in the car.

Tristan asked, "Why aren't you at school? You sick?"

"No. Phillip and my mom are celebrating their engagement."

"Wow!" Tristan exclaimed. "That's great, Zee!"

To punctuate his exclamation even further, Tristan ever-so-casually rested his arm on Zenovia's leg. *You ain't slick*, thought Zenovia with a tiny smile.

"If you say so. So why aren't you and Kyle at school?" Zenovia asked.

"Oh, we only have to go half a day. We get out after our morning vocational classes."

Zenovia wrinkled her nose. "Vocational classes? You mean like wood shop and auto repair?"

"Well, I'm actually in the dental health specialist class. You have a problem with people learning a trade?"

Zenovia bit her lip. She didn't have a problem with vocational programs for people who needed them. But she *did* have an issue with someone as smart and articulate as Tristan blowing his chances at a college education.

"Nah, Tristan. I don't have a problem with it."

Tristan lowered his defenses. "Good, because we've got a great Data Processing program at Carver. You will be going to Carver when Phillip and your mom get married, right?"

Zenovia nodded slowly. She hadn't even thought that far ahead. Switching schools in her senior year of high school was definitely not a part of her plans. But she knew that she could succeed anywhere and the thought of seeing Tristan on a daily basis was enough to make learning fun.

"I guess I will be transferring, but I won't be taking a Data Processing class. I've got too many scholarships riding on my college prep classes."

Tristan looked disappointed. "You still on that college stuff?"

"Yeah. Still on the college stuff."

"Zee..."

"Look, Tristan, let's not have this conversation again. There's nothing you can say that will make me change my mind. If the apocalypse comes while I'm in school, then oh well."

"I wasn't going to try to convince you again."

"Oh. Well, then what were you going to say?"

"Um..."

Kyle tapped on the window. *Dang! Dang! Dang!* Tristan moved his arm from her body as if she were wearing acid blue jeans. And just when Zenovia thought that Tristan was about to declare his love. Or like. Or whatever.

Zenovia hissed, "The door is unlocked, Kyle. Get in the front seat."

Kyle jumped in the front seat and looked from Tristan to Zenovia. He raised a suspicious eyebrow.

"Did I interrupt something?"

"No." Zenovia said. "You didn't."

Tristan added, "Zee's mom is marrying Brother Phillip."

"That's cool. Did you tell her about Justin?"

"I was about to."

With a confused look on her face Zenovia asked, "Tell me what?"

"I think Justin likes you."

Wrong, wrong, wrong, and the total opposite of right. Why in the world would this be happening? Tristan was supposed to be asking her to be his girlfriend.

"Why do y'all think that? Justin is just being nice to me."

Tristan shook his head. "I know my brother. He likes you. But he likes a lot of girls, so I just wanted to warn you."

"So are you gonna talk to him?" Kyle asked with excitement in his eyes.

His question caught Zenovia off guard. "What? N-no."

There was absolutely no conviction in her response. Zenovia was a horrible liar, and she just couldn't promise that she wouldn't *talk* to Justin. Especially if Tristan never made a move.

"Well, you shouldn't, Zee. I don't think he's the one for you," Tristan said.

Zenovia puffed air into her cheeks, feeling utter frustration at Tristan's roundabout way of saying nothing. She decided to change the subject.

"Do y'all know Bryce Goodman?"

Kyle replied, "Yeah. He's a minister. Just gave a sermon at the regional meeting."

"He's friends with Brother Phillip," Tristan added.

"I know. He's going to be the best man in their wedding."

"Well," Kyle said, "I don't like him. He's pretty foul to his wife."

"You don't know that, Kyle."

Kyle frowned deeply and crossed his arms defiantly. "I know what I saw with my own two eyes, Tristan. If I hadn't walked up on him, I think he would have hit her."

"That's so sad," Zenovia said, thinking of her vision. A cheater and an abuser?

"Zee, the Bible says to 'touch not my anointed and do my prophets no harm.' That means that you guys have no right talking bad about Brother Bryce."

Zenovia pressed her lips together tightly to keep from cutting Tristan to shreds with her words. How anointed could Bryce be if he was meeting up with women in alleys and going upside his wife's head?

Audrey and Phillip, apparently finished with their lunch, walked back to the car arm in arm. Zenovia marveled at how normal they looked, or rather how normal Audrey looked. Tristan stepped out of the car and hugged Phillip.

"Congratulations, brother! Zenovia just told us your good news."

"Thanks, man." Phillip glanced over at Zenovia. "You're not thinking of going down the same path, are you?"

Tristan laughed out loud. "Nah, man! Not me. I'm gonna be single and loving it until I'm forty."

"You keep hanging around pretty girls like Zenovia, I'm not sure that's going to happen. Girls like her can be quite tempting."

Zenovia scowled. This was the second time that Phillip had made a comment questioning her chastity.

"Aw, Phillip. Zee and I are just friends. Right, Zee?"

Zenovia could literally feel her blood evaporating from anger. Was this how it was going to be with Tristan? Was he always going to flirt and be sweet to her only when no one was around?

"Yeah. We're just friends. Like siblings almost." The

sarcasm dripped from Zenovia's tone like a melting ice-cream cone.

Then Kyle had to chime in. "And Zenovia is not really Tristan's type."

"I don't have a type, yet," Tristan said.

"Do tell, Kyle," instigated Zenovia. "What is Tristan's type?"

"Well, he likes them stylish with long flowing hair. What did you say, Tristan? When your wife enters the room, everybody is going to stop and look at her. Right?"

Tristan bit his lip sheepishly, "I guess I did say that, but I really wasn't thinking of anyone in particular."

Anyone like who, Tristan? Mia perhaps? Zenovia felt a knot form in her throat and she knew she was on the brink of tears. Could Kyle be any less subtle? But he was just confirming what Zenovia already felt deep down— the Tristans of the world would always be with the girls like Mia.

Audrey's eyes darkened with anger. "Well, Tristan isn't Zenovia's type either. She likes those college boys."

Even though Zenovia was furious with Audrey about the medication drama, she could've jumped up and said, *"Thank you, Mommy!"*

"Okay, right! I'm gonna bring home a doctor from Howard."

Tristan made a facial expression that Zenovia couldn't interpret. He said, "The Brethren could definitely use more doctors."

"Well, we've wasted enough time chatting with y'all," declared Kyle. "There are lives out here to be saved."

As soon as he started the car, Phillip and Audrey

began their inane wedding preparation talk. Zenovia could barely stand to listen to the two of them go on about their lives when she'd just experienced such a blow.

Tristan had dropped the mother lode of definitions. He had broken it down so that it could forever be broke. He had defined their relationship.

There wasn't one.

Chapter Nine

"What are we going to do with your hair?"

Zenovia scrunched her nose into a frown. She didn't like the disgust in Mia's tone when she asked the question, nor did she like the use of the word "we" when referring to a concern that only involved Zenovia.

Alyssa chimed in. "Yeah, Zee. Your hair has to be fly for your mother's wedding."

Zenovia could strangle Audrey for forcing her to attend this slumber party in Tristan's basement rec room. It was the night before the wedding, and Audrey had a lot of last-minute running around to do with Charlotte for the special occasion.

Charlotte had suggested the sleepover so that the girls would be out of their hair, but Zenovia was one hundred percent against it. First of all, Audrey had cut her meds down to once a day, instead of twice a day. So far Zenovia hadn't seen any drastic changes in behavior, but that could change in an instant, and Zenovia wanted to be on hand if it did. If Charlotte said the wrong thing or set Audrey off, it would be tragic.

Second, Zenovia had absolutely nothing in common with Alyssa or Mia—especially Mia. It would almost feel like punishment spending the evening with them, since Zenovia was clueless on their areas of expertise—makeup, clothes, and boys.

"*I'm* going to put curls in it tomorrow. That's why I have it wrapped right now."

"Oh, that's what you call that?" Mia asked. "It's wrapped?"

Zenovia rolled her eyes. Her hair was plastered to her scalp, and she would comb and fluff it in the morning, before adding curls. The definition of a wrap. But of course the two longhairs sitting in front of her had no idea what she was talking about.

Alyssa said, "Oh, yeah. I saw a girl at the salon getting her hair wrapped. It looked hard, like a turtle's shell or something. Why don't you just let your hair grow?"

She might as well have asked Zenovia for the meaning of life. Zenovia rocked that short hairstyle like nobody's business, but truthfully she suffered from a severe case of hair envy. She wanted bouncing and behaving locks that draped across her shoulder or pulled up into a high ponytail.

But Zenovia lied. "I don't let my hair grow because I like it short."

The truth was that her hair was short because of years of chemical processing to try and make "good hair" out of her kinky curls.

"Seriously? Both of my brothers say that boys like girls to have long hair," Alyssa said.

"Well, maybe I don't care about what boys think." Zenovia lied again. "Especially your brothers."

Mia laughed. "I'm sorry, but I do care what they think. Speaking of which, I think I just heard Tristan in the kitchen, so I'm gonna sneak upstairs and say hi."

Alyssa giggled as Mia ran up the stairs. They could hear her saying, "What's up, Tristan?" Zenovia felt her stomach lurch.

"Do you really not like Tristan?" Alyssa whispered.

Zenovia sighed. What would admitting that she liked him prove?

Alyssa continued. "I only ask because I think he really likes you. He might not say it, but I think he does."

"Your brother is not thinking about me, Alyssa, but if he was, I'd probably talk to him."

"You *do* like him! Why didn't you tell me?"

"Because I didn't want you to think I was your friend because of it."

Alyssa laughed as if the thought would've never occurred to her. "Girl, please! I wouldn't think that. A lot of girls like Tristan and Justin."

Mia came back downstairs with Tristan in tow. Zenovia hadn't spoken to him since he'd burst her bubble, and she was in no mood to talk to him now.

Mia gushed, "I asked Tristan if he wanted to play Monopoly with us."

"Do y'all mind?" he asked. Even though he said "y'all," he was looking at Zenovia.

She didn't reply, but Alyssa did, "Of course we don't mind, big broham."

"What about you, Zee?" pressed Tristan. "Do you mind?"

"No."

Zenovia avoided eye contact with Tristan as Alyssa

set up the game pieces. She could feel him smiling in her direction, but she wasn't ready to let him off the hook.

While Zenovia took her time processing what Alyssa had revealed, Mia didn't waste any time with flirting. Zenovia thought she would vomit if Mia batted her eyelashes one more time or tossed her hair any harder.

"So, Tristan," Mia asked, "have you told Zenovia your good news?"

"No. I hadn't gotten a chance."

Alyssa did the honors. "Tristan got accepted to serve at the Brethren headquarters in Boston. Justin did too. Tristan leaves at the end of the school year and Justin leaves in a month."

Zenovia blinked rapidly. Tristan was leaving? She'd gotten baptized and joined a church to make him notice her, but now he was leaving. And Justin too.

"Congratulations," Zenovia said.

"I'll be home on the holidays and stuff like that. But I'm excited. I've been looking forward to this for a long time."

Zenovia nodded, but she didn't smile. She was trying too hard to keep from bursting into tears.

Seeming to sense Zenovia's heartbreak Alyssa said, "But the summer is a long way off. We've got plenty of time to hang with Tristan."

The wedding was simple, elegant, and beautiful. Audrey had floated effortlessly down the aisle looking as if she'd stepped right out of a bridal magazine in her one-hundred-dollar dress and cheap costume jewelry. She was radiant and as much as Phillip had annoyed Zenovia, he'd looked radiant too.

Now everyone was at the Batistes' house for the reception. Charlotte had spent a great deal of time making gourmet appetizers and finger foods. The cake had been done by one of the sisters at the Northeast Devotion Center at no charge.

Zenovia sat in a corner smoothing the skirt of her affordable, handed-down two-piece satin gown. The hunter-green shade was Audrey's favorite color, but it also suited Zenovia well. The smooth material hugged her petite and curvaceous shape in all the right places.

Zenovia had separated herself from the crowd when Bryce Goodman entered the festively decorated recreation room. She was concerned that seeing him and his wife together would trigger another vision. So she watched the action from her seat as she sipped on overly sweet sherbet-filled punch.

She noticed Tristan smile at her from across the room, but she turned away quickly. She still hadn't recovered from hearing his "good news" and still hadn't forgotten about his list of girlfriend qualifications.

But, against her wishes, Tristan crossed the room and sat down next to her. "You don't look like you're having fun."

"I am."

Tristan chuckled lightly. "How long are you going to keep this up?"

"Keep what up?" Zenovia's tone displayed her irritation. She didn't appreciate Tristan taking her feelings lightly.

"The two-word replies to everything. You hardly said anything at all to me last night."

"Well, since you seemed to be engaged by Mia's

incessant chatter, I chose to give my vocal cords a rest."

"Zee, did I do something wrong? I thought we were getting to be friends. I'm looking forward to you coming to Carver."

Zenovia shook her head slowly. Did he really not know why she was upset? Perhaps his flirtations were all in her mind and all Tristan ever really wanted from her was friendship. Maybe her own strong attraction to him was causing her to think otherwise.

"Tristan, you're fine. I've just got a lot going on, I guess. My mother has never been married, so it's going to be an adjustment."

"Well, if you ever want to talk about it, I'm here for you. Even after I go to Boston, we can still write and call one another."

Zenovia managed to give Tristan a smile. "All right. I'd like that."

"It's time to toast the happy couple!" Bryce Goodman's booming voice snatched Zenovia into an unwanted vision.

Bryce sits in a room with two other men, both older than he is. All three of them hold notepads, in which they scribble furiously.

"How many times did this happen?" asks Bryce.

"I'm not sure. I didn't count." This voice belongs to Zenovia.

"If you were truly repentant, you would be more forth-coming with information."

Zenovia rakes her hand through her hair. She looks tired and irritated. Her face is tear-streaked and red. "I'm sorry. I guess I just don't know what you want to hear."

"I'm sorry, too," Bryce says as he closes his notebook.

Tristan touched Zenovia's arm gently. "Zee, you're shaking. Are you okay?"

Zenovia looked down at her hands. She was shaking, and she didn't know for how long. Apparently the toast was finished because people were back to talking and laughing.

She willed her hands to stop trembling, but they did not obey. Up until now, her visions had always been about other people. She'd never had a vision that included her own life, and it was terrifying.

She could still feel the hurt and desperation that her future self was experiencing in the vision. But the vision had been so short and so out of context that she had no idea when or why it would occur. What would she need to be repentant about? And why would she have to prove that to anyone, especially Bryce Goodman?

"I'm going to get you some water, Zee. You look like you're about to faint."

She shook her head. "No, Tristan, don't. I'm fine. Plus Mia is trying to get your attention."

"She is?" Tristan asked, just a bit too happily for Zenovia's liking.

Normally Zenovia would never knowingly send her crush into the arms of another girl, but she needed time to compose herself. She closed her eyes and took deep breaths. Slowly her heart rate returned to normal.

She opened her eyes to Justin, standing in front of her with his arms crossed and grinning mischievously.

"What?" Zenovia asked.

"Are you coming to my going-away party?"

"Sure."

"It's going to be at the Roller Palace."

Zenovia laughed. "You're having a skating party?"

"Yeah. What's wrong with that?"

"You don't seem like a skater."

Justin sat down. "And you don't seem like the type to fall for Tristan, but clearly you have."

"I'm not Tristan's type."

"Tristan doesn't even know what he likes!" Justin replied with a hearty laugh.

"Are you playing matchmaker?"

"Nope. Just wanted to see where your head was at."

Zenovia cringed. "There was a preposition at the end of your sentence, Justin."

He took a flower from the bouquet Zenovia was still clutching and tucked it into her curls. She couldn't contain her smile.

He stood from his seat and leaned to whisper in her ear. "Well, if you're not Tristan's type, he's an idiot."

Chapter Ten

This is your room, Zenovia. I hope you like it."

Zenovia bit her lip and shifted a box of her belongings from one arm to the other. The walls were painted powder blue and there were rainbow borders near the ceiling and floor. It was a child's room.

"Thank you, Phillip."

Phillip beamed. "It took me an entire weekend to decorate this room. Audrey said that you liked blue."

Audrey called from the living room. "Where are you guys?"

"We're in here."

Audrey pushed the door to the room open wide. She laughed out loud. "Phillip, baby, this room is for a five-year-old!"

Phillip looked hurt, so Zenovia tried to intervene, "It's okay, Mom. Before long, I'll be going to college anyway."

Audrey kissed her forehead. "You're right. I guess it doesn't matter too much then."

Phillip frowned deeply. "College? I thought we had talked about this, Audrey."

Zenovia ignored Phillip's comment and continued. "Yep. Howard University. I'm going to be a computer programmer."

Phillip was not pleased. "Audrey, you know how the Brethren feel about a college education."

"And I know how hard my daughter has worked for this. No one is taking this away from her."

"We'll discuss this further. Just the two of us," Phillip replied with anger rising in his voice.

"Ain't nothing to discuss."

Audrey turned sharply and walked out of the room. Phillip's expression was indecisive, but Zenovia knew that this was not a time to pursue an argument with her mother. She'd seen Audrey teetering near the edge of reason before, and this was clearly one of those times.

"Don't go after her," Zenovia stated. It was as much a command as it was a suggestion.

Phillip laughed. "You think I don't know how to handle a woman?"

"I think you don't know how to handle *this* woman. Trust me, Phillip. She's only half-medicated."

"I'm not afraid of your mother."

Zenovia responded with a seriousness that no seventeen-year-old should possess. "Let it go. It's not an argument worth having."

"This time I'll let it go, but you need to know that I'm the man of this house."

"Okay…"

"And now that we've exchanged vows, your mother belongs to me."

"Meaning?"

"Meaning that you don't have a say anymore. You're a child and I'll have you removed from my house if you ever defy me again."

Zenovia blinked rapidly, trying to comprehend this thinly veiled threat. This was the man of Audrey's vision? For the first time Zenovia wondered if the visions came from a source other than God.

Zenovia pulled on the tan rental skates and tied up the worn brown laces. She was at Justin's going-away party, but didn't feel much like partying. Her mood was still somber from witnessing the apparent decline of her mother's mental health. And it was all because Phillip was looking to God for a healing.

Zenovia wasn't the greatest skater in the world and she hadn't been on wheels since she was in middle school. She wobbled to her feet and was struggling to maintain her balance when a thin teenage boy whipped past her and caused her to fall into the lockers. She narrowed her eyes angrily in the boy's direction. He turned on his skates, mouthed the words, "I'm sorry," and flashed Zenovia one of the prettiest smiles she'd ever seen.

Her rage went up in smoke.

Alyssa rushed to help Zenovia to her feet. Echoing Zenovia's thoughts she said, "He's a cutie."

"Yes, he is. Do you know him?" Zenovia asked.

"Are you trying to play my brother, Zee?"

Zenovia laughed out loud. "In order to play him, wouldn't he have to be my boyfriend?"

"I guess so. But you don't want to talk to Emil."

"That's the cutie's name? Emil?" Satisfied that she had regained her balance, Zenovia skated in a little circle.

"Yes, but he's bad news."

"How so?"

"His mom is one of the Brethren, but he refuses to get baptized."

This intrigued Zenovia, since she'd had her own doubts. "I'm sure he has his reasons."

"Well, whatever they are, they can't be good ones."

Tristan and Mia stumbled toward them. They were holding hands and trying not to crash into the lockers. Zenovia involuntarily rolled her eyes. Even though she couldn't control her hopeless attraction to Tristan, he still got on her last nerves.

He asked, "Are you two going to skate or just hold up the wall?"

Alyssa replied for the both of them. "We're skating. We're just trying to build up our nerve."

At that moment, Mia completely lost her balance and fell right into Tristan's arms. She giggled flirtatiously and took her time steadying herself again. Tristan also didn't seem to be in a hurry.

Zenovia blinked back tears and skated away as quickly as possible. She could hear Mia still giggling as she asked, "What's wrong with her?"

Zenovia made a mad dash onto the skate floor and not-so-deftly avoided collisions with several skaters. Justin zoomed past her and grinned. She gave him a weak smile as she safely made her way to the center of the rink. That was where the newbies tried to learn and the "real skaters" perfected their moves.

A worn-out, carpeted bench called to Zenovia and

not a moment too soon. Her knees and ankles felt wobbly and she didn't want to have another wipeout. She fell onto the bench and sighed. She had the perfect seat for people watching because the lights were dimmed on the skate floor and she could see the entire rink.

Justin plopped down next to Zenovia on his next trip around the rink. "Are you having fun?"

"I am," Zenovia replied without any indication in her voice that it was true.

He laughed out loud. "You are so convincing."

"I try so hard, Justin," Zenovia joked with her characteristic sarcasm. "But you just see right through me."

"Are you just gonna let Mia take your man like that?" Justin asked.

"Wow..."

Zenovia tried hard to think of a response that would make any sense. Of course, she wanted to sock Mia in the jaw and lay claim to her "boyfriend," but it wasn't that simple. There was the ever-present pride factor and the little nagging truth that Tristan had made exactly zero verifiable romantic overtures.

Zenovia added, "If she can take him, then he's not mine, right?"

"I am so glad to hear you say that. Now skate with me."

"Thanks anyway, Justin," Zenovia said. "I think I'll just sit right here."

"Suit yourself then. There are many a deserving lady out there looking to skate with me."

Zenovia laughed. "Great! Then go make someone's day."

Justin stroked her face right before he skated away. Normally, Zenovia would've been thinking of the germs left behind by his sweaty hand. But every touch from Justin was full of electricity.

Zenovia refused to let herself think of pursuing Justin. For starters, he was leaving and she didn't want a pen pal for a boyfriend. Second, he enjoyed the girls who fell all over themselves to hook up with him. Zenovia was not planning to become one of those girls.

Since she didn't feel like skating or getting run over, Zenovia decided to watch the "real skaters." She was fascinated by the jumps and twirls although she could never imagine herself doing any of it.

Of particular interest to Zenovia was the Brethren-rebel Emil. He twirled like a figure skater and then dropped to the ground, extended one leg, and continued to spin until he fell flat on his butt. A couple of other skaters clapped and congratulated him on his technique.

Zenovia hadn't realized how hard she was staring at him until they locked eyes. Emil sat right in the middle of the floor and smiled at Zenovia. She quickly looked away, but it didn't stop him from skating over.

Emil hit the toe-stopper on his skates about two inches away from Zenovia. She pretended not to see him, but she couldn't help but return his smile. He was wearing a thick gold herringbone chain with an E dangling from the center.

She looked up at his still-grinning face and asked, "What's the E stand for? Ernest? Earl? Edwin?"

"Earl? Do I look like an Earl?" Emil asked with a laugh.

"Nah. You look like a skinny skater dude. Possibly named Earl."

"The E stands for Emil."

"Good to meet you, Emil."

He sat down on the bench. "So did you just come here to watch or are you skating at all?"

"I'm actually only here because it's a going-away party for my friend," explained Zenovia. "I can't skate."

Emil nodded. "Who's your friend?"

"Justin Batiste."

"Oh, one of them Heights boys." Emil's frown displayed a great amount of disdain.

"Heights boy? Oh, 'cause he lives in Cleveland Heights, right?"

"Yeah. That's your friend?"

Zenovia nodded. "He's pretty cool."

"I didn't take you for a Heights chick, though. You seem kinda down."

Zenovia laughed. "And how did you come to that conclusion?"

"'Cause you looked like you wanted to beat me down when I crashed into you. Heights girls don't fight. That's all hood."

"Wow! I'm definitely not a Heights girl, but I'm not a hood chick either, sir."

Emil seemed thrilled, "Really? Where you stay at?"

"I used to stay in King Kennedy, but we just moved."

"King Kennedy! Yikes, girl, you are more hood than me."

Zenovia shook her head. "The projects do not define me."

"All right then."

Emil stood up and got ready to skate away. Zenovia frowned. "Aren't you forgetting something?"

"What?" Emil asked.

"Aren't you gonna ask me my name?"

He smiled again. "It's Zenovia, right? I already asked around, sweetie."

"Sweetie? You're a little presumptuous, aren't you?"

"Not at all. I can see the future, and I see you and me together."

Zenovia shook her head. "Wow. That was so corny."

Emil winked at Zenovia with one of his big beautiful doe eyes that didn't seem to match his thug persona. He skated off behind a line of boys who were doing a step. They crossed their legs simultaneously, then leaned back and swiveled their hips toward a crowd of screaming girls.

Zenovia's eyes followed Emil around the rink until she caught the gaze of a disapproving Tristan. His eyes were narrowed into little slits and his arms were crossed angrily. Zenovia chuckled at his audacity. No, he did not have the gall to be glaring her down, not when he'd spent the whole evening yukking it up with Mia.

Zenovia took a deep breath and decided that she didn't care about Tristan anymore. He was obviously more susceptible to hair-flinging than intellect. Plus Emil said that he could see the future.

Chapter Eleven

For the first time Zenovia stepped through the doors of Carver High School. It was just a new school, but to Zenovia it felt like another world. The huge center hallway reminded her of a preppy private school from the Disney teen movies with its litter-free floor and freshly painted lockers.

The students were a different breed, too. Everywhere Zenovia looked there were Tommy Hilfiger ensembles and Gap jackets. The black kids at Carver didn't sound like kids from the hood—their dialects had been groomed for college educations that weren't necessitated by an athletic scholarship.

Zenovia felt like a polar bear on a Caribbean isle.

She let out an involuntary sigh of relief when she saw Alyssa walking down the hallway in her direction. Zenovia exhaled again when she noted that Alyssa was alone and not flanked by her two least-favorite people— Mia and Tristan. The three of them seemed to be joined by some invisible preppy umbilical cord.

"Hey, Zee! Are you digging Carver so far?" Alyssa asked.

Zenovia didn't even try to hide the sarcastic smirk that graced her lips. "I'm trying, but it's so different from West Marshall."

"And that's a bad thing?" Alyssa asked as she laughed. "Have you seen Tristan this morning?"

Zenovia shook her head. "Nope. Honestly, I'm just trying to figure out how to get from point A to point B in this maze of a school. I don't have time to check for a boy who isn't checking for me."

"Wow. Where'd all that come from?"

Zenovia shrugged. She couldn't truthfully answer the question because she didn't know where the sour sentiment had come from. Deep down she knew that she wasn't completely through with Tristan—he'd made too much of an impression on her for that. But her pride wasn't going to let her continue to declare her strong like for him when he clearly wasn't interested.

Zenovia finally replied. "Maybe I'm just tripping because Emil called me."

"Skater dude Emil?"

"Yes, Emil from the skating rink," Zenovia corrected, Somehow *skater dude* sounded like a diss.

"What did you guys talk about?"

"Nothing really. We just got to know each other. He's really cool."

Zenovia waited for Alyssa's judgment, but none came. She seemed to ponder the information for a moment and looked as if she had a comment, but she kept it to herself.

"What is your first-period class?" Alyssa asked ending the uncomfortable silence.

"Looks like I have French III first period."

"With Mr. Arnold?"

Zenovia glanced down at her schedule. "Yes, I have Mr. Arnold."

"Tristan and Kyle are in that class," Alyssa said. She punctuated her thought with a sly grin that Zenovia wanted to wipe right off her face.

"Why in the world would either of them be in a French class? I thought they were taking vocational classes."

"They are, but learning a foreign language will help them when they get ready to serve as Brethren missionaries."

"Great. That's just great."

Alyssa giggled and replied, "Your classroom is on the second floor at the end of the hallway."

Zenovia threw her backpack over her shoulder and trudged up the huge center staircase. At her old school she'd never felt self-conscious about her lack of designer clothing, but here Zenovia was bombarded with an endless stream of hundred-dollar jeans and name-brand tennis shoes. She looked at the ground and tried not to bump into anyone on her way to class.

Zenovia entered the classroom as the final bell sounded. Involuntarily she took a quick glance around the room and spotted Tristan. She handed a copy of her schedule to Mr. Arnold and slid into the first available desk.

"Psst!" Tristan signaled from the back of the room. Zenovia pretended not to hear him.

"Zee! Sit back here with us!" Tristan whispered even louder.

Zenovia narrowed her eyes and glared over at Tristan.

She was working on her slow fade into high-school obscurity, and he had picked that one moment in time to become relentless.

Unwilling to move from her seat or give Tristan any satisfaction at all, Zenovia continued to ignore him. While she was glaring she noticed that he was wearing a blue button-down Tommy Hilfiger shirt with a hunter-green sweater vest. He wouldn't have lasted five minutes at her old school with that outfit on. He would've been an instant mark.

Zenovia only half-listened to Mr. Arnold's lesson. As advanced as Carver was supposed to be, they were far behind the Honors French class at West Marshall. Zenovia had been working on translations at her old school, but Carver was still conjugating verbs.

When the bell rang, Zenovia made a mad dash for the door. She had Honors English for her second-period class, and she was relieved. Tristan wasn't taking this class so she wouldn't have to look at him for another fifty-five minutes.

She got halfway down the hallway and thought she was home free. But she was wrong. Tristan and Kyle ran up on either side of her and tried to match her pace for pace.

Tristan said, "Kyle, if I didn't know any better, I'd think that Zee was avoiding us."

"I don't think she's avoiding us," Kyle replied. "I think she's avoiding you."

Zenovia rolled her eyes, "I'm not avoiding either of you."

"Then why did you ignore me when I was trying to get your attention in class?" Tristan asked.

Zenovia blew her swoop bang out of her eye and sighed. How could she explain any of this to him without revealing her feelings? She opened her mouth to respond, but had no idea what words were about to form.

"Listen, Tristan, this is how I am at school. I go to class, I don't talk to anyone, and then I go home. That's what I do. It's not about you or Kyle."

Tristan's beaming smile turned into a wounded frown. "You won't even talk to us? We're your friends."

Zenovia looked at Kyle and then Tristan. How could he be so sincere, but yet be completely oblivious to how she felt about him? How could he not know that she wanted more than friendship? Zenovia thought that her feelings were written all over her face.

"I have to get to class," she finally said as the warning bell sounded.

"What period do you have lunch?" Tristan asked, not giving up.

"Fourth."

"See you in the cafeteria. We sit by the Coke machine in the corner."

Zenovia let out an irritated sigh and jogged the rest of the way to her class. Fortunately, none of the Brethren were in this class, so she was free to disappear at her own leisure.

She spent the entire fifty-five minutes half-listening to her teacher and scribbling doodles in her notebook. She wrote Emil's name in big curlicue letters and smiled wistfully at the thought of him.

Zenovia had grossly misrepresented her and Emil's telephone call, and with good reason. She was not the type of girl to tell everyone her business. Growing up with Audrey had made her an expert at keeping secrets.

The conversation that she'd had with Emil was so real and simple. And so incredible. They related to each other on so many levels. Both of them had grown up with single parents, although his father lived close by and was around from time to time. The best part about talking to Emil was that he was completely unashamed of liking Zenovia.

Unlike some other people.

At lunchtime Zenovia stood at the entrance of the cafeteria and considered not going in. She didn't get the opportunity to ponder for too long, because Mia and Alyssa walked in behind her.

"Come on, girl!" Alyssa exclaimed. "Why are you standing out here?"

"Hi, Zee!" Mia said.

Zenovia replied, "Hello, Mia."

Mia gave Zenovia a tight smile and rushed over to where Kyle and Tristan were sitting. Alyssa hung back with Zenovia who was still taking her time, even though she was pretty hungry.

"Why did you say hi to Mia like that?" Alyssa asked.

Zenovia feigned innocence. "Like what?"

"You were really cold, Zee, like you two have beef or something."

Zenovia glanced at Mia who had her head tossed back in laughter. Surely Tristan couldn't be saying something that was *that* funny.

"No, Alyssa, you're wrong. What could we possibly be beefing about?" Zenovia punctuated her question with a sarcastic grin.

Zenovia and Alyssa joined their Brethren friends at the lunch table. Kyle smiled up at them, but Tristan was engrossed in conversation with Mia.

"And can you believe that she got caught fornicating with Hakeem right in her parents' bedroom?" Mia asked.

Tristan replied, "Wow. These young people obviously don't understand that we are living in the end times."

"I know!" Mia exclaimed. "If the end doesn't come before I'm grown, I can wait until I get married. Fornication is not worth my life."

Zenovia shook her head and rolled her eyes. Were they really saying "fornicating" instead of "having sex"? Who talked like that?

"Looks like somebody has a crush," Kyle said as he flipped through the pages of Zenovia's notebook.

"Give me that!" Zenovia replied as she snatched her notebook away from him.

Tristan's eyes lit up. "Who does Zee have a crush on?"

Zenovia felt her nostrils flare angrily. Did Tristan think she was doodling about his unresponsive self?

She replied, "None of your business."

"Emil!" Alyssa blurted.

Tristan's face contorted into a fatherly frown. "The hood character from the skating rink, right? He's not baptized."

"So what?" Zenovia asked. Her attitude was apparent in her tone and in her stance.

"Baptized members of the Brethren," Tristan explained, "are held to a higher standard. If the end comes before Emil goes down in the water, it's too late for him."

Alyssa interjected, "That's right, Zenovia, but you're safe. You've been baptized."

"She's safe as long as she stays sin-free," Kyle said.

Zenovia's mind reeled. No one had told her before she got baptized as a Brethren that she would only be able to talk to boys who were baptized. No one had told her about the higher standard. And who could ever remain sin-free? Had the Brethren not heard the scripture at Romans 3:23? She'd learned it in Sunday school.

Zenovia asked, "Don't you know your Bible, Kyle? It says in Romans that all have sinned and fall short of the glory of God."

"Oh, that's your life before you become a Brethren," Tristan says. "But now you've been purified. Don't mess it up dealing with a guy like Emil."

The entire conversation weighed heavily on Zenovia's mind for the rest of the day. She was still pondering it all when she met Emil after school for burgers. They'd chosen the mall in her old hood, because she didn't want to run into any of her Brethren friends.

While they stood in line at Burger King, Zenovia stole glances at Emil. She wanted to take him all in without being obvious. His outfit was all hood, not prep school like Tristan. He had on layered T-shirts, jeans with a bit of a sag, and Timberland boots. Of course, he was rocking his gold herringbone chain.

When their food was ready they sat down at one of the mall tables. They were right out in the open—in full view of anyone that might walk by, including members of the Brethren. Emil didn't look over his shoulder, like Tristan did. He didn't care who saw them together. Thinking about her closet friendship with Tristan made Zenovia's mood melancholy.

"What's wrong, baby girl?" Emil asked as he took a huge bite out of his hamburger.

"What's wrong with you, ordering a burger with no pickles or onions?"

Emil rewarded Zenovia's joke with his slow and sexy smile. "You listened to my order? Well, you can remember that because soon you'll be getting my food."

Zenovia laughed out loud. "Boy, please! Do I look like your butler?"

"No, but that's what a good woman does. She takes care of her man."

"You Brethren guys are male chauvinists!"

Emil frowned and turned serious. "I am not a Brethren guy."

"You're not?"

"Nah, but I didn't know that mattered to you. I should've guessed, right? You hang with some of the biggest Brethren drones in Cleveland."

"Why do you call them drones?"

Emil's smile returned. "A drone is a worker bee. Their entire purpose in life is to get food for the queen and build the nest. They work themselves to death, never stopping once to enjoy the flowers they touch everyday."

Zenovia gazed at Emil for a moment, then she burst into laughter. "Wow, Emil! You're so deep!"

"Shut up! You know what I mean," replied Emil as he threw a French fry at Zenovia.

"I do understand. Is that why you're not baptized? You don't want to become a drone too?"

Emil explained, "Listen, I'll do it when it's right for me. I love God, but I'm not about to get baptized because

the masses are doing it, or because my mother is hounding me."

"Is your mother hounding you?" Zenovia asked.

"Man, is she ever. She wants her little friends at the
Devotion Center to pay her some attention."

"That must tire her out, you know, trying to impress
people," Zenovia said.

Emil shook his head. "She never gets tired of it."

The mood had gotten heavy, so Zenovia tried to
lighten it up. "Are we going to get these roller skates or
what?"

Emil smiled and rubbed his palms together. "Yes, absolutely. Let's go upstairs to Nickle's Sporting Goods."

They started upstairs to the sporting goods store, and
Emil casually took Zenovia's hand. The touch was sweet,
spontaneous, and out of the blue. It seemed like nothing, but it was enough to hurtle Zenovia into a vision.

*She lay naked across a small bed, with a sheet draped over
her body. Emil strokes her face as she slowly wakes.*

"Is it morning?" she asks.

*Emil smiles and sings part of a Shirley Murdock song,
"It's morning."*

*She scrunches her nose into a frown. "That song is about
adultery. We're not adulterers."*

*"Nah, but we're fornicators, though. Your Brethren
friends won't be happy about this."*

"I don't care what they think," Zenovia says.

"Yes, you do, but it's okay. We won't tell them."

*Emil takes Zenovia's face in his hands and covers her lips
with his own. It's a deep lover's kiss, and it sends shock waves
through her entire body.*

It was a short vision, but it was enough to rattle Zenovia. She didn't feel herself squeezing Emil's hand as they walked into the sporting goods store.

"Are you all right, baby girl?" Emil asked as he shook his hand free.

Zenovia was annoyed that she couldn't pull herself together quickly. "I'm fine."

"You sure? 'Cause you're kind of blushing. If you can't handle holding hands with me, I'll understand."

"You're so funny, Emil."

He leaned over and kissed her on the cheek. "And I'm magically delicious."

"Ewww!"

Zenovia laughed nervously at his joke, knowing that at some point in time she might actually get a taste of Emil. Oddly enough, the nervousness Zenovia felt didn't come from the act of losing her virginity. It came from worrying what would happen if the Brethren found out.

Chapter Twelve

Do you believe in fate?" Zenovia asked Tristan.

They were sitting at the game table in the Batistes' basement, waiting for Mia and Alyssa to decide on which board game they were going to play. The choices were among Monopoly, Scrabble, and Taboo. Zenovia was partial to Scrabble. She was a *beast* in Scrabble. All that studying for the SAT test gave her a vocabulary advantage over most other teenagers.

Zenovia was still thinking of the vision she'd had of herself and Emil. She knew that having sex with Emil would be wrong, and she had no inclination to sin against God. But if the visions were to be trusted, something was going to change. Something was going to drive her to a place she didn't want to be. She wondered if it was truly inevitable.

"I don't believe in fate," Tristan replied after pondering the question. "I do believe in destiny, though."

Zenovia nodded slowly and said, "Don't you think they're pretty much the same thing?"

"Nah. You don't have any control over fate, right?"

"Right."

"But destiny...I think destiny is like God's divine plan for your life. But you can choose to accept it or not."

Zenovia let Tristan's explanation sink in. She couldn't think of how she could be destined to sleep with Emil out of wedlock. Certainly that would not be God's plan for her life.

Before she got a chance to counter Tristan's idea, Mia and Alyssa came back downstairs with their game choice. Zenovia rolled her eyes when she saw the turquoise-colored box in Mia's hand. They were playing Taboo.

"Tristan, Kyle called when we were upstairs," Alyssa said.

When she didn't relay any message, Tristan asked, "And?"

"Oh. He's not coming over tonight."

Mia gave a fake frown. "Aw...that's too bad. Did he say why?"

Kyle sits in the middle of a bedroom floor, gripping a Bible and a letter in his hands. Tears rush down his cheeks and drip onto the leather-bound book. His arms are also dripping. With blood.

"Tristan, why don't we go check on Kyle?" Zenovia asked.

The three other teenagers looked at her strangely. Perhaps it was the desperation in her tone, or maybe it had been apparent when she'd zoned out. The vision seemed to only last a few seconds, but Zenovia never knew how she appeared to others when she was having one.

Mia whined, "Kyle's cool. He's just being antisocial! I want to play Taboo."

Something about Zenovia's demeanor must've struck a chord with Tristan, because he said, "Mia, you and Alyssa can stay here and play Taboo. We'll just run over and see what's up with Kyle."

"I want to go!" Alyssa said.

Tristan shook his head. "No. Just stay here with Mia. We'll be right back."

Zenovia and Tristan dashed up the basement stairs and into the kitchen. Justin was there and making a turkey sandwich. He looked up from his snack with questions in his eyes.

"Where are y'all going?" he asked as Tristan grabbed his keys from a hook on the wall.

"To Kyle's house," Zenovia replied.

"What's going on over there?" Justin inquired.

Tristan responded, "Nothing. Well, Zenovia just had a feeling that we should go over there."

Justin laughed. "A feeling? Like some kind of sixth sense or something? Wow."

Zenovia narrowed her eyes and frowned at Justin. "Don't be a jerk, Justin. It doesn't suit you at all."

A faint smile appeared on Tristan's lips. He seemed to enjoy Zenovia sparring with Justin.

Justin smiled as well. "You're right, Zee. I apologize."

Zenovia could tell that he was teasing her, and spontaneous butterflies appeared in her stomach. Even when Justin was irritating her, he was still fine as all get out.

"Let's go, Zee," Tristan said.

Zenovia wondered if Tristan intuitively knew what she felt when she dealt with Justin. He always got extra protective of her around his brother. It was like Tristan was a caveman guarding the woman he'd dragged home to his bearskin, except that he hadn't actually claimed her or dragged her anywhere.

As they drove down the street, something occurred to Zenovia. "Tristan, why did you say I had a *feeling* we should go and check on Kyle?"

"You did, right? Have a feeling or something?" Tristan explained.

Well, of course, the answer was yes, but how could Tristan have known? And if he could tell, did that mean Mia and Alyssa could tell, too? Did they think she was some kind of *Twilight Zone* weirdo?

Zenovia asked carefully, "Why do you think that?"

"I guess it was the look on your face when you said it. Like you were worried or something. I don't know."

Zenovia exhaled slowly. So it was nothing too out of the ordinary. Like her eyes didn't roll up into the back of her head during the vision or anything like that. It was just that she'd seemed worried.

They pulled up to Kyle's house in a matter of minutes. He lived only a few streets away from the Batistes but it seemed like it was two different worlds. While the Batistes lived on a street with pretty little bungalows and colonials with manicured lawns, Kyle's street was quite the opposite. On both sides of the street were apartment buildings. Some were nice, but many were in varied states of disrepair. The one Kyle lived in looked no better than the projects she and Audrey had moved from.

Tristan knocked on the downstairs apartment door. No one responded immediately, so Tristan knocked again.

"I know someone's at home, because Kyle's mom's car

is here," Tristan said as he pointed out the rusted brown Chevy Cavalier.

After a third knock, someone was coming down the stairs. Zenovia could hear the heavy footsteps even if she couldn't see who it was behind the heavy oak door.

Kyle's mother opened the door. "Hello, Tristan. Hello, Zenovia. Are y'all here to see Kyle?"

Tristan replied, "Yes, ma'am. He was supposed to come over tonight, but he called and said he couldn't make it. May we come in?"

There was a pregnant pause before she responded. "I guess so. Come on in."

Tristan must've heard the hesitation in her voice too, because he glanced at Zenovia with one of his eyebrows lifted in question form. Zenovia wondered what they were walking themselves into.

They stepped into the apartment and Kyle's mother called out, "Kyle! Tristan is here!"

Zenovia guessed that it wasn't important to Kyle's mother to announce her presence. Since it was such a little thing, Zenovia decided to let it go. She just wanted to see if Kyle was all right.

Kyle walked out of a room in the rear of the apartment. As soon as Zenovia saw him, she knew that everything was not all right. His eyes were puffy and his nose was red, obviously from crying. He was also wearing the same shirt from the vision.

"What's up, dude!" Tristan exclaimed in a too-happy tone. He seemed oblivious to Kyle's distraught state.

"Hey, Tristan. Hey, Zee," Kyle replied.

Kyle walked slowly into the living room where Tristan and Zenovia stood. He seemed to wince with pain on each step and he was still clutching the envelope that Zenovia had also seen in her vision.

"What's that in your hand, Kyle? A college acceptance letter?" Zenovia asked.

Even though she sincerely wanted to know what was contained in the envelope, Zenovia's question was a joke. Probably ill-timed, but a joke nonetheless. Of course she knew that he wasn't applying to any colleges. He and Tristan had made it abundantly clear that they were dedicating their lives to the Brethren.

"No," Kyle replied. "It's just a letter from the Brethren headquarters, telling me what I already knew."

Tristan's eyes dropped to the floor. He must've guessed, like Zenovia had, that the Brethren headquarters had rejected Kyle's application for volunteer service.

Zenovia waited for Tristan to say something comforting, but when he remained silent she said, "You can serve God some other way, Kyle. You don't have to go to the Brethren headquarters to do that."

"That's what I keep telling him," Kyle's mother interjected. "But he just keeps sitting in there on the floor, slicing up his arms...."

An expression of horror and embarrassment covered Kyle's face. He dropped the letter to the floor, turned and ran out of the room.

Tristan looked helplessly at Zenovia, who, of course, was not at all shocked by the revelation. Zenovia sighed and found herself whispering a silent prayer for Kyle. A sidelong glance at Tristan's bowed head told Zenovia he was doing the same.

"Y'all might as well go," Kyle's mother said. "He won't be coming over to your house tonight."

"I wouldn't either," Zenovia replied. "Do you think that embarrassing him will help him with his problem? You should try to get him some help."

Kyle's mother answered, "What do you know? God will heal him if we pray hard enough. It's nothing but demonic forces."

Zenovia took a slow, slow breath in, trying to control her anger. Kyle's mental health was not her burden, but after living with a nonmedicated Audrey for years, she knew the difference a little Thorazine or Prozac could make.

Tristan tried to smooth things over by saying, "That's what she meant. Maybe we can take Kyle to the Council of Elders for help. They'll know what to do, and if there's a demon, maybe they can help cast it out."

"That's not what I meant," Zenovia retorted. She didn't need anyone explaining her words for her, especially not Tristan.

Zenovia strode furiously toward the door. As she ran down the apartment stairs, she heard Tristan saying goodbye to Kyle's mother. Zenovia didn't think that she could stay in that apartment for a moment longer without saying something really hurtful to that woman.

She and Tristan drove in silence. Zenovia blew frost on the window and scribbled it away. Tristan wore a tight frown on his face, as if he was searching his mind for something to say.

Zenovia finally broke the silence. "I'm right, you know. Kyle probably needs a good antidepressant."

"He needs a true healing that won't come from pills."

Zenovia rolled her eyes at what she was starting to recognize as Brethren rhetoric. Why didn't anyone believe that God gave the doctors the knowledge to prescribe medication? Why couldn't pills be a part of their healing?

"Tell me something, Tristan," Zenovia said in a calmer tone, "if you fell and broke your arm, would you just go home and wait for a divine healing?"

"That's not the same thing."

"Answer the question, Tristan. Would you go home and wait for your healing?"

"No," Tristan replied quietly.

"What would you do?" Zenovia pressed.

He sighed. "I would go to the emergency room and let them treat me."

"Really? Couldn't it have been demonic forces that made you fall? Why not call on the Council of Elders?"

Tristan seemed irritated by Zenovia's sarcastic logic. "Zee, when people have mental issues, it's the demons. Even Christ, when he walked the earth, healed men and women who were demon-possessed."

"He healed lepers and blind folk too, but I don't see the Brethren shooting down antibiotics and cataract surgery," Zenovia argued. "It doesn't make any sense."

"Zenovia, you shouldn't question the accurate knowledge that's given to us by the Council of Elders. Your questions just show your immaturity as a Christian. With more study, you'll learn to accept the will of God."

Zenovia closed her eyes and let her head fall against the headrest. Tristan was too smart for this. He was too smart to not examine an idea for himself. He was too intelligent to allow his logic to give way to utter foolishness.

As Tristan drove he drummed his fingers on the steering wheel and hummed a Brethren worship song.

Chapter Thirteen

It was a cold and bleak Sunday morning when Zenovia's carefully constructed card house started to crumble.

She awoke with a start to the overpowering smell of bleach. It was so strong that it burned her nostrils as she inhaled. She sat up straight in her bed as a sense of dread chilled her insides. Normally she got a similar feeling when she was about to have a vision. But this time the feeling had more to do with reliving the past.

Zenovia pulled on her bathrobe and walked barefoot into the kitchen. The sun had not yet risen but the house was bright, because every light was on. Zenovia rubbed the sleep from both her eyes and peered into the kitchen.

Audrey was on the floor with a bucket and a scrub brush. A white scouring powder was everywhere—on the counters, in the sink, all over the walls. And the stench of bleach was even stronger, bringing tears to Zenovia's eyes.

"Mom, what are you doing?"

Audrey looked up at Zenovia with a wild look in her eyes. "It stinks in here. Can't you smell it?"

Zenovia replied, "All I can smell is bleach."

"I think someone was in here while we were sleeping. Somebody's been here, 'cause I can smell 'em. They smell like they should be in the zoo."

Zenovia turned away from her mother and pulled her lips in tightly to keep the sobs from escaping. Her mother's delusions had started again and it was as bad as, if not worse than, ever.

"What is all this racket?" Phillip asked as he stumbled from his and Audrey's bedroom.

"You can't smell it either?" Audrey asked. "What's wrong with y'all? Y'all noses must be messed up if you can't smell that!"

Phillip looked to Zenovia, his eyes begging for an explanation. She chuckled as tears ran down her cheeks. "Why are you looking at me, Phillip? You're the boss, right?"

"What should I do?" he asked.

The fear in his voice touched Zenovia. She understood how he felt.

Audrey was perfectly fine the night before. They had played a game of Scrabble in which Zenovia beat them both brutally. Audrey was laughing, joking, and baking cookies.

But this was how it always happened. Without her medication, it was only a matter of time before Audrey slipped into her delusional world.

Zenovia decided to answer Phillip's question. "You should give her the medication."

"No!" said Audrey. "I ain't taking them damn pills.

They stop my nose up and I can't smell what they're putting in the food."

Surprisingly, Phillip concurred with Audrey. "I'm not giving her those pills, Zenovia. She doesn't want them, and I think she could get well without them."

"It's going to get worse, and then you'll wish you had listened to me."

Audrey using the word "damn" was only a precursor to the vile things that would come from her mouth if she was allowed to go much longer without her medication. Her disease took every semblance of decorum and transformed her into something ugly.

Audrey looked up from the floor at Zenovia and said, "Why don't you just shut up and help me clean up in here?"

Zenovia trudged into the kitchen and got down on her knees. She took a scrub brush and started to move the scouring powder and water paste around. Tears dropped to the floor and mixed with the cleaning products.

"Not like that!" Audrey fussed. "Do it in circles. That way you get all of the smell."

"Mom, that doesn't make any sense."

Zenovia thought she saw a moment of clarity flash across Audrey's face. Then Audrey said, "How you gone tell me what makes sense? You can't even smell nothing."

Zenovia drew in a long and labored breath and released it slowly. Then she took the scrub brush and made little circles on the floor.

Audrey's episode had lasted two days. She spent the entire time cleaning the house with bleach and scouring powder. In every room, and on every surface, bleach was used to rid the house of Audrey's phantom odor. Even things that should've never been bleached, like couches and rugs and clothing.

When the house was bleached to Audrey's satisfaction, the episode subsided.

After the worst of it seemed to be over, Phillip took Audrey and Zenovia to a meeting at the Devotion Center as if chaos had not visited their home for two days straight. Zenovia was used to this reaction. She had done it for twelve years of her life, until Audrey had broken down and started taking medication.

As it stood, living with a nonmedicated Audrey was not Zenovia's choice. And since she had no say in Phillip's house, she had started a countdown to when she would leave for college.

Zenovia sat through the meeting feeling disconnected from what she heard. She remembered going to church before she and Audrey joined the Brethren and hearing words that would help her make it through the drama of living with her mother. She would listen to the minister preach about the grace of God, and say, "His grace is sufficient for thee." And then in that same message hear how, "I can do all things through Christ who strengthens me."

She remembered learning the power of prayer, and how if two or three agreed on a matter and prayed on it, how God would be in their midst. But the Brethren talked about none of these things. The evening message was about how blessed the Brethren were to know the "truth" and that it was their mission to share their truth with the world.

But Zenovia wanted to know what to do about her mother.

Zenovia watched Audrey's expression go dark as she sat in her seat. Someone's child was sitting behind her and the toddler kept kicking the back of her chair. Phillip was completely oblivious to the change in Audrey; he held her hand tightly and had his eyes on the podium.

"Somebody better get this brat," Audrey mumbled under her breath.

Zenovia tried to motion to the child's mother, but she was preoccupied with a smaller baby who fussed in its carrier. Then the toddler took a small toy, like something out of a Happy Meal, and launched it into the air. Zenovia gasped as the hard toy landed on Audrey's neck.

Audrey jumped up from her seat, grabbed her oversize purse, and marched angrily to the bathroom.

Phillip asked Zenovia, "What's the matter?"

Zenovia frowned and faced forward, ignoring Phillip's question. The answer was too complex to whisper in a Brethren meeting. In Zenovia's mind, *everything* was the matter. She just hoped she could hold it all together until she graduated from high school and went away to college. Then she would begin her own life, and leave the burden of caring for her mother to Phillip.

Chapter Fourteen

You're not concentrating," Emil said sternly as Zenovia fell flat on her behind for the umpteenth time.

He was trying to teach her the line step that all the really good skaters knew. It was a crossover and then a swivel of the hips. The male and female skaters both did the move; the guys adding stomps, kicks, and jumps and the girls adding squeals and finger snaps.

Emil was being truthful: Zenovia was not concentrating. She had too many things on her mind. She was, of course, concerned about Audrey's deteriorating mind. But she also worried about her friendship with Tristan, which seemed to be unraveling as quickly as Audrey's mental state.

"I can't do it, Emil. I'm not ready yet," Zenovia whined.

Emil said, "You've got about an hour left in this practice skate, and then the adult session starts. All of your friends are going to be here. Don't you want them to see you do this step?"

Zenovia looked up at Emil and felt a smile tickle her lips. Even though he was frowning, Emil was devastatingly gorgeous. It was taking every bit of self-control she could muster to not pull him into her arms and kiss him.

"I don't think I'm going to get this tonight, Emil. I need more practice."

Zenovia pleaded with him with her eyes, and his face softened. He held out his hand to help her up.

"Okay, you don't have to do the step tonight. Do you want to practice couple skating?"

"No, Emil. I'm tired. Plus I'll probably just make you fall."

He skated behind her and took her left hand in his and placed his other hand on her right hip.

Emil said, "Just relax, and let me do all of the work."

Zenovia allowed Emil to guide her onto the skate floor. "Candlelight and You" by Chante Moore was blaring from the speakers, and the floor was crowded with other couples. But to Zenovia, it felt like she and Emil were the only ones there. Emil's warm breath on her neck and his strong protective grip on her hand made her feel something that she'd never felt before.

Safe.

Zenovia had no idea why Emil made her feel protected. If anything, after having that vision about him, she probably should have felt afraid. But there was nothing sexual or immoral about this feeling. Even though she'd only known him a couple of weeks she felt closer to him than she'd ever felt to any other male. This feeling was quickly erasing any and all puppy love feelings that she felt for Tristan.

The song ended and Emil led Zenovia over to the concession area. Zenovia happily sat down at one of the tables, relieved that she could finally rest her feet.

"What do you want to eat, baby girl?" Emil asked.

Zenovia twisted her lips to one side. "I don't know. What is there?"

"Pizza, fries, nachos. You know. The typical stuff."

"Fries, then, I guess," Zenovia replied.

"Coming right up."

Emil went to stand in line for their food. Zenovia watched as girls looked at him with longing in their eyes. They did not seem to care that he had a girlfriend sitting nearby.

One of the girls left the concession line and skated over to Zenovia. The skinny girl was wearing greasy lip gloss and a long synthetic ponytail that she'd whipped over one of her shoulders. In Zenovia's opinion, she was the personification of hoochie.

The girl said, "You are so lucky. I heard Emil knows how to put it down."

Zenovia's eyes widened. *Put it down* was hood slang for someone who was good in bed. Zenovia had already figured out that Emil was no virgin, but she didn't know that he had a reputation. She wondered how many girls he'd been with.

Emil carried a tray to the table and sat down. In addition to Zenovia's fries, there was a huge order of chili cheese nachos and a large beverage. Zenovia wondered how Emil stayed so thin. With the amount of junk food he devoured, he should've been big as a house.

"I hope you don't mind sharing a cherry slush," Emil said.

Zenovia replied, "It all depends on where your mouth has been lately."

"What are you trying to say?" Emil asked. "You think I'm some kind of freak or something?"

"Some girl just came up to me and told me I was lucky for being your girl."

Emil grinned. "You are lucky."

"So it's true then. You know how to put it down?"

Emil took a long sip of the slush and smiled. "Sienna is a hoe, Zenovia. She was just trying to get you mad. She's been trying to get with me for months and I'm not feeling her."

"Have you ever felt her?" Zenovia asked, not entirely sure if she wanted the answer.

Emil's nostrils flared angrily and he seemed offended. "Are you asking me if I had sex with her?"

"Yeah, that's exactly what I'm asking."

"Nah, she's not my type. She's probably got a disease or something."

Zenovia quietly munched her ketchup-covered fries. She didn't want to continue the heated conversation because she much preferred Emil when he was smiling. He was also quiet, but it was a brooding and uneasy silence.

Finally Emil spoke. "Do you think that just because I'm not baptized, that I'm running around like some dog in heat, humping everything in a skirt?"

"No, I really don't." Zenovia was completely caught off guard. Besides, his assumption couldn't be any farther from the truth.

Emil sighed wearily. "Listen, I'm not going to be like those Heights dudes, all right? But that doesn't mean I'm a bad person. And it doesn't mean I'm gonna play you for somebody like Sienna."

"I believe you, Emil," Zenovia replied. "I just wanted to know if what she said was true."

A slow smile replaced Emil's haggard look. "Well, you'll just have to see for yourself."

"Emil…"

"Just kidding!" he said with a giggle.

The practice skating session was finally over and the adult skaters started to trickle into the skating rink. Tristan, Alyssa, Mia, and Kyle were some of the first to walk through the door. Alyssa saw Zenovia and Emil and rushed over to their table.

"Hey, Alyssa," Zenovia said. "Have you met Emil?"

Alyssa smiled and replied, "I've heard of him, but never met him. What's up?"

"Not a thing. Nice to meet you, Alyssa," Emil answered with very little emotion in his tone. He seemed somewhat annoyed by Alyssa's presence, but Zenovia couldn't be sure.

"Same here!" Alyssa said as she plopped down at Emil and Zenovia's table.

Tristan, Mia, and Kyle made their way over to the table as well. Tristan made brief eye contact with Zenovia. She looked away quickly, as if she had done something wrong. But she had not. Whatever Tristan felt for her was irrelevant because he hadn't shouted it from the rooftops like Emil had done.

Still Zenovia felt her heart lurch when Tristan put his arm around Mia and pulled her into a friendly embrace. Mia seemed to be in heaven from the spontaneous public display, but Zenovia frowned. If he was trying to make her jealous, it was working. But why would he care to make her jealous?

"So, Zee, are you learning all the skater moves?" Kyle asked.

Zenovia was surprised that Kyle was at the skating rink. She was glad to see him in high spirits again, but she wondered how long it would last.

Mia chimed in, "I'm sure she's going to have us all looking stupid."

"I know, right?" Alyssa said. "Are you twirling and jumping yet?"

"No," Zenovia answered with a laugh. "I'm barely keeping my balance."

Tristan and Emil conspicuously refrained from the lighthearted banter. It was as if they were each sizing up an opponent. No one seemed to notice the tension except Zenovia. Her eyes darted back and forth from Tristan to Emil, praying neither of them said anything out of pocket.

She should've prayed harder.

"So, Emil, did you get baptized at the last regional meeting? Did I miss you going down in the water?" Tristan asked.

Emil balled up his fist in front of his mouth and exhaled. It probably wasn't the first time he'd been asked the question by an overzealous Brethren member. Zenovia hoped that Tristan would end his inquisition with one question.

Emil replied, "Nah, man. You didn't miss nothing. I didn't get baptized."

"That's what I thought," Tristan said. After a long pause he continued. "You know Zenovia got baptized, right?"

"Yeah, I know."

Much to Zenovia's displeasure, Tristan went on with his verbal barrage. "So you know you can't do the things with her that you're used to doing. If she fornicates, you know she'll be cast out."

Zenovia knew this was a conversation between two rivals, but she had to interject. "What do you mean cast out?"

"They didn't tell you about that before you got baptized?" Emil asked with a little chuckle. "Of course they didn't tell you about that."

Zenovia reminded herself of everything she'd been taught. She'd been told she could live forever in a paradise. She'd been told that the churches were in error. She'd been told she was living in the end times.

She couldn't remember being told anything about being cast out.

Tristan retorted, "Remember in the baptism sermon when they talk about the chastening rod?"

Zenovia remembered the word. Chasten. To punish by suffering.

"I vaguely remember that," Zenovia replied.

Kyle explained, "It's part of the vow to the Brethren that you take when you go in the water. If you are caught in a sinful and unrepentant state, then you are cast out."

"But what does it mean to be cast out?" Zenovia asked.

Emil did the honors. "It means that none of your Brethren friends will talk to you. Actually, they'll treat you like you don't exist."

Zenovia looked up at Tristan with questions in her

eyes. "Is this true, Tristan? Is this how the Brethren treat people when they make mistakes?"

"It's how the Brethren treat unrepentant sinners. It's in the Bible, Zee. A little leaven spoils the whole loaf."

Zenovia shook her head slowly, not wanting to believe what she'd just heard. She analyzed this new information. After she took a vow to the Brethren, they were allowed to cast her out if she sinned? They were allowed to take her friends and just make them disappear? She felt like she'd just bought a used car and found out that it didn't have an engine.

Swindled.

Bamboozled.

One of Emil's skating partners flew past the table. He did a little twist and called out, "E! Man, are you skating tonight or hanging with your little girlfriend?"

Emil glanced at Zenovia and asked, "Do you mind?"

"Of course not. Get your skate on!" Zenovia tried to sound chipper and upbeat as if the new Brethren revelation hadn't chilled her to her core.

Alyssa sat down in Emil's vacated seat and put her arm around Zenovia. She said, "Zee, you know you don't have to worry about being cast out. They save that only for the worst of the worst."

Zenovia didn't reply. Tristan had implied that she could be cast out for fornicating. She knew many, many people who had made that mistake. Too many. But none of them were Brethren.

Of course, she couldn't help but think of the vision she'd had about herself and Emil. Was she doomed to be cast out of the Brethren? If she trusted the visions as

Audrey did, she would have to say yes. Maybe it was for the best that Tristan didn't pay her any attention. They seemed to have different destinies.

"What, are we at a funeral or something?" Mia asked. "Can we go and skate? I like that song."

"Emil tired me out with all of that practicing. I'm just going to sit here and chill," Zenovia said.

Tristan asked, "Do you want some company?"

Zenovia looked out at the skate floor. Emil was in his element. He was skating with his friends, doing the step they'd made up during the practice session.

"Sure," Zenovia replied. "Sit yourself on down."

Zenovia was irritated with herself for her conflicting feelings. No matter how much Tristan ignored her or tried to make her jealous with hair-flinging Mia, something about him still tugged at her heart.

Kyle, Mia, and Alyssa clumsily made their way onto the skate floor. They held on to each other for dear life, and were actually quite hilarious to behold.

"They are an accident ready to happen," Tristan said with a chuckle.

Zenovia replied, "Why don't you go help them? Your girlfriend is about to fall on her booty."

"Who, Mia?"

"Yeah. Y'all been real chummy. And here I thought you were going off to the Brethren headquarters to serve the Lord. Sounds like you might end up with a little Brethren wife."

Tristan's smile faded and was replaced with an expression that Zenovia couldn't read. She looked away from his intense gaze and focused her vision onto the skate floor. She watched Emil attempt an intricate jump that he'd tried during the practice session. He didn't quite make it though, and caused a four-person pileup.

"Looks like your friend took a spill," Tristan remarked with a sarcastic sneer.

Zenovia narrowed her eyes angrily. "Well, he takes chances. That's how you and he differ."

"What do you mean?"

"Nothing, Tristan. Nothing at all."

Zenovia felt that Tristan got the deeper meaning of her words because he'd grown silent once again. But she could never be sure what he was thinking. His body language would have Zenovia thinking one way and then his actions would be the complete opposite.

Tristan sighed and gazed deeply into Zenovia's face. "Zenovia…I…"

"Come on, baby girl!" Emil exclaimed as he crash-landed into the table. "You're not going to let all that practice go to waste, are you?"

Was Tristan on the verge of spilling his guts again? Zenovia wasn't going to find out. She was standing from the table and ready to skate with Emil.

Emil continued, "Sorry, Heights boy, she's coming with me."

Zenovia and Emil both cracked up laughing. Emil's comment was so unexpected, spontaneous, and silly that Zenovia couldn't help it. Even if it left Tristan looking and perhaps feeling rather foolish.

Maybe it was a sign that each time Zenovia thought Tristan was about to reveal his inner feelings, he was interrupted. She hadn't had any visions about him yet, which according to Audrey meant that Zenovia should just forget about him and move on with her life.

Zenovia glanced back over her shoulder as she stepped onto the skate floor and accidentally locked eyes with Tristan. A tiny smile played on his lips and he gave her a slight wave, as if he was saying goodbye.

Chapter Fifteen

Zenovia was petrified.

She stood elbow to elbow with Emil in the small sanctuary of the Northeast Devotion Center. The service had just ended, and most of the congregation milled around, holding random conversations. Emil's mother, Gladys, was seated in the second row with her arms folded and wearing an ugly frown on her face.

According to Emil, Gladys had insisted on visiting the Northeast Devotion Center so that she could meet Zenovia in person. But to Zenovia she didn't look too happy about it.

"Don't worry," Emil said cheerfully, "Gladys is cool."

"Cool" was the last word Zenovia would've used to describe the woman. Her hair was pulled back into a severe bun at the nape of her neck. Zenovia thought that the bun was made of fake hair, but it was pulled so tight that Gladys's eyes were stretched into little slits.

"She doesn't look cool, Emil. She looks like she will hurt me," Zenovia replied.

Emil chuckled. "Don't be afraid. She won't get too out of pocket here at the Devotion Center."

Zenovia wasn't at all convinced, but she followed Emil to Gladys's seat. Gladys looked at Zenovia and Emil and her frown deepened. This made Zenovia's heart sink.

"Mom, I want you to meet my friend Zenovia," Emil said as he bent over to kiss his mother on the cheek.

She assessed Zenovia with a quick glance up and down. "So you're the girl I've been hearing so much about."

"Yes, ma'am," Zenovia replied. She stuck out her hand to shake Gladys's but the woman ignored her.

Gladys cleared her throat. Then in a calm, quiet, and steady tone said, "You know he has hoe blood."

"I'm sorry. Come again?" Zenovia was confused and Emil had a look of sheer embarrassment on his face.

"I said he's got hoe blood. His daddy is a hoe, and Emil is just like him."

Zenovia chuckled nervously, "Um, I don't know what to say."

"You don't have to say anything. Just remember what I'm telling you. He's a hoe and he does what hoes do."

As if on cue, Audrey walked up to join the conversation. Her red curls bounced as she walked and she looked years younger than Gladys, even though Zenovia was sure they were close to the same age.

Audrey had been relatively stable for the past week. She'd only bleached the house once, and she'd allowed Phillip to share a bed with her. But still Zenovia was concerned that she would soon be looking as embarrassed as Emil.

"Hey there, Emil. Is this your mama?" Audrey asked.

Gladys responded for him with an irritated edge to her voice. "Yes, I am Emil's mother. Who are you?"

"Who peed in her Cheerios?" Audrey asked Zenovia. "Mom!"

Audrey looked around and realized she was in the sanctuary. She hunched her shoulders, covered her mouth with her hand, and laughed. "Oops. Excuse me y'all. Who *urinated* in her Cheerios?"

Zenovia closed her eyes and sighed. She didn't believe this was happening. "This is my mother, Audrey."

"Well, Audrey, are you aware that our children are dating?" Gladys asked, conveniently ignoring Audrey's shoulders that were still trembling with laughter.

Audrey mimicked Gladys's stern, robotic monotone. "Yes, I am aware that they are dating."

"Well, don't you think it's a bit much? They're too young to date, don't you agree?" Gladys continued her questions as if she was dealing with someone reasonable.

Unfortunately, she was in a conversation with Audrey.

Audrey threw her head back and let out a hearty laugh. "Woman, you need to chill out! They're just kids. You act like they fixing to get married or have some babies or something. Just chill!"

Audrey walked away, still laughing. Gladys wore an indignant expression on her face. Meeting Emil's mother had not gone well.

Emil whispered to Zenovia, "Okay, sorry, Zee. This was a bad idea."

"You think?"

Chapter Sixteen

All of the young people from the Northeast Devotion Center were huddled in the Batistes' driveway to see Justin off to the Brethren headquarters. It was the weekend before Thanksgiving, and although the temperature was a frigid thirty degrees, everyone was wearing a smile.

Everyone except Zenovia.

Standing there watching Justin pack his bags into the van just reminded Zenovia that at the end of the school year, Tristan would be following his brother. In the face of losing the first real friend she'd found, the only things that gave her comfort were Emil's arms wrapped around her. He stood behind her wearing a thick down coat. Casually he rested his head on her shoulder. He was so close that his breath warmed the back of Zenovia's neck.

"When are we going to get out of here?" Emil whispered.

Zenovia replied, "In a little bit. We don't have to stay long."

Alyssa walked up to the couple and said, "Dag, you guys are all hugged up! Can I get some warmth?"

"Get yourself a boyfriend," Zenovia replied with a grin.

"I didn't know I had achieved boyfriend status," Emil stated.

Zenovia grinned harder. "You're almost there. If you conduct yourself appropriately, you might make it in a year or so."

Alyssa and Zenovia burst into laughter, and after a moment Emil joined them too. While they were laughing, Kyle walked up to the trio who were situated at the rear of the crowd of teenagers. He looked to be on a mission and was clearly not amused.

"Kyle, why are you looking so sour?" Alyssa asked, beating Zenovia to the punch.

"If I'm looking sour, it's because sin leaves a bad taste in my mouth."

Zenovia raised a warning eyebrow at Kyle. She knew he wasn't about to stand up here and try to front on her and Emil when she had plenty of reasons to have a bad taste in her mouth about him. It never ceased to amaze Zenovia how the people who needed the most help seemed to always be the ones looking to judge someone else.

"Just chill, Kyle," Alyssa said.

But Kyle chose to continue. "I mean, come on, Emil. This is a Brethren gathering and you're practically groping Zenovia."

Zenovia turned to Emil to see his reaction. His head was tilted back and he bit his bottom lip. She watched his chest ease up and down slowly in his down coat. She hoped that he was trying to hold his temper.

Zenovia had learned from his skating buddies that Emil was not only known for his prowess with the ladies, but he was known for his fighting ability. Kyle's sheltered life in the Brethren would leave him completely unprepared for a thug like Emil.

Alyssa must have also heard the rumors about Emil because she grabbed Kyle by the arm and dragged him to the other side of the driveway.

"Be easy, Emil," Zenovia begged.

"For you, I'll be cool, but dude betta not step to me in the street."

Zenovia highly doubted that Kyle would have the guts to even make eye contact with Emil without the safety net of his Brethren friends.

Emil added, "Can we get out of here now?"

"Let me go give Justin a hug and say goodbye. Then we can be out."

"All right, I'll be waiting at the corner."

"Tristan will take us home."

Emil let out a disgusted snort which let Zenovia know she said the wrong thing. She hadn't meant to insult Emil, but it was cold and she wasn't trying to stand outside waiting on the bus.

She smiled, "If we ride the bus, you're going to have to keep me warm."

"That is not a problem, baby girl," Emil said with a grin.

She watched Emil start off down the street and quickly scanned the crowd for Justin. It should've been easy to find him since he should've been packing his own belongings into the Batistes' van. But leaving to serve at the Brethren headquarters had given Justin an almost celebrity status and everyone was trying to get his ear.

Zenovia finally spotted him talking to one of the older ladies from the congregation. She pinched Justin's cheeks and then kissed them. He endured the affection like a gentleman, and it made Zenovia smile.

She followed him into the side door of the house, where he'd disappeared. She cleared her throat as he was about to dash up the steps into the kitchen. Her small noise made him halt in his tracks and turn around.

Zenovia said, "You are such a ladies' man, Justin. That little old lady just couldn't keep her hands off of you."

"Zee. I didn't know you were here."

"Yeah, me and Emil have been kinda on the outskirts."

Justin grinned. "Emil. That's the guy you're seeing, right?"

"Yes. I just wanted to congratulate you, Justin, and get a hug. Then I'm getting out of here."

Justin continued to smile and Zenovia thought his eyes would pierce her soul. He held out both his arms. "Come here, Zee."

Zenovia stepped forward and allowed Justin to encircle her with his arms. He held her close...too close, but she didn't pull away.

Finally he let Zenovia go. "You take care, Zee."

"You too, Justin." Zenovia managed to croak out her response. There was a knot in her throat that threatened to steal any words she wanted to speak.

"And don't worry about Tristan. If he doesn't come around, then he doesn't deserve you."

Zenovia smiled, suddenly feeling more relaxed. "I think I've probably already given up on Tristan."

"Good. Maybe you'll still have a crush on me when I come home," Justin said presumptuously.

Zenovia burst into laughter. "You are hilarious, Justin. I am going to miss you though! Take care."

Zenovia turned to walk back down the steps, but Justin grabbed her arm. He spun her around quickly and before she could object they were standing nose to nose.

"Justin..."

He didn't reply, but planted a warm and sweet kiss on Zenovia's lips. He didn't put his tongue in her mouth, but gently bit her bottom lip as he pulled away. Zenovia felt weak, then immediately guilty for having that feeling. She pulled away from Justin and fled.

She quickly moved through the crowd that had grown considerably since she'd been inside. Down the street, at the corner, she could see Emil waiting for the bus. If she could just get away from the house, and from Justin and his reckless lips, she'd be able to compose herself.

Just when she thought she was home free, Tristan called to her, "Zee, are you leaving? You just got here!"

Instead of stopping, she waved at him and sped off down the street without anyone else really noticing. She wasn't the center of attention, so no one cared whether she stayed or went, except maybe Tristan who seemed to want to follow her, but didn't.

Zenovia jogged down the street and noticed Emil waving frantically. She wondered what his problem was, until she saw the bus approaching. She sprinted the rest of the way, because it was Saturday and the next bus wouldn't be coming for forty-five minutes.

She made it to the bus, but had to stop and catch her breath. Zenovia was not the athletic type—she was more into books than running track. Her body was not used to exerting any extra effort. She squatted with both hands on her thighs and took slow breaths.

The bus driver opened the door and fussed. "Are you two coming or not?"

Emil looked at Zenovia and she nodded. They stepped onto the bus and Emil paid both their fares while Zenovia found a seat. Emil preferred sitting near the back of the bus, especially for the thirty-five-minute ride to his side of town.

They were going to Randall Park Mall—the hood mall. It was more of a hangout spot than a shopping area, especially since they had converted the movie theater into a one-dollar show that only had old movies.

Emil plopped down next to Zenovia. "I thought you weren't going to make it."

"I know! I haven't run that hard in a long time. I think I may have pulled a muscle."

A slow grin started on Emil's face. "Which muscle is it? Do you want a massage?"

"Ha, ha. No, I do not want a massage from you!"

"Why not?" Emil asked, an offended tone in his voice.

"Because you are just trying to turn me into a sinner."

"You been hanging around those Brethren for too long. There is nothing sinful about a massage."

Zenovia leaned forward in her seat and looked out of the window. She figured that it would be pointless to explain to Emil that she was joking, and that she really didn't think a massage was a sin. He seemed so sensitive when it came to the Brethren and sin. So much so that it got Zenovia thinking that maybe he believed in the Brethren's teachings more than she did.

She continued to look out of the window and watched the landscape change from suburban to ghetto almost immediately. The pretty little bungalows and colonials were soon replaced by raggedy storefront churches and corner check-cashing stores.

"So are you ignoring me now?" Emil asked since Zenovia did not reply to his last comment.

Still turned toward the window, Zenovia replied, "No, I'm not ignoring you. I'm thinking about what you said."

That was only partially true. She *was* thinking about Emil's massage, but she was thinking more about the kiss that left a tingle on her lips. Of course, it was foolish for her to be thinking of a stolen kiss from Justin. He was leaving and so was Tristan. They were going to be soldiers in the Brethren army and she would be left behind as a childhood memory.

She turned to face Emil. With his eyes he smiled, but there was also something else in his expression. Was it insecurity? Zenovia wasn't sure.

"You know I'm never going to be like Tristan or Kyle."

"I know. I don't want you to be like them."

Emil's heavy exhale made Zenovia think he was relieved. He said, "Sometimes I think...well...never mind."

"Tell me. Tell me what you think, Emil."

"Sometimes I think that I should just leave you alone. You deserve somebody like Tristan, I guess."

The sadness in his voice touched Zenovia. She put her hand over his and squeezed tightly. "I do deserve the best. That's why I don't want you to leave me alone."

Emil leaned in and tentatively planted a light kiss on Zenovia's cheek. As sweet and innocent as it was, the kiss was just as thrilling and electric as the one Justin had stolen. Zenovia smiled what must've been an encouraging smile because Emil took a chance and placed a more skilled kiss on her lips.

"Can I be your boyfriend?" he asked.

"I don't know...can you?"

Chapter Seventeen

Girl, what is up with that giant gold necklace?" Alyssa asked, spying out Emil's gold chain that Zenovia was sporting.

They stood in front of Zenovia's locker as she quickly grabbed her French textbook. There had been homework in that class but Zenovia had not completed it. She'd spent the entire weekend hanging with Emil.

Zenovia reached up and ran her fingers over the thick, heavy jewelry. "Emil wanted me to wear it."

Zenovia smiled wistfully as she remembered how she came to be in possession of the chain. After Emil had kissed her out in public on the bus, he'd put the chain around her neck.

He'd said, "Do you want to wear my chain?"

"I don't know," Zenovia had replied. "Is this to let everyone know that I belong to you?"

"Not everyone," he'd responded without a hint of hesitation. "Just Tristan."

Mia interrupted Zenovia's reminiscence by asking, "Is he your official boyfriend now?"

"Yes. It's official."

Mia locked eyes with Alyssa and then they both looked at the floor. Zenovia was confused by their uncomfortable body language.

She asked, "Is there a problem?"

Alyssa replied, "No...I guess not. He's really cool."

"He's ghetto," Mia stated. "But if that's what you like, I guess you should go with it."

Zenovia paused on ripping into Mia because Tristan was walking toward them with a smile on his face. Mia beamed a smile at Tristan in return.

"Hey, y'all!"

"Hey, Tristan," Mia replied, still smiling, "take a look at Zenovia's gangster chain!"

Tristan peered at the glistening chain with the huge letter E dangling from the center. His smile instantly faded.

"You're kidding, right? You're not wearing that dude's chain around like you're his girlfriend."

Zenovia was beyond offended. "I'm dead serious, Tristan. Emil doesn't have any problem claiming me, so why should I be ashamed of him?"

"Well, if he's letting you wear his jewelry, you must be giving him something he can feel."

Zenovia slammed her locker shut, and strode away from Tristan and his smug facial expression. Only a preppy Brethren guy would think that quoting a Curtis Mayfield song was an acceptable diss. As she walked away she could hear the ripples of laughter from Mia. How could Tristan say that he was her friend, yet be so cruel?

She dashed into the classroom and took her seat before Tristan had the chance to catch up with her and offer a fake apology. But contrary to what Zenovia thought would happen, Tristan walked into the room and right past Zenovia. He snubbed her as if she was the one who had offended him.

Kyle sits on the floor in his kitchen, eyes glazed, head drooping, and still wearing his pajamas from the night before. The pajama shirt is long-sleeved, but the sleeves stick to his arms. The beige color of the shirt is stained dark red and a knife lies on the floor next to him.

He isn't moving.

His body, which is supported by the kitchen cabinets, slides down into the pool of blood that surrounds him. Somewhere in the distance a woman screams.

Zenovia abruptly snapped out of her vision and said aloud, "Where's Kyle?"

"*Excusez-moi, mademoiselle?*" the French teacher asked.

Zenovia closed her eyes tightly and shook her head. She gave a desperate glance to Tristan and mouthed her question again. "Where's Kyle?"

Tristan's attitude immediately melted. He said, "I don't know."

Zenovia stood from her seat, grabbed her things, and started for the door. She didn't wait for permission, a hall pass, or for Tristan. The vision had seemed more urgent than any she'd ever had.

She was halfway down the hallway before she realized that Tristan was right behind her.

"Zee, where are you going?" Tristan asked.

"To Kyle's house."

"How are you getting there?"

Zenovia hadn't thought about that. "On foot, I guess."

"Come on. I'll drive."

They drove in silence. Not because of Tristan's ridiculous outburst from before, but because Zenovia had more on her mind than that. The vision had been ghastly; all in black and white except for Kyle's blood.

As they approached Kyle's street, the sound of sirens drowned out Zenovia's thoughts. In front of Kyle's apartment building were two fire trucks and an ambulance.

"We're too late," Zenovia said, not knowing if it was the truth although she felt it was so.

Tristan didn't reply, but parked his car as close as possible. He ran out and toward the apartment building, leaving Zenovia to follow.

Zenovia stopped in her tracks as two paramedics pushed a stretcher from the apartment building. The white sheet that covered it was soaked through with blood in several places. Tristan, who had continued on to the apartment, was stopped by two firemen.

Kyle's mother ran from the building, screaming. It was the same scream Zenovia had heard in her vision. She caught sight of Tristan and staggered over in his direction.

"Tristan!" the distraught mother howled. "All he wanted was to serve the Brethren! That's all he ever wanted."

Involuntary tears started down Zenovia's cheeks. She wiped them away angrily. What good were her visions? Audrey always told her they were a gift from God, but what kind of gift was this! Seeing things when there was no time to stop them was not a gift.

Kyle's mother continued her sorrowful crying. "He j-just wanted to serve the Brethren!"

Zenovia had been staring at the ground, but the sound of Kyle's mother's voice caused her head to snap upward. Actually it wasn't the sound of her voice. It was her words.

She'd said that Kyle had wanted to serve the Brethren.

Not God.

The Brethren.

Chapter Eighteen

Zenovia watched sullenly as Audrey made a mess of their kitchen. She was making fried chicken, spaghetti, and banana pudding. Her trademark funeral foods.

She was cooking for Kyle's funeral.

Phillip walked up and stood next to Zenovia. She looked at him, acknowledging his presence, but said nothing.

"Are you all right?" he asked.

Zenovia didn't know how to answer that question. She *did* feel all right, or rather at peace. Kyle had made a choice to take his own life and there was nothing she could do about that. But somehow she felt that she *shouldn't* be all right. She thought that she should be traumatized.

Phillip didn't wait for her to reply. He said, "Kyle was troubled. I believe the Holy Spirit revealed that to the Council of Elders at the Brethren headquarters. That's why they didn't accept him."

Audrey said, "Whoever revealed what, the boy is still dead and gone."

"You're right. He is gone," Phillip said. "What are you cooking anyway? It's breakfast time. Why are you frying chicken?"

"The Brethren don't take food to the family when someone dies?" Zenovia asked.

Phillip replied, "Yes, when there is a funeral. But Kyle...well he committed suicide. There won't be a funeral."

"Well, that's all the more reason for me to take something over there."

Phillip said, "I can't allow you to do that, Audrey. The Brethren are pretty steadfast on this."

Audrey's expression instantly darkened. She was holding a chicken wing that she had just floured and was about to drop it into the heated skillet. She took that piece of chicken and hurled it across the room at Phillip.

Zenovia sighed and stepped out of Audrey's line of fire, while Phillip ducked. She walked toward her bedroom and didn't even look back when she heard pots and pans being thrown around the kitchen. Without her medication, it took so little to set Audrey off.

When Audrey wasn't having an episode she was fine. Almost normal. She was funny and vibrant. She was affectionate with Phillip, cooking huge elaborate meals and keeping him in the bedroom for hours at a time.

But once she was set off, it was a nightmare. And Zenovia was tired. Control had been taken away from Zenovia and she did not feel equipped to handle the aftermath.

Once she closed her bedroom door, her pager buzzed on her hip. She looked down at it, and it was the Batistes' phone number.

She picked up the phone in her bedroom and dialed. Tristan answered, "Hello?"

"Hey, Tristan. It's me, Zee. Did you page me?"

"Hi, Zee. I did page you. Are you going to school?"

"No...are you?"

"Yes. I was checking to see if you needed a ride."

Zenovia frowned. "Your best friend just committed suicide yesterday and you're going to school?"

"There's no reason for sorrow."

"There's no reason for sorrow? Tristan! What do you mean? How could you say that?"

"Kyle will be resurrected in the end. The Bible says to let the dead bury the dead. The fact that Kyle was so troubled in his mind shows that the demonic forces in this world are busy."

Zenovia screamed, "Demonic forces? He was depressed! And you know what else? The Brethren pushed him over the edge. Who rejects a boy trying to volunteer?"

"Zenovia." Tristan's voice quieted to a whisper. "Don't talk like that about the Brethren. Don't invite God's wrath on your life."

Zenovia slammed the phone down. She couldn't listen to a nanosecond more of Tristan's Brethren rhetoric. She wanted to let loose like Audrey and throw some things at someone.

Her phone rang again. "Hello!"

"Zee, what's up?"

Zenovia sighed. "Emil. Hey. Why aren't you at school?"

"Told Moms I wasn't feeling good."

"Oh, I'm home too."

Emil laughed. "Obviously. I'm talking to you, right?"

"Ha ha. I'm not exactly myself, you know."

"I heard about Kyle. That's messed up."

"Yeah."

"So do you want to come over?"

Zenovia nearly dropped the phone. "Um…I don't think that's a good idea, Emil."

"You scared?"

Zenovia chuckled. She *was* scared, but she was glad that Emil had taken her mind away from Kyle.

"I'm not scared, but I'm a little emotional right now."

"Well, let's go to the skating rink then."

"This early in the day? Won't they ask why we aren't at school?"

"Nah. They're cool at Roller Palace. Don't worry about it."

Zenovia said, "Okay. Do you want to meet at the rink?"

"I'll catch the bus down by you. Meet me at Lee and Mayfield at about noon. We'll get something to eat and then ride on out to the rink."

Zenovia hung up the phone and smiled. She looked forward to spending the entire day with Emil. She showered, and then picked out a sweater and jeans.

"Zenovia!" Phillip called from the living room. "Tristan, Alyssa, and Mia are here."

So they decided to stay out of school after all. Zenovia walked into the living room with her arms folded. She was still disgusted with Tristan and his "no reason for sorrow" speech.

Audrey was seated at the kitchen table. There was flour everywhere, including in her hair and on her face. Neither she nor Phillip had attempted to clean up the pieces of chicken that were on the floor or the pots and pans that were tossed onto the floor. Zenovia wondered why Phillip had let them in when Audrey was in mid-episode.

"Hey, y'all," Zenovia said.

Alyssa and Mia did not try to hide their shock at Audrey's state. Tristan, though, averted his eyes and looked directly at Zenovia.

He said, "We decided you were right, Zee. We're staying out of school today to remember Kyle. Do you want to hang at our house?"

Zenovia exhaled slowly. "I'm going to hang with Emil, at the rink."

"Wow! Tristan, I thought you said she was sad!" Mia exclaimed.

Tristan asked, "Zenovia, what's up?"

Audrey laughed. No, it was more like a cackle. She cackled. Then she said, "She ain't trying to hang with y'all. She going to be with her boo! You messed up, Tristan."

"How did he mess up?" Mia asked.

"He had his chance, but now Zee ain't even thinking about him. It's all about that Emil. You see she's wearing his necklace."

Mia laughed. "Well, Tristan was never interested in Zenovia that way, so it's cool."

Zenovia, Alyssa, and Tristan all gave Mia please-shut-up stares. Zenovia didn't want to talk about whatever chances Tristan might have had and she was sure he didn't want to either.

"Why don't you guys go to the rink with us?" Zenovia asked. "We can all hang out together and remember Kyle."

Alyssa replied, "That sounds really cool. Let's go."

They all piled into Tristan's car. Mia was in the front seat with Tristan, leaving Alyssa and Zenovia to sit in the back. Zenovia was cool with the seating arrangement because she didn't want to make eye contact with Tristan after Audrey's uncomfortable revelation.

"Were you meeting Emil at the rink?" Tristan asked.

"No. We planned to meet at Lee and Mayfield at noon. He usually catches the bus down here."

Alyssa said, "Well, it's almost noon, so we can just go that way."

Tristan pulled away from the house slowly. There had been a light snow the night before, so the ground was somewhat slippery.

"So what's up with your mom?" Mia asked.

"Just be quiet, Mia," Tristan fussed.

"No, it's cool. I'm not ashamed of my mother. She's sick."

"Sick how?" Alyssa asked.

"She's schizophrenic," Zenovia explained. "Before she married Phillip she took medication, but now she doesn't."

Zenovia's no-holds-barred explanation seemed to satisfy Mia's curiosity. She tossed her hair and smiled in Tristan's direction. "Are you doing okay, Tristan? You can cry if you want. I'm here...we're here for you."

Alyssa and Zenovia shared one glance that transferred more than a thousand words. They both went through contortions to hold in their laughter. Mia was so transparent, but Tristan either didn't notice Mia's overtures or he didn't care.

They reached the bus stop at Mayfield and Lee just as Emil's bus was pulling up. Zenovia jumped out of the car. She wanted to talk to him and explain before he saw Tristan and immediately got angry.

"Hi, Emil!" Zenovia wrapped her arms around his neck and kissed him on the cheek.

Emil saw Tristan's car and frowned. "Why is he here?"

Zenovia explained how they'd come to her house and how she'd ended up inviting them to the rink. He did not look happy.

"Be cool for me. Okay?" Zenovia asked.

"All right, but Tristan better not say nothing reckless."

"He won't. Come on."

Emil got into the backseat with Zenovia and Alyssa. He grunted hellos to everyone in the car and then put his arm around Zenovia. She watched Tristan glance at them through the rearview mirror. He wore a straight face, neither angry nor sad.

Zenovia gave him a little smile and he looked away. She snuggled in close to Emil and inhaled his masculine scent. She almost wished she'd accepted his invitation and come to his house for some alone time.

But when she felt the hot stream of breath into her ear and the tingles it sent through her body, she was convinced, more than ever, that being with Emil was dangerous.

Chapter Nineteen

Zenovia spread her college brochures out on the table. It was January of her senior year, and she had already completed her admissions packages and scholarships. She was mostly waiting on responses. Audrey walked up to the table holding a sandwich and a glass of Kool-Aid.

"Are you hungry?"

"Not really, but thanks, Mom."

"You've been sitting at this table all morning. When do you plan on taking a break?"

Zenovia took the plate from Audrey's hand which smelled strongly of bleach. Audrey had been up since before sunrise, giving the house a good bleaching. This time she smelled animal feces. She'd accused Phillip of letting a raccoon in the house during the night, and she even thought that the animal had given birth in her kitchen.

Then, a few hours later she was making ham sandwiches like everything was everything.

Zenovia had already chosen her school. She was going to Howard University without a doubt. Her guidance counselor told her that it was almost certain that she'd get a full ride, with her academic achievements and her extracurricular activities, but she was leaving nothing to chance.

A lack of funds was not going to trap her in hell with Audrey and Phillip.

Audrey handed Zenovia a piece of mail. "I forgot to give you this. It looks like a letter from Justin."

Zenovia took the letter gingerly. He'd only been gone a month, and she didn't miss him. Not seeing him had cured her of her incurable crush, but the letter took her mind back to his stolen kiss.

She tore the envelope open slowly and read the words written in cursive in green ink.

> *Hey Zee,*
>
> *How are you? Do you miss me yet? Go ahead and smile. You know you want to. It is beyond cold here in Boston. I never thought I'd be wishing for Cleveland weather, but this is a different brand of chill-you-to-your-bones cold. Hope you're studying hard! I expect to hear about you leaving for college soon.*
>
> *I hear you and Emil are still going strong. I thought that was a temporary, puppy love kind of thing. I should've paid closer attention and threw more salt in his game.*
>
> *Make sure you watch over Tristan for me. He's still really broken up about Kyle, even if he doesn't let on. Hope you're not too sad. Maybe see Kyle one day again. I'm praying for all of y'all.*
>
> *But it's almost time for group Bible study. Here at headquarters we all study together. It's kind of nice,*

*having all these volunteers here with our minds on serving
the organization. It's a beautiful thing.*

Well, even if you don't miss me, I miss you!

Live free . . . give free,

Justin

Zenovia folded the letter and placed it back in its envelope. What a character Justin was. But he was right, she and Emil had grown even closer. Zenovia could see herself with him for the rest of her life, and he'd completely obliterated any feelings that she'd had for Tristan.

It was like the closer they got to graduation, the more she put the thought of him away. They were still friends, of course, but Emil's charming way of claiming her before the world caused Zenovia to be completely enamored with him.

They were still on winter break, but it had been an uneventful vacation. The Brethren's Christmas celebration consisted of a worship service where they thanked God for sending Jesus to earth. No parties, no decorations, no tree. It hadn't really bothered Zenovia to have these things missing, though. It wasn't like she and Audrey had merry holidays before the Brethren.

Zenovia's pager buzzed on her hip. It read 149—Emil's code. It was the street he lived on. She picked up the phone and dialed his number, smiling even before she heard his voice.

"Hey, baby girl," said Emil. "You ready for your driving lesson?"

"Ha! No, I'm not ready at all. I don't want to get my license."

"It's easy! My dad is letting me borrow his car, and

there is no snow on the ground. This is the perfect chance."

Zenovia laughed. "The perfect chance for us to wind up wrapped around a tree."

"Baby, I will not let that happen. I promise. I'm on my way to pick you up. Be ready in fifteen minutes."

"Okay, okay. I'll be ready."

Emil actually pulled up in about twelve minutes, but Zenovia didn't care. She would've been happy if he'd just beamed over, as long as he showed up. She could hear him on the front porch, and knew he was about to ring the doorbell. Emil never just honked his horn. He came into the house and said hello to Audrey, no matter what state she was in. He acted as if Audrey's affliction was just a part of her personality and Zenovia loved him for that.

Audrey opened the door as Zenovia pulled on her coat and boots. "Hey, Emil. What ya know good?"

Emil hugged Audrey and kissed her cheek. "Ain't nothing going on, Sister Audrey. How you feeling?"

"I'm good, baby!"

Audrey turned up the volume on the television. She was watching her favorite thing—videos on BET.

"Look at his fine chocolate self!" she said to the screen.

"Ooh, Sister Audrey! Brother Phillip is gonna get you," teased Emil.

"What he don't know won't hurt him!" Audrey replied as she did a modified version of the Monorail line dance.

Zenovia laughed and pulled Emil outside. Zenovia put her hand over her mouth when she saw Emil's father's car. It was a nineteen-eighty-something Thunderbird with more rust on it than paint.

"This is your father's car?"

Emil laughed. "This is his old car. He drives a van."

"It is old... very old," Zenovia remarked.

Perhaps sensing Zenovia's tentativeness he said, "It drives and it has heat. Come on."

Emil drove to a park near his house and stopped in the parking lot. He turned to Zenovia and said, "Are you ready?"

Zenovia wasn't afraid to drive, but the fact that she'd never done it before left her feeling a bit nervous. And if she was going to get her lessons in that raggedy automobile, she'd just as soon pass.

"I'm not ready, Emil. It's quiet here. Why don't we just sit and talk."

Emil's eyes lit up. "In the backseat?"

"Sure, but we're not going to do anything freaky, so don't get any ideas."

Zenovia didn't sound serious at all, especially since she and Emil had had this conversation several times before. She'd swear that they weren't going to do anything at all, but once in close proximity of one another they'd start kissing and petting, each time going a bit further.

Once they had settled into the spacious backseat, Zenovia asked, "Emil, have you thought about what you're gonna do after high school?"

"No! That's a long way off."

"Six months is not a long way off."

Emil got a thoughtful-looking expression on his face. "Well, I'm just going to get a job. Nothing special. How much planning do I need?"

"You're not going to college?" Zenovia asked.

"Brethren don't go to college."

"When did you become a Brethren drone?"

"Well, I…"

Emil started his reply, but was cut off by a loud knock on the car window. He wiped away the fog and standing outside with a menacing expression on her face was Sienna—the girl from the skating rink.

"Aw, man," Emil said.

"Aw, man, what?" Zenovia asked.

Sienna frowned and knocked on the window again, her thick honey blond braids flapping around her head like tentacles. "Get out of the car, Emil! I've been following you all day."

Zenovia waited for an explanation from Emil, but he was silent. The only thing he did was give Zenovia an apologetic look.

Sienna would not be ignored. "Emil, you better get out of that car before I tell your girlfriend our little secret."

"What secret, Emil?" Zenovia asked finally finding words.

Emil sighed. "She might be pregnant."

"With your baby?"

Sienna answered from outside. "Yes, with *his* baby! I'm five months pregnant with his baby!"

Zenovia did the math, adding and subtracting months in her mind. She'd definitely gotten pregnant before she and Emil had started dating. But was he still messing with her?

"Emil—" Zenovia started.

"Not since we've been together, Zee. I swear."

"But when I asked you if you'd slept with her you said no."

"I lied."

"But why? Why would you lie about that?"

"Would you have talked to me if you'd known? Would your Brethren friends have approved?"

Emil's big brown eyes pleaded for the truth, but Zenovia had to look away. The Brethren would not have approved of him, and she probably wouldn't have either. But now that her heart belonged to Emil, his transgressions didn't seem like a deal breaker. They simply seemed like transgressions.

"Why don't you get out of the car and see what she wants," Zenovia said.

Sienna laughed. "Yeah, Emil, quit trying to lie to your bald-headed girlfriend and come see about your son!"

Self-consciously, Zenovia's hand went to her hair which was styled in a layered, curly cut and tapered at the neckline. Sienna's long braids were real, even though they looked like the synthetic hair that came in packages at the beauty supply store.

Emil ignored Sienna's rant and wiped a tear from Zenovia's face. "I love your hair, Zee. I love you, too. No matter what happens, I want you to know that."

He kissed both her cheeks and her mouth before he stepped out of the car. He slammed the door angrily, and walked up on Sienna swiftly and threateningly.

"What? What do you want?" he asked.

Sienna's wicked smile melted and she burst into tears. "I want you to stop playing, Emil! I'm having your baby and you act like you don't care anything about me."

"When we get a paternity test, then we'll figure it out. But until then, stop calling me and following me. I'm not your boyfriend."

Sienna's friend who had stayed in the car jumped out and said, "Come on, girl. This dog ain't worth it."

The girl led the sobbing Sienna back to their car. Emil got into the front seat of his father's car and left Zenovia sitting in the backseat.

"You cool?" he asked.

Zenovia didn't reply. She couldn't. Emil had said that he loved her, but he had a baby on the way, with Sienna. It was unreal, and Zenovia couldn't form words that would describe her feelings.

Zenovia could hear Emil's mother, Gladys's, voice in her head. *He's got hoe blood.*

She should've listened to Gladys. Then she wouldn't be sitting in the backseat of a rusty Thunderbird with a broken heart. All because Emil was a fornicator.

Emil started driving, but Zenovia didn't ask where he was taking her. He said, "This doesn't change anything with us, Zee."

"How can you say that, Emil? It changes everything."

He slammed on the breaks, placed the car in park, and turned all the way around in his seat. "It doesn't change that I love you. Sienna is just a hood rat having a baby. That's all."

Zenovia looked into Emil's eyes which were glazed over with tears. She wanted so badly to believe him. But how could she?

Emil wasn't like Tristan. He wasn't pure and chaste. How could she stay in a relationship with him? One day soon, he'd ask her to do what Sienna had done, and if she refused he'd get it elsewhere. He'd do it no matter how much he loved her.

Because he's got hoe blood.

Emil started driving again. They were going toward his house, but Zenovia didn't object. She was still reflecting on his words.

He'd said that he loved her. It was the first time she'd ever heard that from a man. Well, Emil wasn't quite a man, but he wasn't a boy, either. He was about to be a father.

Emil stopped the car in the driveway of his house. "Are you going to come in?" he asked.

"I don't think your mother would approve."

Emil paused before replying. "You're right. Let's go to my dad's house."

"Your dad? Does he live nearby?"

"Yep. Around the corner. He's cool, and I have my own room over there."

"Okay."

Emil guided Zenovia to the side door of his father's house. "Be quiet, because my grandmother lives downstairs and I don't want to have to talk to her."

Zenovia nodded and followed Emil up the two flights of stairs. Downstairs a creaky door opened.

"Dag," whispered Emil. He held his finger to his lips, telling Zenovia to stay quiet.

"Who is that?" Zenovia smiled at the old woman's saucy tone.

"It's me, Grandma."

"Emil! Ain't no school today?"

Emil laughed, "I'm on winter break, Grandma."

"Oh. You want something to eat? I just made some okra."

"No thanks, Grandma. I'm cool. I'm 'bout to watch some TV."

"All right, baby."

Emil covered his mouth to keep from giggling and showed Zenovia into his father's house.

"I didn't know your parents were divorced," Zenovia said.

"They aren't. They just don't live together."

Zenovia was confused. "So they're legally separated?"

"Not exactly. My dad visits Gladys when he wants to get some, like on their anniversary or his birthday."

Zenovia laughed. "That's crazy!"

"No, it's not. They love each other, but they don't get along so well."

Zenovia glanced around the room. There were pictures of scantily clad women on all of the walls. Some of the pictures were torn from magazines, some were posters, and some were Polaroids.

"This is a bachelor pad," Emil explained.

"Obviously."

Emil went to the small refrigerator in the even tinier kitchen. "Do you want something to drink?"

"What do you have?"

"Beer, wine coolers..."

Zenovia laughed. "How about Kool-Aid?"

Emil shook his head. "No can do. There's some ginger ale in here, though."

"I'll take it."

Emil took Zenovia to the living room area which was very sparsely furnished. There was a big soft recliner, and that was it.

Zenovia looked around the room. "Where are we supposed to sit?"

"We can share! It's a big chair, Zee."

Zenovia grinned at the mischievous look in Emil's eyes. She wondered how Emil did it. How was he able to make her forget about his pregnant fling with one smile?

It was chilly in the house, so Emil dashed into his bedroom and emerged with a blanket. He and Zenovia snuggled into the recliner, him with a Molson Ice and her with a can of ginger ale. He turned on the TV with a remote and started flicking through the channels, settling on *Star Trek* reruns.

"Are you kidding me?" Zenovia asked. "You're a Trekkie?"

"Yes, I'm a Trekkie. Does that surprise you?"

"Yeah, it kinda does. You don't seem like a guy who would like sci-fi."

Emil cleared his throat. "Well, I do. I mean, don't you ever think about the universe?"

Zenovia burst into laughter. "The universe? Emil..."

"I'm serious. Like what if there is some parallel universe out there where we're living alternate lives?"

Zenovia's laughter had turned into a full-fledged giggle fit. Tears were running from her eyes. And it wasn't because what Emil was saying was so funny. It was because he was dead serious about it.

Emil continued, "Check it out. You could be in some other time continuum...."

"Time continuum?"

"Yes. Time continuum. And you might not have met me. You could be kicking it with your little Brethren drone Tristan, slaving for the organization."

"I'm not liking that," Zenovia said with a scrunched-up nose. "I'm glad I'm in this dimension."

"Me, too," replied Emil. He punctuated his sentiment with a kiss on Zenovia's nose.

She shrank away from his touch, because a picture of Sienna and her wild braids flashed before her eyes. But Emil was persistent. He kissed her again on her cheek and this time she didn't resist.

Their kissing turned into petting which quickly turned into blouses and shirts being removed. Before Zenovia could resist properly, she was in Emil's bedroom and in his bed, acting out the vision she'd already seen.

The truth was she didn't want to resist. She wanted this boy who said he loved her, and she wanted to rebel against the Brethren who did not care about another boy who killed himself because he wanted to serve them. She wanted Emil all for herself and she knew that she couldn't compete with the Siennas of the world.

Girls like Mia got Tristan, and girls like Sienna ended up with Emil.

She wasn't Mia or Sienna, but she didn't want to lose Emil. Even if she ended up being just another jump-off to him. She wanted to give him her virginity, because what else did she have that he wanted?

Guys like Tristan wanted girls with brains, but Emil...no matter what he said, he wanted the body.

Chapter Twenty

What's wrong with you?" Audrey asked.

She was referring to Zenovia and the ridiculous funk of a mood she found herself in. It all started the day after she'd given her virginity to Emil. It wasn't anything that he'd done or said, because he'd been especially attentive, sweet, and everything a recently satisfied boyfriend should be.

It wasn't that she was bothered about Sienna, because she simply wasn't. She had exed Sienna right out of her mind as if her or Emil's supposed baby didn't exist.

It was more about her vision. The vision she'd had of her and Emil fornicating and how she'd casually fulfilled it as if it was fate. She couldn't believe that God would predestine her to sin against Him, but how else could she explain the vision?

She thought back on her conversation with Tristan about destiny and fate. Did she have a choice, once she saw a vision? Or did God know what path she'd choose even if He wished her to do otherwise? It was all confusing, and she didn't know what to think.

What she did know was that the Brethren didn't have the answers.

They'd gone to a Brethren Bible study the day after she'd sinned with Emil, and she was definitely on edge. She wondered if the Holy Spirit was going to reveal something to the Council of Elders or to Tristan. Would her secret be written all over her face?

To make things even worse, Bryce Goodman had stood before the congregation giving a lecture about immorality. He talked about the stench of sin and how God chastises those He loves.

The whole eight minutes he was before the congregation irritated Zenovia to no end. The man was either having or planning to have a flagrant affair on his wife, and he stood up there talking about the stench of sin.

The scripture that kept playing in Zenovia's mind was, "For all have sinned and come short of the glory of God."

So wouldn't that mean everyone in the congregation was covered in the stench of sin? The Brethren never talked about forgiveness, grace, mercy, or God's love. Only about what would happen if you got caught sinning.

In his sermon, Bryce even encouraged people to snitch on those that they knew were engaged in some kind of sin. He'd said that it was ideal for a believer to confess his sins, but that not everyone had the strength to do that, and that it was of utmost importance to keep the congregation clean.

From the stench of sin.

It all bothered Zenovia, because she wondered what kind of Christian she was. She wasn't repentant. She wasn't even sad about what she'd done. So what did that mean?

Did she not love God?

The thought of God thinking that *she* didn't love *Him* affected her more than anything that the Brethren preached across the pulpit. She had come home from the Bible study and prayed. She had asked God to forgive her even though she wasn't sorry. She didn't know if that was right or if God even heard it.

But she prayed it anyway.

Zenovia snapped out of her recollection and peered at her mother, who seemed to be looking right through her. "Nothing is wrong, Mom. I'm okay."

"Listen," she said, "I know what you're going through. Sometimes the things we do against the Lord help to make our lives a testimony for someone else."

Zenovia smiled. Audrey giving advice was rare, and it was even less likely that she would say anything lucid. Zenovia wondered if she'd seen a vision of her and Emil. The thought of it made her skin crawl.

She decided that she didn't want to know, so she took Audrey's advice at face value.

Audrey wasn't big on lectures. She'd say what she had to say and let it go. Zenovia appreciated her for this, especially since Audrey could start off on one subject and end up somewhere totally different and cursing you out when you didn't even know you were arguing.

Zenovia's pager buzzed on her hip. It read 149-911. It was Emil and it was an emergency. Immediately she picked up the phone and called him. It crossed her mind to ask him why he always paged her instead of just calling her!

"Hello," said Emil.

"Hi there," said Zenovia. "Can I ask you a question?"

"Yes..."

"Why don't you ever call me? Why do you always page me?"

Emil took a long pause before responding. "I never know what's going on with Audrey, so I just let you call me back. Is that cool?"

Zenovia smiled. "Yes. I was hoping that it wasn't some kind of ego thing."

"Um...no," Emil replied.

She asked, "Is there something wrong?"

He sighed. "Yeah, kinda. Can we meet?"

"Sure. At the rink?"

"No. Let's do the mall."

"Okay, when?"

"Now."

"Okay, I'll see you there."

Zenovia hung up the phone feeling alarmed. She didn't need a vision to let her know that whatever Emil had to say it was going to be all bad.

The telephone startled her when it rang. "Hello."

"Hey, Zee!"

She thought it was Emil calling her back, so she was surprised to hear Tristan's voice.

"Oh, hey, Tristan. What's up?"

"We haven't seen you all vacation! I know you've been hanging with Emil and all, but can you show your friends a little love?"

In spite of herself, Zenovia grinned. Even with the impending doom of whatever Emil wanted to meet with her about, she couldn't help but get a little excited when hearing Tristan's voice.

"Well, I have to meet Emil at the mall, but after that I'm free."

"How are you getting to the mall?"

"The bus."

"It's a little chilly to be waiting on a bus. Do you want a ride?"

Zenovia considered the request. It would probably annoy the heck out of Emil to see Tristan drop her off at the mall. But Zenovia had the sneaky suspicion that she was going to be beyond annoyed after their conversation.

"Yes, Tristan. I'd love a ride. But you can't drop me off in front of the food court."

Tristan chuckled. "Of course. I don't want your thug life boyfriend coming after me."

"You're funny, Tristan. And what do you mean thug life? Is Tupac acceptable listening for one of the Brethren elite?"

"Ha, ha. I still have to take a shower—can I pick you up in forty-five minutes?"

It would take over an hour for the bus to get her there, so Zenovia replied, "Absolutely. Thanks, Tristan."

"My pleasure."

Tristan was right on time, and Zenovia went outside to meet him. She didn't want to give him the opportunity to come inside and chat with Audrey, because she was in one of her moods. Unlike Emil, Tristan didn't have a safe comfort level with Audrey's mental illness.

"What's up, dude?" Zenovia asked as she got into the car. She was trying to pretend like everything was all good, and that she wasn't worried about meeting with Emil.

"What's up with Zee?" Tristan asked.

He put an extreme emphasis on the word Zee, like he hadn't seen her in ages and was just that excited to hear about her life. Zenovia thought it was cute.

"Hmm...let me see. I've picked my school."

"Your college? Is it somewhere near Boston?"

A look of shock came across Zenovia's face. Tristan played entirely too much. Why would he be asking her such a thing?

"Um...no, I didn't apply to any schools in New England. I actually plan on attending Howard University."

"Where's that? Is that an Ivy League school?"

Zenovia's jaw dropped. "You're kidding me, right? Howard is a historically black university. It's in Washington, D.C."

"I'm not kidding, but I'm interested in what you're doing."

Zenovia felt completely bizarre about the conversation. "Why do you care so much about my choice of college?"

"I thought it would be cool if we were near each other. I could serve at the Brethren headquarters, and you could go to class. Then we could hang on the weekends."

Zenovia shook her head and looked at Tristan as if he'd lost his mind. "Tristan, I don't get you."

"What?"

She'd opened the door yet again for him to really say how he felt, but he refused to walk through. It was frustrating because as much as she dug Emil, she didn't know if there was a future with him. She could envision him with illegitimate children all across America, but she couldn't see herself being their stepmother.

But Tristan. He could be her husband when he got done with all of his volunteer work. They could build a little happy Brethren family and have a house with a dog.

Well ... maybe they could've had it before she decided to fornicate with Emil. What would he think of her now that she was no longer pure?

Tristan said, "It just seems like we're losing you."

"We who? Who is losing me?"

"The Brethren, our crew, I don't know. Maybe I'm just tripping because Kyle's gone and my brother is in Boston. You're my only other friend."

Zenovia nodded slowly. This was the closest Tristan had ever come to spilling any emotions over her.

"What about Mia?" Zenovia tempted fate with her question. "She's your friend."

"Mia? She's not even a real person! She's just ... I don't know, but she's not like you."

"What am I like, Tristan?" Zenovia asked, trying to lead him to the water.

"I mean, you're passionate about everything! You think about stuff, and you don't just agree because you should agree."

Zenovia bit her lip and sighed. It was those things that Tristan loved about her that made her so wary of the Brethren. Her analytical thinking, her passion, her rebelliousness; all of that was being stolen from her as one of the Brethren.

"You're not losing me, Tristan. I'm still your friend."

Tristan turned and blessed her with a beautiful smile. "I hope that's always the case, Zee. I really do."

"You're the only one who can mess it up!"

"Wow. So can I tell you something...a secret?"

Zenovia's eyebrows went all the way up. "A secret? I didn't know you had secrets."

"I do. I do have secrets."

"Do tell."

"You're not going to tell anyone are you?"

Zenovia was immediately serious. "Tristan, I would keep your secrets forever. Even if we're not friends anymore."

"I believe you. So I'm going to tell you. But in pieces, because it's hard for me to just tell this kind of thing, but I have to tell you."

"Okay, now you've got me stoked! What is it, for crying out loud?"

Tristan took a deep breath. "See, it's hard for me to do this, because I'm not supposed to have these feelings."

"Oh, good grief, Tristan! Spill it or zip it!"

Tristan laughed. "Okay, well, I kind of have a crush on someone."

"Do I know her?" Zenovia asked.

He paused for a moment as if deciding whether or not to continue. "Yes. You know her."

"Okay, is she one of the Brethren?"

"Of course!"

"Forgive me. I don't know what I was thinking. Are you going to tell me who?"

Tristan looked at the ceiling. "Not yet. When I pick you up from the mall. When should I pick you up?"

They were at the mall entrance and Zenovia was about to explode! She could tell that Tristan was on the verge of professing his love. She knew it!

But why now? Why after she'd met, fallen for, and given it up to Emil! Why couldn't he have been up-front from the beginning? Why wasn't she more patient?

Why wasn't she getting out of the car to go meet her boyfriend?

"Tristan, I'll page you when I'm ready."

"Okay. See you in a bit."

Chapter Twenty-one

Zenovia was early for her meeting with Emil. She was glad to have the moment to catch her breath and analyze her conversation with Tristan. Because Tristan was completely out of control.

First of all, what did he mean when he said they were losing her? Perhaps her inner critique of the Brethren was outwardly apparent, although she went through great pains to hide her feelings.

She switched gears for a moment, to what Emil could want to meet her about. What if he had some kind of disease? She could see that dusty Sienna being the carrier of multiple illnesses. What if he had something that a condom couldn't protect her from? A shiver went up her spine. She hoped that it was anything but that.

Well, almost anything.

She sat at a table in the center of the food court and watched Emil as he walked in the door. He trudged slowly ahead like he was on his way to his execution. Zenovia waved at him and he nodded slightly.

He sat down in front of Zenovia and the first thing she noted was how tired he looked. His eyes were puffy and red and there were huge dark circles under them. Normally, Emil was always on the verge of a smile, even when he was being serious, but his mouth was down-turned and his expression sullen.

"What's wrong, Emil? And don't say nothing, because it's written all over your face."

Emil sighed. "I don't even know how to start."

"That doesn't sound good Emil."

Zenovia felt her stomach lurch when Emil's eyes misted.

He said, "It's just that this might be our last conversation, so I don't want to rush into it."

When the first tear dropped from Emil's big doe eyes onto the table, Zenovia's own waterworks started.

"Why would we be having our last conversation right now? Are you breaking up with me?"

Emil nodded. Zenovia shook her head violently, "Why are you breaking up with me? Is it because I gave it up?"

"No! It's Gladys. She said she saw us go into my father's house and knew that we didn't come out for hours. She said that she'd go to the Council of Elders if I didn't break it off with you."

"I don't care about that!"

"I do. I can't have them cast you out because of me. You don't know what it'll be like. None of your friends, not even your mother, will be allowed to talk to you."

"Nothing will stop my mother from talking to me."

"But it's not just that, Zee. I'm corrupting you. You can do better than me."

Zenovia took a sip of her soda and said, "I don't believe this. I really don't believe this."

How convenient it was that Emil decided to care about corrupting her, after he'd already ultimately corrupted her.

"Plus, my dad...I mean, we take care of ours. If Sienna's baby is mine, I need to handle my business."

Zenovia laughed, but the sound was more sorrowful than amused. "This is a joke, right?"

"No, Zee. I didn't lie when I said that I loved you. I do. That's why I'm listening to my mother and not messing with you anymore."

The reality of what he was saying finally sank in, and even though she'd thought this was the inevitable end, it still hurt. She laid her head on the table and sobbed openly, not caring about the strangers staring at her.

She cried over losing Emil. She cried over losing her virginity. She cried over her own stupidity.

"Don't do that, Zee. Don't cry like that," Emil said, his own voice still wavering.

"Just leave, Emil," Zenovia said through the sobs. "There's nothing more to say."

Emil stood, but instead of walking away he kneeled in front of Zenovia, hugged her midsection, and sobbed into her lap. She found herself stroking his back, trying to comfort him when he was the one who was doing the hurting.

After he composed himself, Emil said, "I'm so sorry, Zee. I need you to believe me."

"I believe you."

As if it had just dawned on Emil that his emotional display was completely the opposite of his gangsta facade, he quickly stood to his feet and wiped his eyes. Zenovia stared at him with so much disbelief in her eyes along with her tears. He was supposed to be rebellious with her. They were the anti-drones that were going to let their love win out in the end.

Right.

Her Emil, her rebel, thugged-out Emil had let his mother end their relationship.

She did believe that he was sorry, though. It didn't change the fact that she'd given him her most precious thing, and he hadn't deserved it at all. Her purity was ruined and wasted, and it was all for naught.

Chapter Twenty-two

After finally bringing the torrential flood of tears under control, Zenovia paged Tristan to pick her up from the mall. She didn't want to see him any more than she wanted to continue her conversation with Emil, but she needed to get home, and the twenty-degree January weather wasn't very inviting for riding the bus.

She rushed through the steadily falling snowflakes and jumped into Tristan's car. The cold wind turned her cheeks red which, thankfully, masked the streaks that her tears left.

"That was quick!" Tristan said. "I wasn't expecting to hear from you for a few hours."

Zenovia nodded and gave Tristan a tiny smile. She hesitated to open her mouth to speak, afraid that her voice would crack and reveal her distress.

"So...did you eat something?"

Zenovia shook her head. She almost lost it when she thought of her and Emil's usual mall food court meal. They'd always shared a big messy tray of chili fries and a large cherry slush. She swallowed hard, but was unable to dislodge the knot in her throat.

"Are you hungry?" Tristan asked.

She felt a small tear leak from one of her eyes. She shook her head quickly, wishing that Tristan would just be quiet.

"Zee..."

"Don't."

Zenovia was only able to utter that one word before she broke down again. This time there were no sobs, just a flood of tears.

Tristan pulled his car over and parked on the street. Zenovia was relieved that he didn't try to comfort her. She didn't want to be comforted by him.

As she sobbed, she silently prayed. *God, I feel too ashamed to speak with you right now. It took Emil breaking up with me to even feel sad about being disobedient to you. I deliberately sinned against you and now I'm here crying. I just hope that you're patient with me, even though I don't have the right to ask for patience. I pray that you're merciful, though I don't have the right to ask for mercy. I love you, Lord, and I'm sorry for what I've done.*

"Are you sure you want to do this?" Tristan asked as he pulled into the driveway of his house. "Maybe you need some time to think about it."

After her prayer, Zenovia knew what she needed to do. She had to confess her reckless sins with Emil. She had to somehow make things right again. And confessing her sins seemed to be the first step.

"No, Tristan. I need to do this now. Isn't confession part of what we believe as the Brethren?"

Tristan nodded. "Yes, of course, but not everyone does it. Some people are content to just confess their sins to God and be through with it."

"Are you telling me to go against what we believe?" Zenovia asked.

"I'm telling you to think about it before you do it, Zee. I'm telling you to think of the consequences."

"What could be worse than losing my salvation, Tristan?"

Tristan stared down at his hands. "Zee, I don't know what you've done, but I do know that the Brethren will not go easy on you."

"What do you mean, *go easy?*" Zenovia asked, confusion etching lines into her forehead. "I don't want anyone to go easy on me. I just want to confess, have God forgive me, and move on with the rest of my life."

"I think you should confess, Zee, but I don't want to lose you."

Zenovia blinked back a tear caused by Tristan's sudden sentimentality. "You're not going to lose me."

Tristan sighed. "Do you know that serving the Brethren is the most important thing in my life?"

"Yes, I know that."

"Well, when I tell you that I will lose you behind this, I'm not being dramatic. I'm saying that if you do this, things will never be the same between us."

Zenovia shook her head. She should've assumed this much without Tristan saying a word. If he was too worried about what the Brethren would say about him loaning her his suit jacket, of course he wouldn't want to be associated with a sinner. Especially not a sinful, loose girl who might hurt his chances of serving at the Brethren headquarters.

But it didn't matter. Her confession was not about Tristan or even the Brethren. It was about God. She'd just poured her heart out in prayer, and believed that she needed to take it a step further.

"Tristan, I need to do this. I think your father is the only one I could tell about this."

Tristan sighed. "All right, Zenovia. I'm going to pray that this is the right decision."

"It is the right decision, Tristan. I can feel it."

Chapter Twenty-three

Zenovia heard the doorbell followed by the knock on their front door, but made absolutely no effort to get out of her bed to answer it. After the forced break up with Emil, she had retreated to her bedroom, only leaving for school, meals, and to use the bathroom.

Between bouts of tears, she prayed and thought about calling Emil. She was desperately fighting the urge to call him, and she died a thousand deaths checking her buzzing pager and hoping that it was Emil. The blouse that she wore during their break-up meeting was draped across her pillow, because it held Emil's scent.

Confessing her sins to Brother Batiste had not had the desired effect. Zenovia had hoped to feel as if a burden had been lifted, but it was quite the opposite. Tristan's father had been very cold and clinical, taking notes as if he was a court stenographer recording the confession of a murderer.

She had not left their home feeling renewed or refreshed. To the contrary, she'd felt soiled and damaged.

Tristan was not allowed to drive her home or even to say goodbye to her as she left. She was driven home in silence by Sister Batiste. The woman who helped plan Audrey's wedding didn't even wait until Zenovia got into the house before burning rubber to get away.

She was told by Brother Batiste that the confession was not the end, and that more of the Council of Elders would be contacting her soon. So instead of feeling closer to God for confessing her sins, she felt apprehensive and terrified.

She listened to the voices in the living room after the doorbell stopped ringing and the knocking ceased.

She heard Audrey open the door and say a greeting. "Hey, Brother Bryce! Phillip didn't tell me you were coming over. I would've cooked something."

"Hello there, Audrey," Bryce Goodman replied. "Phillip didn't know we were dropping by."

"He didn't?" Audrey asked. "Then why are y'all here?"

Bryce replied, "We're here to see Zenovia. Is she here?"

Zenovia sat straight up in her bed. She hadn't known that someone would come to their home to further interrogate her. She hadn't mentioned any of this to Audrey. Not her fornication with Emil, or her subsequent confession to Brother Batiste.

She felt a deep rumble in the pit of her stomach.

"Zee!" Audrey called from the living room. "You've got company."

Zenovia looked in her mirror and dabbed the tears from her face with a tissue. Then, she walked into the living room with hesitation in her steps. Bryce and another one of the Council of Elders were seated on their leather sectional.

"Hello, Zenovia," Bryce said.

"Hi."

"Do you know Brother Wilkinson?"

Zenovia shook her head. "Why are you here?"

Bryce held his hand out to the couch. "Have a seat. We're just here to talk to you for a bit about what you told Brother Batiste. Is that okay?"

Zenovia said nothing in response, but sat down next to Bryce. He continued, "You confessed that you were intimate with Emil Buchanon, but you didn't give any details."

"Details?"

"Yes. We'll need details in order to know if we should schedule an elder tribunal."

Zenovia gave incredulous glances to each of the men. She had no intention of answering any questions until she looked over into the kitchen at Audrey. Her mother was clearly nervous, wringing her hands and pacing back and forth.

"Is there reason for us to call an elder tribunal?" Bryce asked.

Zenovia raised an eyebrow at the man. He seemed way too excited about the very idea of calling the elder tribunal. He sat on the edge of the couch holding a pen and notebook and licking his lips.

"Well, I don't know the reasons for calling an elder tribunal, Brother Goodman, so you're going to have to fill me in."

Brother Wilkinson responded, "Any improper sexual activities would require an elder tribunal."

"Have you all talked to Emil?" Zenovia asked.

Bryce asked, "Why? So you can corroborate your stories?"

"No. I was just curious," said Zenovia. She could feel her temperature rise, but for Audrey's sake, she tried to keep her cool.

"Well, for your information, we're not authorized to approach Emil. He isn't baptized as one of the Brethren," Brother Wilkinson stated. He was clearly the less blood-thirsty of the two.

"What happens if I refuse to answer you?" Zenovia asked.

"Then we will assume that you were committing for-nication. We will also assume that since you refused to tell us that you have absolutely no remorse or repen-tance..."

"...And you will be cast out at the next Bible study," Brother Wilkinson said.

"Just like that?"

Bryce nodded slowly. "Exactly like that."

Zenovia weighed her options. Immediately being cast out of the Brethren meant no more friendship with her best friend Tristan and no more letters from Justin. It meant that Audrey would be embarrassed in front of all her new Brethren friends.

Did it mean that she'd be cast away from God? She didn't know, but as much as she doubted that it was true, she didn't want to take any chances.

Zenovia deeply inhaled; calmly exhaled. "I suppose you need to call your elder tribunal."

In the kitchen, Audrey howled. It was painful for Zenovia to listen to her making that noise and knowing that it was because of her sin.

Looking satisfied, Bryce got to his feet. "Zenovia,

we'll contact you with further information. I have an appointment."

He and Brother Wilkinson started toward the door, but Bryce touched Zenovia on her shoulder before walking away. She recoiled from his touch, but it was too late.

"*I can't leave her. You know that,*" *Bryce roars at the woman in the red coat.*

"*Well, then, I'm getting married to Scott. He loves me.*"

Bryce grabs the woman by her arm. "*Don't even think about it, Leah. I won't let it happen.*"

Leah says, "*I have to, Bryce. I'm pregnant with your baby. I'll be cast out if I don't have a husband.*"

Bryce paces the sidewalk and throws his arms into the air. "*So what if you get cast out? Then we can be together and there won't be another man raising my child!*"

"*You want me to be cast out? Well, let's confess and get cast out together.*"

"*I can't do that, Leah.*"

Leah slaps Bryce across the face, "*You selfish bastard.*"

Zenovia shivered. She glared at Bryce and said, "Tell Leah I said hello."

Bryce's face turned a ghastly shade of ash. He replied, "Brenda. My wife's name is Brenda."

"I know."

Chapter Twenty-four

"How could you?" Audrey wailed.

She was still standing in the middle of the kitchen, even though Bryce and company had been gone for half an hour. Zenovia felt that it was time to tell Audrey about her and Emil in case she found out from one of the Brethren.

"How could I what?"

"How could you get in trouble, Zee? I've been so proud of you!"

Audrey's words felt like punches. "I'm sorry, Mom."

"Now Phillip is going to trip! He's gonna want to put you out of his house when you get cast out!"

"*When* I get cast out?"

"Yes, when! I've seen it, Zenovia. God gave me a vision."

Zenovia frowned. So even if she had this tribunal with the Council of Elders, she was still going to be cast out.

So what was the point?

She paged Emil 911. There was no way she was calling

his house when Gladys had decided it was her duty to inform the Brethren of her indiscretion.

The phone rang less than a minute after she sent the page.

"What's up, Zee? What's the emergency?"

"Um...I just wanted to tell you that I have to go before an elder tribunal."

There was silence on the line.

"Emil, are you there?" Zenovia asked.

"Yes, I'm here, Zee. Why do you have to meet with the Council of Elders?"

"I confessed to Brother Batiste, about us sleeping together, and I guess they want more details now."

"My mother is going to kill me," Emil hissed.

"Is that all you care about? Don't you care what God might do?"

Emil sighed. "Right now, I'm more afraid of my mother than God. Gladys swings a mean frying pan."

"Well, I just wanted to tell you, Emil, in case anyone questions you."

"They won't. They can't punish me for anything, so they won't waste their time."

Was it only about punishment? The more Zenovia shared her decision to confess with others, the more it felt like she'd made a grave decision. But how could doing the right thing come back to haunt her? She didn't believe that God worked that way.

She believed there were rewards for doing the right thing.

Emil said, "I'm sorry about the elder tribunal. Do you want me to say it was my fault? I'll do that, you know."

"No, Emil. You've done enough."

Chapter Twenty-five

Zenovia's chest heaved up and down. She was sure that the three men sitting in front of her could hear her heart beating, because to her it sounded like an entire marching band drum line was playing in her ear. They were in the library of the Devotion Center, and although it was a nippy early spring day outside, the temperature inside the room was stifling hot.

Bryce Goodman smiled at her. Zenovia got the impression that there was some nervousness behind his grin. She couldn't blame him for that, though. She had intentionally spooked him about his mistress.

Zenovia had no plans to reveal his indiscretion, though. How could she? Would she just tell everyone that she'd had a vision that Bryce Goodman had a pregnant mistress? Zenovia knew that no one would believe her after her own sordid confession.

"Zenovia, if you cooperate, this shouldn't take long at all," Bryce said.

Brother Wilkinson added, "It's unfortunate that we are here with you only a few months after your baptism."

The other member of the tribunal was Brother Jennings. He said, "Most of the time, the newly baptized are more zealous. It keeps them from returning to their former lives of sin."

"None of that matters now," Bryce said. "Because we're here and we have to handle this matter. I will ask the questions and these two brothers here will take notes, so that we can be sure to have an accurate account."

Zenovia thought that Bryce was announcing the beginning of the tribunal and she bowed her head, anticipating a prayer.

Bryce said, "So, Zenovia. Would you like to tell us what you and Emil Buchanon were doing in his father's house alone?"

Zenovia snapped her head up. So there would be no prayer.

"Well, he invited me over for a visit."

"Were the two of you dating?" Bryce asked, his tone clipped and unfriendly.

"Yes."

"What did you do once inside the house?"

"He gave me something to drink."

Bryce's eyebrows shot up. "Alcohol?"

"No. It was ginger ale."

"So you weren't impaired or in a drunken state?"

"No..." Zenovia hoped that this was a good thing, her not being drunk, but she couldn't interpret Bryce's facial expression.

"You were fully aware of your actions?"

"Yes."

All three of the tribunal members stopped and looked at each other. The two scribes wrote something down in their notebooks. Zenovia tried to deduce their thoughts, but she was at a loss.

"What happened next?"

Zenovia paused before replying. "There was only one place to sit, so we shared the recliner and started to watch television."

"Is this when the fornication took place?"

"No. That was later."

"So there was fornication?"

Zenovia wondered if the Brethren ever said *have sex*. She replied, "Yes."

"Was this the first time?"

"Yes."

"Did he take you right there in the recliner?"

"No. In his bedroom."

"Did you climax?"

"Excuse me?" Zenovia just knew she'd heard wrong.

"Don't act as if you don't know what I'm talking about. You are far from innocent, Zenovia. I'll ask the question again. Did you come?"

"I-I don't think that's pertinent information."

Bryce frowned. "We decide what's pertinent. Elders, please note that she refused to answer the question. Was there protection used?"

"Protection?"

"Yes, contraceptives. A condom, perhaps?"

"Oh yes. Yes, we were safe. We used a condom." Zenovia sighed. This had to be a mark in her favor. She hadn't wanted a baby or a disease, two things that would complicate this situation even further.

"Did you bring it with you?"

"Did I bring what with me?"

"The condom. Were you carrying it in your purse when you got to Emil's house?"

"No. It was in his room."

"Do you ever carry contraceptives with you? Are you on birth control pills?" Bryce asked.

"No, of course not. I'm not on birth control."

Zenovia looked to the other tribunal members, to try and determine if this line of questioning was out of the ordinary. They scribbled madly into their notebooks, all three men seeming to get some kind of sick pleasure from her sordid deeds.

Bryce ignored her anxiety and asked another question. "How many times did you fornicate that day?"

"What?"

"How many times did this happen?"

"I'm not sure," Zenovia replied honestly. "I didn't count."

"Are you pregnant?"

"No," replied Zenovia wearily.

"How do you know you're not pregnant?" Bryce asked.

Zenovia rolled her eyes. "How does *any* woman know she's not pregnant?"

"If you're not pregnant, what prompted your confession? Do you have some kind of disease that could be spread to other men in the congregation?"

Zenovia angrily stood to her feet. "No! I confessed because I want to be right with God."

Bryce and the other two members of the tribunal frowned deeply. Zenovia could feel their judgmental stares boring a hole to her core. Their questions made her feel naked and exposed.

Bryce said, "If you were truly repentant, you would have a better attitude. You haven't shed one tear."

"I'm sorry. I guess I just don't know what you want to hear."

"I'm sorry, too," Bryce said as he closed his notebook. "When we're done deliberating we'll get back to you."

Brother Wilkinson said, "Let us close in prayer."

Finally, a prayer. After traumatizing her beyond reason and raping her with intimate unnecessary questions, they wanted to send up a prayer.

Brother Wilkinson prayed, "Dear heavenly Father, we come before you today asking that your will be done. We ask that your loving, chastening rod be used to make straight what is crooked and to correct what is disgusting. We know that your attributes are love, wisdom, justice, and power, but the greatest of these is justice. Your holy word says an eye for an eye, and we exact justice in your name. We pray in the name of Jesus, Amen."

The other two members of the tribunal said "Amen" but Zenovia could not force herself to agree with the venom that had just been masked as a prayer. Not one mention of God's mercy or grace. Not one mention of the blood that was shed on Calvary for the sins of mankind. Just fire, brimstone, punishment, and chastening.

Bryce looked pleased with himself, or maybe he'd just enjoyed interrogating a young girl about her sex life. Perhaps he'd been trying to get revenge for Zenovia's jab concerning his mistress. Whatever it was, Zenovia decided that he looked purely evil. There was no way the Holy Spirit had ever touched this man, much less communicated with him.

Zenovia walked out of the library where Audrey and Phillip were waiting to take her home. Phillip had a deep frown on his face and Audrey's face was puffy and tear-streaked, probably because she dreaded the worst.

Zenovia put on a courageous facade for her mother. Since the entire tribunal process started, Audrey's mental state had steadily worsened. In a week's time she had bleached their house about twenty times.

Audrey and Phillip had even gotten into an argument because she'd splashed bleach onto one of his favorite suits. After their fight, instead of splashing bleach like it was holy water, she took to sitting little teacups and saucers of bleach all around the house. They were on the tables, mantelpieces, lamp stands, and counters. The house smelled so strongly of bleach fumes that Zenovia could smell it in her nasal passages even when she was elsewhere.

Zenovia hugged her mother tightly, but Audrey was unresponsive. She seemed to look right through Zenovia and at Phillip. The three members of the tribunal emerged from the library right after Zenovia. The older two men went on to the parking lot of the Devotion Center, but Bryce stayed inside.

Bryce walked up to Phillip and patted him on the back. "It's going to be all right, bro. Don't worry."

"I didn't know we would have these kinds of problems from her," Phillip replied. "I thought she was a nice girl. And to think we let her spend so much time with Tristan and Justin."

"It would've been tragic if she had seduced Tristan instead of that thug Emil Buchanon," Bryce said. "His Brethren career would be over."

Zenovia had to swallow hard to keep from spewing venomous words at Bryce and Phillip. They acted as if she was a complete whore who had seduced Emil. And even if she was without morals, shouldn't they be worried about her salvation? Who cared about Tristan's career with the Brethren?

Chapter Twenty-six

Zenovia had received the results of the tribunal by telephone. She was to be severely chastened but not "cast out." Her chastening would include having her name read before the congregation along with a scripture about sin. According to Bryce, the details of her transgression were private and would not be shared beyond the tribunal.

She sat rigidly in her seat at the Devotion Center. She knew that her chastening would occur at this meeting, but she didn't know where in the service it would take place. Her friends all avoided eye contact with her as if they knew what was coming. Alyssa, who usually sat next to Zenovia, was stationed next to her mother and Tristan was seated at the back of the auditorium with his nose in his Bible.

Even Audrey had opted to sit next to Phillip on the other side of the Devotion Center, leaving her daughter alone to endure whatever horror was to come. The tribunal meeting had happened over a week before, and Zenovia could sense a distinct change in Audrey's attitude toward her.

Audrey had almost seemed to travel back in time to

when she was a teenage mother. She'd started calling Zenovia "Babylon" and "Jezebel." She'd even told her that she had a vision of her being gang-raped by one hundred men. Zenovia attributed the vileness to Audrey's declining mental state, but it hurt nonetheless.

Audrey had become increasingly dependent upon Phillip as well. She couldn't seem to be comforted by anyone but him, and only wore a smile on her face when he was in the room. He doted on her as well, planting kisses on her and indulging her quirky suspicions and even the bleachings. It was as if Zenovia's sin had brought them closer together.

At about the midpoint of the meeting, Bryce took to the podium. It seemed as if he wanted to look solemn, but couldn't hide the hint of glee that was on his face. He looked across the congregation and opened his Bible.

"Congregation. Please open your Bibles to Hebrews Chapter Twelve, Verse Eleven."

When the rustling of pages died down, he continued, "Please follow along as I read. 'Now no chastening for the present seemeth to be joyous, but grievous: nevertheless afterward it yieldeth the peaceable fruit of righteousness unto them which are exercised thereby.'"

Zenovia followed along carefully in her Bible. She wondered what fruit would come from her Brethren punishment. Would she end up practicing righteousness?

Bryce continued, "Congregation, it always saddens me to make these announcements. But we know that it is important for the cleanliness of our congregation."

Zenovia inhaled and held her breath. How long was he going to drag this out?

Bryce sighed dramatically and said, "Zenovia Sinclair

has been severely chastened and should be treated as such. Please take care to guard your families and remember to adhere to the restrictions set forth in the Brethren code. Thank you."

Zenovia had been informed by Phillip what her restrictions would be under her chastening. While everyone was still allowed to say hello to her, she wouldn't be allowed to associate with any of the other young people in an unsupervised setting. She wouldn't be included in any spiritual conversations, either. The punishment was to go on for between six months and a year.

Initially, Zenovia hadn't thought that it would be that bad. But she felt everyone's eyes on her after the announcement was read. Some gave disapproving glances, even people who hadn't met her before that night.

A single tear slid down Zenovia's cheek as she looked at the floor. She swiftly wiped it away, wanting to maintain her dignity, as difficult as it was. Besides, she had cried so many days over Emil that it seemed she didn't have many tears left.

She remembered her first time walking into the Devotion Center. She had been determined to fade away into the background, but surprisingly the opposite had happened. Her life had taken center stage.

She looked back down in her Bible and reread the verse that Bryce had read. Then her eyes traveled to the previous verse. Hebrews 12:10 said, "For they verily for a few days chastened us after their own pleasure; but he for our profit, that we might be partakers of his holiness."

The words of this verse sank in as Bryce left the podium with a smirk on his face.

They chastened us after their own pleasure.

Chapter Twenty-seven

The end of the school year and graduation couldn't come fast enough for Zenovia. There was no senior prom for her. She had no date, nor did she have any friends at the school who weren't members of the Brethren. She saw no point in spending any of her precious college dollars on a dance with strangers.

It seemed that her life had yet again changed drastically overnight. She'd gone from a lonely existence with Audrey to a bustling social calendar when they'd joined the Brethren. Now, she was alone again, without even Audrey at her side.

Audrey had completely turned against Zenovia. She refused to even speak to her daughter. Zenovia thought it was all for the best, especially when she received news that she'd received a full scholarship to Howard University.

Immediately after receiving her acceptance letter, she got a part-time job, so that whatever wasn't covered by her scholarship, she'd have on her own. Phillip was dead set against her attending college, so she expected no help from him. Audrey had nothing that Phillip didn't provide.

Zenovia stood in her bedroom admiring herself in her cap and gown. No matter what the Brethren did to her, they couldn't take away her 4.0 grade point average and salutatorian honors.

Her bedroom door slowly opened, and there stood Audrey wearing her favorite green dress and her hair was flat ironed pin straight. Zenovia waited for her to speak, so that she would know which Audrey she was dealing with at that moment.

"Phillip said to hurry up or you're going to be late for your graduation."

Zenovia was shocked. She'd assumed she'd be riding the bus downtown to the Convention Center. No one in the house had spoken a word about the ceremony. She hadn't offered any invitations and there had been no inquiries about it.

Audrey continued, "Do you have tickets?"

"Yes, of course." Zenovia dashed to her backpack and pulled out the square red tickets that she didn't think she'd need. She handed them to Audrey.

"You have a cousin in Washington, D.C.," Audrey stated flatly as if she wasn't giving a major revelation. "That's where your college is, right?"

"Yes. A cousin?"

"Her name is Corrine. She's my niece. Maybe you could look her up when you get there."

Zenovia said nothing. Not because she was at a loss for words, but she wanted to give Audrey the floor in case there were any other revelations. It could possibly be their last lucid conversation before she left for school.

Audrey, however, seemed to be done with her revelations. She left the room gripping the tickets in her hand.

At the graduation, Zenovia searched the preparation area for Tristan. There were only high school seniors in that part of the building and they were the only two Brethren members in their class. Kyle would've been the third.

They found each other, simultaneously, it seemed. After an awkward moment, Tristan's smile blazed across his face. He dashed over to Zenovia and hugged her. Nothing had changed about Tristan—he was always a different person away from the watchful eyes of the Brethren.

Tristan spoke first. "Class of 1995! Go, Seniors!"

"Wow," said Zenovia. "We haven't spoken since..."

"I know. My parents..."

Zenovia shook her head. "Don't explain, Tristan."

Tristan opened his mouth, then closed it again. Zenovia was glad he decided not to defend himself, because there was no excuse for his actions. Of course, he would've avoided her when there were other Brethren members present, but nothing had stopped him from smiling at her in passing or saying hello in their classes where there were no other Brethren present.

Zenovia wanted to make him more uncomfortable, but decided against it. Even though he had erased their friendship, he was not the cause of her pain.

"So you'll be leaving soon, right?" she asked.

"Yeah. Two weeks after we graduate I'll be on my way to the Brethren headquarters. You're leaving too, right? I heard my mom saying that you'd gotten into that college."

Zenovia raised an eyebrow. She wondered what else Sister Batiste had said about her, but then thought it would probably be better not to know.

"Yes. I got into Howard. I'll be working for the next few weeks, and then I leave too."

Tristan's smile faded. "Will you find a Brethren congregation in Washington, D.C.? There are several of them you know."

Zenovia hoped that her blank stare was enough of an answer. She was not going to seek out the Brethren; she planned to avoid them like the plague. As a matter of fact, she was hoping to never have to deal with the Brethren again once she left home.

"It wasn't that bad, was it?" Tristan asked.

"What wasn't that bad?"

"The chastening."

Zenovia exhaled slowly, trying to compose her thoughts. It had been the worst experience of her life. It was even worse than Audrey's tirades, because she was used to the craziness. The complete alienation she felt at the hands of the Brethren was indescribable.

She thought about how even Alyssa had acted as if she was invisible. She had expected it from Mia who she'd never really counted as a friend, and from Tristan because of his excessive holiness. Alyssa, though, had never seemed as rigid as the others. But in the end, her loyalties were the same as the rest of the congregation.

Zenovia finally replied, "No, Tristan. It wasn't very bad at all. It was for my own good, right?"

Tristan looked relieved. "I'm so glad you realize that, Zee."

Zenovia turned to walk away from Tristan. She

doubted if they'd ever speak again. It seemed crazy. She'd had her first and second loves all at once, in Tristan and Emil, and they'd vanished just as quickly.

Tristan called after Zenovia. "Zee! I never got to tell you my secret."

"What secret?"

"My secret crush."

Zenovia let out a soft chuckle. Now, of all times, Tristan wanted to come clean. Now when it wouldn't mean anything at all?

Zenovia asked, "It doesn't really matter anymore, does it?"

"No," Tristan replied as his eyes dropped to the floor. "I guess it doesn't."

Part Two

I waited patiently for the LORD; and he inclined unto me, and heard my cry.

He brought me up also out of an horrible pit, out of the miry clay, and set my feet upon a rock, and established my goings.

And he hath put a new song in my mouth, even praise unto our God: many shall see it, and fear, and shall trust in the LORD.

Psalm 40:1–3

Chapter Twenty-eight

That guy is definitely checking you out."

Zenovia rolled her eyes at her cousin, Corrine. Corrine, who was ten years older than Zenovia, was obsessed with finding her a husband. It was practically unbearable.

Zenovia had not wanted to contact her cousin when she'd started school, but kept the information that she'd found in the telephone book. Her freshman year, Zenovia realized that she had nowhere to go for the holidays and took a chance. Fortunately, her cousin was just as lonely as she was and they'd been friends ever since their first conversation.

"He was not looking at me! Will you stop it?"

"Stop what? It doesn't make sense that my beautiful, almost-graduated, magna cum laude cousin hasn't had one date in four years."

Zenovia couldn't hide her smile. She knew that Corrine was just worried about her. And she was right. Zenovia hadn't had a date in four years.

It wasn't as if Zenovia had avoided men completely. There were a few who had caught her interest, but as soon as they'd started asking questions about her family, and her religion, she'd retreated.

"I could've had plenty of dates! I was just focusing on school. I didn't come here to meet a husband."

"You should've!" Corrine scoffed. "Wait until you're my age. You'll wish you'd scored a man in college."

Zenovia tossed her long two-stranded twists over her shoulder and slyly glanced at the man Corrine had spotted. He was tall, thin, and had very light skin. His low haircut looked stunningly attractive on him. And he *was* staring in Zenovia's direction. She looked away quickly.

"He's not my type, Corrine."

"Seriously, Zenovia."

Zenovia smiled and took a bite out of her burger. She wasn't sure she had a type anymore. After Tristan and then Emil had stolen her heart four years ago, she hadn't given herself the opportunity to find out.

"I bet I could find you a boyfriend at my church."

Zenovia closed her eyes and sighed. Corrine's second favorite pastime, behind finding her a boyfriend, was trying to convert her back to Christianity. Zenovia had given up on being a church member. She hadn't entirely given up on believing in God—but she was close.

God seemed to be only a concept, and Christianity a set of rules and consequences. At least that was the Brethren way. Even though she'd only been a member of the Brethren for a brief period, it had seemed like a lifetime. All of her other religious experiences seemed foggy and forgettable.

"Can we talk about something else?" Zenovia asked.

Corrine leaned back in her chair and folded her arms. "Okay. When is the last time you spoke to your mother?"

"It's been a few months. New Year's, I think."

It was New Year's. She had called to wish her mother a good year. She remembered that after she'd hung up the phone, she'd wished she hadn't called.

Zenovia found it very hard to keep in contact with Audrey and simultaneously leave her past behind. After Zenovia left, Audrey had become even more thoroughly indoctrinated with the Brethren teachings. Every conversation they had was about Zenovia turning back from her sinful ways and returning to the Brethren.

Audrey also managed to inform her of all of the comings and goings of her former friends. Emil had married the mother of his child and had two more. Alyssa was engaged to some nice young man from a neighboring congregation. Tristan was still happily serving at the Brethren headquarters.

Hearing about their happy vanilla-flavored Brethren lives had almost launched Zenovia into a bout of depression.

Corrine leaned forward and lovingly said, "You should try to reach her, you know. It can't be healthy for her, being trapped in that cult."

Zenovia frowned thoughtfully. She couldn't decide if the Brethren were healthy for Audrey. Her mental state seemed nearly stable, even though she hadn't taken any medication for years. But Zenovia couldn't be sure about Audrey's schizophrenia because Phillip refused to speak with her. They'd had one conversation since she'd left for school, in which he'd told her two things. One, that her mother had been healed by God. And two, that she was an apostate.

She'd been shocked at that term—apostate. It seemed so vile coming from Phillip's mouth. He'd hurled it at her as if it was the worst insult he could think of.

Zenovia knew the definition of the word. It meant someone who forsook his or her religion. She supposed it was appropriate, if by religion he meant the Brethren. But she hadn't forsaken her belief in God, not completely, and that was more important.

"I think my mother is fine," Zenovia finally replied. "She's got her husband, and he loves her."

Corrine said, "Well, your mother always *was* happiest when she had a man in her life! I remember when she dated your father. Grandpa was ready to use one of those shotguns on her."

Zenovia grinned. She enjoyed hearing stories about the father and grandparents she'd never known. She wished she could've met them, but her grandparents had both passed on when she was little and no one knew where her father was.

"So are you going to come to church with me tomorrow or not?" Corrine asked. "We're having Friends and Family Day."

Zenovia wrinkled her nose. "I don't think so. I've got other plans."

"No, you do not have other plans. The only thing you do besides study is play in that nappy hair of yours!"

"I am happily nappy, thank you very much."

"Whatever. They have perms for five dollars at the Korean store on the corner."

Zenovia laughed. Her first week of school, she had

done what the natural hair sistas on campus called "the big chop." She'd cut off every inch of distressed and chemically repressed hair from her head leaving her with a teeny-weeny afro.

After a year or so, her tiny afro was giant, curly, and breathtaking. She'd never known that her hair was curly and it was a welcome discovery. When she didn't feel like picking it out and pinning a flower behind her ear, she made small two-stranded twists that cascaded down her neck like curly ropes.

"Will there be food after service?" Zenovia asked.

Corrine sucked her teeth. "Just like a heathen. Yes, we will be having fried chicken, macaroni and cheese, yams, collard greens, and Mother Sylvia's peach cobbler."

Zenovia's mouth watered. "Okay, then. Count me in."

Chapter Twenty-nine

Zenovia stayed close to Corrine as they entered the church. She let out a breath of relief when she saw that Reaching the Masses was a normal church. Zenovia was ready to buck toward the exit if it even remotely reminded her of a Brethren sanctuary.

Reaching the Masses had all of the comfortable church effects that she'd forgotten: long wooden pews with red velveteen pillows, a big white pulpit with an area for the choir, and a "Do this in remembrance of me" table all decked out in white for communion.

"Are you all taking communion today?" Zenovia whispered to her cousin.

"Yes. It's first Sunday."

Zenovia swallowed hard. It was the first Sunday in May. Communion Sunday and Friends and Family Day all wrapped into one. She was going to look like such a sinner when she didn't partake of the bread (crackers) and wine (probably grape juice).

Corrine seemed to notice Zenovia's hesitation. "You take communion, right?"

"I *have* taken communion, but I don't think I will today."

"And why not?"

How could she voice the words that she felt in her heart? Zenovia didn't feel worthy of putting anything holy in her body, even if it was only symbolic. In her heart she'd rebelled against the Brethren's chastening. And what if they were right? What if she didn't deserve this?

"I just haven't been to church in a long time, Corrine. Don't you think I need to start off kind of slow?"

Corrine frowned. "You have let those Brethren damage you, Zenovia. You need to leave that guilt on the altar."

"What does that look like, Corrine? Leaving something on the altar? It just sounds like church talk."

Corrine shook her head and led Zenovia up the aisle. Zenovia objected. "Do we have to sit all the way in the front? I like to blend."

"There is no way you're going to blend in that outfit, sweetie. Plus I want some of the single brothers to get a good look at you."

Zenovia looked down at the pink suit that Corrine had loaned her. It did fit her perfectly, hugging every curve. The skirt was a little on the short side, but it showed off Zenovia's flawless caramel legs. She'd styled the front of her hair in pretty, shiny Bantu knots and the back was a free-flowing afro.

Corrine was right. There would absolutely not be any blending.

They took a seat in the third pew from the front. "Wow. I'll be sure to get a dose of the Holy Ghost sitting up this close."

"That's what I'm hoping. You need it! You're too young to be this burdened down."

Again, Corrine had spoken truthful words. Zenovia didn't feel like she was twenty-one years old. All of her life, she'd seemed older and wiser than her years. But this was different. It wasn't about maturity at all.

It was all about carrying a heavy load. She would love to leave it somewhere—at the altar or anywhere else. On her lowest days, she stood in the mirror with tears streaming down her face, wondering what happened to Kyle after he'd taken his life.

Was he at peace or was he somewhere roasting in eternal torment? Usually, after having a good cry she decided that she didn't want to find out.

"Where's the bathroom, Corrine? I don't want to have to walk down the aisle with one finger pointed in the air in the middle of service."

Corrine laughed. "So you do remember something about church! It's through those double doors on the left. And please don't use the handicapped stalls. I don't want you getting cussed out by anyone on the Mother's board."

Zenovia walked up the side aisle, trying to wipe the smile from her face. Corrine was so funny, and most of the time she didn't even know it.

"Zee?"

Zenovia stopped in her tracks. She'd recognize that voice anywhere, but she was too afraid to turn around. What if she was hearing things? What if this was a vision, which would be even worse, because it wouldn't be tangible and real. And she couldn't hear that voice without it being tangible.

And then she felt a light touch on her arm. "Zenovia, it is you." Now the silky smooth voice was all up in her personal space.

She turned slowly, hoping that this was someone from campus who she'd met in passing. But it was not. The voice belonged to Justin.

"What are you doing here?" Zenovia asked with a panic-stricken tone.

Justin laughed in ripples. The same beautiful laugh she'd remembered. "Aren't you just a little bit happy to see me?"

She was more than a little bit happy to see him, but she was afraid to say so. Memories of their last encounter flooded her brain, and she could almost taste his stolen kiss still lingering on her lips.

Zenovia did not offer a response, so Justin continued, "I'm here with a friend. It's Friends and Family Day."

"No. I mean why are you *here* in D.C.? And why aren't you at a Devotion Center? I hear there are plenty in town." Zenovia gathered herself long enough to pose the questions on her mind.

"I'm here because I live in Baltimore and my friend invited me. I could ask you the same thing about the Devotion Center."

Zenovia narrowed her eyes. She knew that there was more to Justin's tale, but she didn't want to probe. She had no intention of sharing her horror story, or even talking to him for thirty more seconds.

"Well," Zenovia said, "it was good seeing you, Justin. Have a nice life."

She tried to walk away from him, but Justin grabbed her arm again. "Zee…"

How fortunate for Zenovia that Justin's *friend* decided to walk up to them at that very moment.

"Justin, baby, who is this?" She made sure to emphasize the word baby as if sending a message to Zenovia.

Justin beamed at the young, curvaceous woman. Her jealous glare melted away. "This is my friend Zenovia, from back home. The last time I saw her, she was in high school."

The woman's eyes swept up and down Zenovia's outfit, and rested exactly where Justin's eyes were resting—on her legs. Zenovia wished the Lord would singe them both with a lightning bolt. The nerve!

"Welcome to Reaching the Masses. I don't think I've seen you here before. I'm Lynora." She extended a stiff hand toward Zenovia.

Zenovia shook the hand gingerly. "Thank you. My name is Zenovia, and Corrine is my cousin."

"Oh, Sister Corrine is a sweetie. Tell her I said hello." This time Lynora gave Zenovia a warmer smile.

An uncomfortable silence hung in the air, so Zenovia said, "Well, like I said before, good seeing you, Justin and nice meeting you, Lynora."

Zenovia half-stumbled the rest of the way to the bathroom. What were the odds that the first time she set foot inside a church in four years she'd see one of the Brethren? Especially Justin.

Hopefully, it was a coincidence, but it felt like an omen.

And wasn't there a rule that the Brethren had about visiting other churches? Zenovia thought that it wasn't allowed, but that was years ago. Maybe the rules had changed.

Or maybe Justin was breaking the rules.

Zenovia refused to let her mind linger there. She didn't want to know if Justin was in rebellion or a former Brethren member. Either way, it was too close to home.

She walked back to her seat next to Corrine just in time for service to start. "What took you so long?" Corrine whispered. "I wanted to introduce you to a few people."

Zenovia knew that she meant a few men. "I guess I just took my time."

"Are you okay? You look a little rattled. Did someone say something crazy to you about that skirt? I knew I should've given you something longer to wear." Corrine snatched a scarf out of her purse and threw it on Zenovia's lap.

Zenovia smiled. "No one said anything. I'm fine."

"Okay, but you let me know if someone offends you. We're supposed to show love to our visitors."

The service started with a small group of very talented singers, but they were unable to hold Zenovia's attention for more than thirty seconds. She forced herself not to turn around in her seat to locate Justin, but it was as if she could feel his eyes burning a hole into the back of her head. She wished she'd convinced her cousin to sit somewhere in the back, so that she could escape if need be.

Zenovia caught bits and pieces of the sermon. It was about how humans cannot have a relationship with God without the Holy Spirit. The church really seemed to be receiving the message, as evidenced by the nodding of heads and the random "Hallelujahs" being shouted across the sanctuary.

But as captivating as the message was, Zenovia felt distracted. At first, she attributed her lack of focus to Justin. But, for some reason, she felt drawn to a woman sitting in the very front pew. The woman's shoulders were hunched and she was trembling. The trembling was almost unrecognizable, but Zenovia was concentrating so hard on the woman that her movements seemed exaggerated.

At the moment of Zenovia's greatest concentration, the woman suddenly turned around and looked over her shoulder.

The woman is standing in the center of a room and surrounding her are men sitting in folding chairs. She is scantily clad and wearing a long flowing wig. One of the men yells something, and she starts to dance and gyrate. The men throw money at her—dollar bills.

A single tear rolls down her cheek.

The vision ended as quickly as it started. Zenovia gasped for air; it felt like she was suffocating. The woman from the front pew was the woman in her vision minus the wig. She had not had a vision since she'd left home for college, and thought that maybe she'd been healed of her affliction.

She breathed deeply and waited for her heart rate to slow to its normal pace. It was a good thing that Corrine was in the midst of a full-fledged praise break, because she would have definitely noticed that something was not right with Zenovia.

"Go to her."

Zenovia nearly jumped to her feet. She looked around to see if anyone else had heard the voice or if it was as she suspected and only in her mind. Since no one looked alarmed—and that deep booming voice would have alarmed *someone*—she assumed that it was in her head.

That assumption made her heart start racing again. She'd never heard voices outside of the visions. Was she losing it? All her life Zenovia had been terrified that some latent schizophrenia gene was going to surface.

"Tell her what you saw in your vision, and tell her that I forgive her."

Zenovia shivered. Maybe she really was unraveling. She was sitting in church, having visions and hearing the voice of...God?

She decided to make an appointment with a psychiatrist on Monday.

"Zenovia, you are not insane, but you are to be My mouthpiece in this house. Go to the woman...tell her what you saw."

There was something so calming and so peaceful about the voice that she believed it. She felt no fear either, just a compelling need to move over to where the woman still shook with sobs.

Since there were no empty seats in the woman's row, it was hard for Zenovia to get to her. She stepped on a few pairs of toes and stumbled over a variety of purses. She smiled at the elderly woman sitting next to her target and squeezed between the two of them.

The young woman stopped crying long enough to stare at Zenovia with wonder in her eyes. "Do I know you?" she asked.

Zenovia replied, "No, but I need to tell you something."

"What is it?"

Zenovia whispered to the young woman what she'd seen in the vision and then the exact words that she'd heard after her vision. She couldn't wrap her mind around the idea that the voice might actually be God talking.

The young woman's eyes opened wide. She covered her mouth with her hand and fresh tears poured from her eyes. Then she shocked Zenovia by dashing from the pew and running up to the altar.

Everyone in the congregation looked at her strangely, because the pastor was still preaching. But the young woman didn't care. She wept at the altar and called out the name of Jesus.

After their initial astonishment, several members of the church rushed up to the girl and prayed with her. One of the people praying with the young woman was Corrine.

The pastor said, "Obviously, the Lord has laid it on this woman's heart to lay her burdens on the altar. I want everyone in here to point in her direction and pray with her. Pray that the Holy Spirit blesses her with a healing touch."

Zenovia didn't know if that instruction included her, so she left her hands folded neatly in her lap. There was something unsettling about how joyful and sorrowful the woman seemed at the same time.

Corrine and the other praying ladies led the young woman out of the sanctuary when she finally calmed.

At the Friends and Family dinner, Zenovia was glad that Corrine had chosen a seat on the opposite side of the fellowship hall as Lynora and Justin. She had tried to talk Corrine into going out for dinner, but she wasn't having it. She wanted to brag about her little cousin to the rest of her church.

The bragging rights came from what the young woman—her name was Penny—had told the prayer team. She'd told them that Zenovia was a prophet and that Zenovia had told her things about herself that she couldn't possibly know because they'd never met.

Of course, it was all true, but Zenovia was uncomfortable with the attention being given to her by the church members. She'd never viewed her visions as prophecies, but as mere annoyances that made her feel like an outsider.

"What did you tell that girl?" Corrine whispered after yet another one of the church members stopped at the table to meet Zenovia.

"Nothing, really. I could just tell that she was upset, and I told her that God would forgive her for whatever she'd done."

Zenovia took a deep breath. It wasn't exactly a lie, but Corrine looked at her as if she knew there was something being left out.

Corrine sucked her teeth. "Mmm-hmm. You're holding out on me, little cousin."

"Why do you think that?"

"Not only because that girl, Penny, was acting like she'd seen Moses, Abraham, and all twelve of the apostles, but because that scrumptious-looking chocolate dream has been staring you down since we got in here."

Zenovia shot a quick glance in Justin's direction. "He's someone I know from Cleveland. Nobody really. His parents go to church with Audrey."

"He's a member of that Brethren cult?" Corrine asked, not trying to hide the contempt in her voice.

Zenovia shrugged. "Well, he was. I haven't talked to him, so I can't say for sure."

"I will tell you one thing. He's over there looking at you like he wants to reconnect."

Zenovia ventured another peek in Justin's direction, but he was no longer seated. She was astonished to find that her stomach dropped when she noticed his absence.

"Good afternoon, young man. Are you visiting with us today?" Corrine said.

Zenovia didn't even need to turn around in her seat to know who was standing behind her. Corrine's bright and inviting smile completely told the story.

Even though she wasn't surprised by Justin's presence, Zenovia still jumped when he placed his hand on her back.

"Yes, I am visiting. Sister Lynora is an acquaintance of mine, but so is Zenovia. You look like her mother. Are you related?"

Corrine beamed. "Yes, we are related! I'm Zenovia's cousin."

Zenovia glared at Corrine. "Why don't you just ask me, Justin? I'm sitting right here."

Justin sat down in the empty seat next to Zenovia. "I would have, but you didn't seem to want to talk to me earlier."

"Why wouldn't she want to talk to such a charming young man?" Corrine asked.

Zenovia rolled her eyes. She could tell that she was completely alone on this one. Corrine had no doubt been won over by Justin's stunning good looks and silky smooth voice.

Justin replied, "I've always had trouble with Zee. I tried, with no avail, to get her to pay me some attention years ago."

Zenovia burst into laughter. "Stop it, Justin. I'll have a conversation with you, but please stop the madness!"

"Thank you!" Justin exclaimed. "That's all I wanted in the first place."

Zenovia turned toward Justin and deliberately looked him dead in his eyes. "Go ahead, talk. From the looks of the buffet line, you've got about two minutes before they start feeding us, and I happen to be hungry."

"I'll need more than two minutes."

"That's all you've got."

Justin tilted his head to one side and grinned mischievously. "Not if you have dinner with me tomorrow night."

"Absolutely not," Zenovia replied adamantly.

She was in no hurry to revisit her past. Actually, the past was very safely behind her until Justin decided to show up with all of his grinning.

"Lunch?" he asked.

"I don't think so."

"What about a midmorning snack?" Justin pleaded.

Corrine interjected, "Zenovia, what is wrong with you? Don't make this man beg!"

"Because I will beg, you know," Justin said. "I just want to catch up and maybe finish some unfinished business."

"Ha! We did *not* have any unfinished business," Zenovia replied.

Zenovia was becoming more and more annoyed with the conversation. Yes, she'd been insanely attracted to Justin. But unfinished business? No. They did not have unfinished business.

He finished very nicely when he stole a kiss from her and went away to the Brethren headquarters.

But even though she was irritated, Zenovia was curious. Why was Justin pressing so hard to spend time with her, right in the face of his acquaintance Lynora? Did his feelings run deeper than Zenovia had imagined?

She dismissed the thought immediately. That was impossible. Justin was being Justin. A ridiculous tease.

"Would you look at that?" Zenovia asked. "They're calling our table right now."

Zenovia stood to her feet and Justin did the same. "I'll stand in line with you," he said. "We can talk now if you want."

Zenovia sighed. "Won't your friend be angry? What was that she called you earlier? Baby?"

"Nobody over here is worried about Lynora," Corrine said. "You two have your conversation and I'll handle her."

Zenovia trudged grimly toward the buffet line. "Go ahead, Justin. I'm listening."

"I have some questions," Justin said. "I'll leave you alone if you answer them. Is that fair?"

"Okay, I'll answer your questions. But you better not ask me anything crazy."

"Why didn't you write to me?" he asked.

"Are you serious with that question? Why would I write to you?"

Justin narrowed his eyes. "Number one, because I

wrote you a very nice letter. Number two, because you kissed me back, Zee. I thought we were going to get together one day."

"First of all, I did not kiss you back. I ran away from you. If you're gonna reminisce, please do it properly. Next question."

"I see you still want to live in denial. But, okay, next question. Were you in love with Tristan?"

Zenovia crossed her arms angrily. He had no right to ask her that. Because if she had been in love with Tristan, then he'd violated that love and probably some unspoken code for brothers.

"Are you going to answer me?" he asked after Zenovia hesitated further.

She had asked herself the same question during her freshman year of college, when she'd found it almost impossible to accept a date from any of the men on campus. She'd wondered if she still carried a torch for an inaccessible man who she would probably never see again.

The answer she'd discovered was a complex one.

She'd admired Tristan, and found him mature, compelling, and attractive all at the same time. But his lack of reciprocation left her feeling empty, so the feelings had eventually faded into nothingness.

Justin should've been asking about Emil. Her heart was still missing the piece that he'd stolen. She had no doubt that if she saw Emil again, her heart would do flip-flops.

She answered him. "I was not in love with Tristan. I had a crush on him and then he became my best friend. And then..."

"Then what?" Justin asked.

"Then nothing. I left the Brethren and never talked to him again."

Justin nodded slowly. "Maybe it's you and Tristan who have unfinished business."

"No, I don't think so. Tristan made every choice for the perfect life that he wanted to live, and I didn't fit into that picture."

"Well, you'd fit perfectly into my picture...."

Zenovia had no idea how to respond to Justin's statement. She was so relieved to see Corrine walking toward them even if she did have her pastor in tow. Anything would be better than answering Justin.

"So this is the young lady that everyone is raving about!" the pastor said in his booming voice.

Corrine looked so proud. "This is my little cousin, Zenovia Sinclair. Zenovia, meet Bishop Wilcox."

Zenovia reached for the outstretched hand and shook it. "Hello, Bishop Wilcox. It's an honor to meet you. Your sermon was awesome."

"Thank you, but I believe the Lord was doing more work from the pews this morning than from the pulpit. I hear you shared an awesome prophetic word with our newest member, Sister Penny."

Justin's eyes grew large. Zenovia panicked and said, "Bishop Wilcox, have you met Justin Batiste? He's also visiting today."

Bishop Wilcox patted Justin on the shoulder. "We have met, thank you. Justin visits us quite regularly. I keep wondering when he's going to join."

"One Sunday I'll do it, Bishop. You know I've got some demons to face first," Justin replied.

"Don't wait too long, son, Jesus is coming back!" Bishop Wilcox said. He sounded on the verge of launching into a sermon right in the buffet line.

"I won't, Bishop."

Bishop Wilcox smiled again at Zenovia. "But back to you, woman of God! I feel an awesome shifting in the atmosphere! Something is happening in the spirit realm and you are a part of it."

Bishop Wilcox shook Zenovia's hand again, but didn't wait for her to reply.

Zenovia shook her head slowly as a look of sheer wonder covered her face. Something was happening in the spirit realm? And *she* was a part of it? She didn't know what that looked like.

But it sounded like something she'd been waiting to hear her entire life.

Chapter Thirty

Zenovia couldn't believe she'd said yes to a date with Justin Batiste. She tried to replay the whole conversation in her mind to see where she'd gone wrong and lost the upper hand. But Justin had always been able to do that. He completely disarmed every one of her defenses.

She also couldn't believe how nervous she felt. It was Justin. She knew him, so it shouldn't feel like this. She shouldn't be getting sweaty palms and an upset stomach.

But even though she shouldn't be feeling any of those things, she absolutely was.

Zenovia had decided against telling Corrine about the date. What if it went nowhere? What if all of Justin's charm now came across as cocky and unbearable? She didn't want to get Corrine's hopes up, because it was a first date that might end up being a last date.

When she heard the knock on her door, Zenovia's stomach dropped. She took one last self-appraising glance in the mirror. She liked her hair—it was styled in a wild twist out that framed her face. Her long Bohemian skirt and peasant blouse completed her look. Before she went to the door, Zenovia grabbed a few silver bangle bracelets and slipped them over her wrist.

On the second knock, Zenovia opened the door. "Hey, Justin."

Justin caught her completely off guard by hugging her tightly. It felt way too intimate for the first contact on their first date. Zenovia gently pushed him away.

"What's up with that?" she asked.

Justin smiled. "You really don't know how happy I am to see you? It felt like you disappeared off the face of the earth."

Zenovia blinked rapidly and struggled to catch her breath. "Uh...do you want to come in or something?"

"I'm pretty hungry," Justin said as he patted his tight abdomen. "How does chicken and waffles sound?"

Justin's simple statement made the air feel less thick. Zenovia exhaled gratefully. "It sounds really good, Justin. I'm hungry too."

As they walked to the car, Justin made all the correct chivalrous gestures—opening doors and walking on the proper side of the sidewalk. His extra effort was cute to Zenovia, because she'd never known that Justin worked this hard with women. He seemed like the type that just had the girls falling at his feet.

"I didn't disappear. It was more like being banished." Zenovia did not want there to be any uncomfortable silences while they drove to the restaurant so she responded to Justin's comment.

"You mean banished from the Brethren? But I thought you were only chastened, right? You didn't get cast out of from the congregation."

"It felt like exile to Siberia. Tristan barely even spoke to me after it happened. I think that hurt the most."

Justin sighed. "Well, Tristan is a company man. He's going to be loyal to the Brethren, no questions asked, for the rest of his life."

"What about you?" Zenovia asked. "I thought you were a company man, too."

"It all changed for me when I went to serve at the headquarters. I saw some things I didn't agree with, and I had the audacity to open my mouth about them."

"Really? What happened then? Were you chastened?"

Justin smiled a grim smile. "No, not exactly."

"Well then, what's the problem, and what are you doing down here?"

"Actually, I was cast out. And I moved to Baltimore just because it was the first city that came to mind."

"And you probably left a trail of crying women behind you."

"I wasn't the womanizer you thought I was, Zee."

"Yeah, okay. You had me hemmed up in a corner at your house kissing on me and a date outside," Zenovia countered. "Justin, don't try to play. Maybe you've changed, but I know what you were back then."

"All right, I did date a few ladies."

"This is what I don't understand. Why did you serve at the Brethren headquarters? You didn't really seem dedicated like..."

"Like my brother? Like Tristan?"

Zenovia hadn't meant to make the comparison between Justin and Tristan. But it was obvious how different they were. It was almost impossible to believe they shared the same gene pool.

Justin continued, "I went to serve at the Brethren headquarters because it was a status thing. It made me a better catch to the ladies."

"Are you serious?" Zenovia asked. "Please tell me that's not the truth."

"Isn't that what you think?"

Zenovia sighed and looked out of the window. They were approaching the restaurant and it was a good thing. She would've preferred an uncomfortable silence to a really awkward conversation.

Justin found a parking spot close to the building and came around to open her door. "I'm still a gentleman, even when I'm being insulted," Justin said with a slight grin on his face.

"I didn't mean to offend you."

"It's okay, Zenovia. Your offensiveness has always been part of what attracted me to you."

Zenovia laughed. "You weren't attracted to me. You toyed with me."

Justin smiled but kept his response to himself. The restaurant's hostess led them to a table in the rear of the restaurant. Justin ordered beverages for both of them.

Zenovia endured his silent appraisal as his eyes slowly took her in. She watched the smile replace his serious facial expression, so she assumed that he no longer felt offended.

"So you went to college and got all earthy on me, huh?" Justin asked.

Zenovia's hand went self-consciously to her hair. "This had nothing to do with college."

"Well, whatever the reason, I like it. It fits you."

"Thank you. I wish that you'd changed too, but you look exactly the same. You're taking me all the way back, you know. Right back to the back row of the Devotion Center."

Justin nodded. "I know how you feel. I started having flashbacks as soon as I saw you at your cousin's church. But at least you weren't born into the Brethren."

"What difference does it make when you join?" Zenovia asked.

"The way the Brethren serve God...or the way they serve the organization, it was the only way I knew how to worship. Everything else seemed strange to me."

Zenovia nodded. "I can understand that. The Fellowship of the Brethren was just another church when Audrey and I first joined. Have you talked to your mom and dad? How are they doing?"

"I've called once since I've been here. My mother told me I was better off dead, and my father attached several different four-letter words with his new name for me—his apostate son. But outside of that...I guess they're fine."

"That's harsh. I thought Audrey was bad."

Justin clasped his hands and leaned forward in his seat. "Audrey is...well...she's not okay, but I guess you know that."

Zenovia took in one deep breath and blew it out through her nose. "I know, but she hasn't ever been okay. I try not to think about it too much, because there's nothing I can do about it."

The waitress finally came up to the table to take their orders. Justin said, "We'll both have the chicken and waffles special. Thank you."

Zenovia covered her mouth to smother her chuckle as the waitress smiled sweetly at Justin. He had that effect on most women, and he wasn't the least bit modest about it.

"What is so funny?" Justin asked after the waitress walked away.

"You. You're funny. You had that girl all twisted."

Justin smiled, "That wasn't on purpose."

"I know. That's why it's so funny."

"All right. Just keep laughing then. I can't wait to tell Alyssa about this."

"You all talk?"

"Mmm-hmm. I talked to her yesterday evening; told her I was going out with you."

"What? Why'd you do that?"

"I thought she'd be happy to hear it."

"Was she?"

"Yes."

Zenovia tried to imagine Alyssa being happy about anything that was going on in her life. She couldn't. After her chastening, Alyssa hadn't said two words to Zenovia. So to think she'd care abut Zenovia's life post-Brethren was unimaginable.

"Have you talked to Tristan?"

Justin looked at the floor. "No. He won't talk to me. Not while he's still at the headquarters. Maybe after he leaves."

Zenovia completely understood the pain-filled expression on Justin's face. She wondered what Justin could've learned about the Brethren that made him have doubts.

She asked, "Justin, how do you feel about church now? I'm asking because I almost don't want to be a part of it. I believe in God, but I just want to believe in Him and not have to answer to people, do you know what I mean?"

"I know exactly what you mean," Justin replied with an emphatic nod. "It's why I haven't joined any churches since I left the Brethren. I've visited them, but I just can't join."

"The Sunday you saw me at Reaching the Masses is the first time I've walked into a church since I left for college."

"What a coincidence."

Zenovia smiled in response, although she didn't agree with Justin. She didn't think it was a coincidence that she ran into Justin at church. Something told her that God was up to something, but she had no idea what it could be.

And she didn't need a vision to tell her that.

Chapter Thirty-one

Zenovia glanced around Bishop Wilcox's office while he finished a telephone call. Almost every wall was lined with books and Bibles, but one of the walls was covered with pictures. Zenovia guessed that the woman in the big hats was Bishop's wife and the little boy was their son.

When Bishop ended his phone call, Zenovia asked, "Is that First Lady Wilcox?"

"Yes," Bishop said as he turned to look at the wall. "She was a beautiful woman, wasn't she?"

Zenovia bit her bottom lip. "I'm sorry, Bishop. I didn't know...."

"No need to apologize. She and our son passed on six years ago. They died in a car accident."

"Well, I'm sorry for your loss then," Zenovia said solemnly.

"Thank you. Would you like something to drink? The nurses usually keep my mini-refrigerator stocked."

"No, thank you."

What Zenovia really wanted was to hurry and get

finished with the meeting. She'd only agreed to it after Corrine had twisted her arm and made a boatload of promises. She knew it had something to do with what happened on Friends and Family Sunday with Penny, but other than that, she had no idea why Bishop Wilcox had requested the meeting.

"Zenovia, I know you want to know why I wanted to meet with you, especially since you're not one of our members."

Zenovia nodded. "Yes, Bishop. I definitely am curious."

"First, let me ask you a question. Have you ever heard of anyone having a prophetic gifting?"

Zenovia scrunched her nose. "You mean like a psychic? I've seen them on television and I think they're mostly fake."

"I'm not referring to psychics, Zenovia. If any of them have powers, they are not ordained by God. The Bible speaks against such things and calls it witchcraft."

Zenovia sighed. Bishop's statement was one of the reasons that she and Audrey had never shared their abilities with anyone. It was the one lesson that Audrey had taught Zenovia daily, and even though Audrey was mentally unstable, on the subject of the visions, Zenovia took her advice.

"Well then, what do you mean by prophetic gifting? Do you mean like the prophets in the Bible?"

Bishop Wilcox nodded. "Yes. I mean people chosen by God and anointed with His Holy Spirit to edify the body of Christ with the gift of prophecy."

"Like God's mouthpiece?"

Bishop Wilcox's face lit up. "Exactly! A mouthpiece."

Zenovia felt like she was watching a movie of her life,

some fictional representation of what could not possibly be happening. The visions were one thing. Zenovia *knew* that they were real. But hearing the voice of God and being His mouthpiece was something entirely different, and entirely unbelievable. She planned to cure the voices next week with a low dose of an antipsychotic drug.

"Bishop, excuse me for being skeptical about this. But I'm not sure if God has ever spoken to me, much less anointed me with His Holy Spirit. I'm not worthy of anything like that, I'm afraid. You're going to have to find another prophet for your church."

"None of us are worthy of the free gifts we receive from God. Not even salvation. Why do you believe you're less worthy than anyone else?"

Zenovia's mind raced back to all of the sins she'd committed as one of the Brethren. She believed that God had forgiven her, but she never wanted to be in a position to be judged by church members, or bishops, or anyone else. Besides, forgiveness did not exactly equal making a person your personal mouthpiece.

"I've done a lot of things I'm not proud of, Bishop. I don't think I'm the one you're looking for."

Bishop Wilcox gave Zenovia a fatherly smile. "I'm not looking for you, God is. He's waiting to wrap you up in His loving arms."

Zenovia looked away from Bishop Wilcox's gaze. She could tell that he was sincere, and if she hadn't been so jaded by the Brethren, she might have enjoyed having Bishop Wilcox as a pastor.

"Maybe we're getting ahead of ourselves. Why don't we just talk about what happened on Sunday," Bishop Wilcox suggested.

"I told Sister Penny that God had forgiven her for her sins."

"How did you know about Sister Penny's sins?"

Zenovia paused before responding. "I could tell she was distraught. Most of the time people cry in church because they feel guilty about something they've done."

"There were lots of people in tears on Sunday," Bishop countered. "What made you get up out of your seat to go to Sister Penny?"

"She looked at me, and I just felt compelled to go to her."

Bishop Wilcox took his glasses off and rubbed his hands together thoughtfully. "You know, Zenovia, nothing you tell me will leave this room."

"I know. Corrine told me that I could trust you."

"Then why don't you trust me? It's time for you to let God carry your yoke."

Zenovia tried to think of some excuse to give to Bishop when she heard that voice again in her head.

Tell him.

Zenovia felt her heart start to race. Not the voice. Not again. She'd been hoping that it was a one-time foray into madness, but the voice was back, clear as day and once again giving her instructions.

Lay down your burden. Tell him.

It was a burden. Her secret was weighing her down right along with the guilt she carried around from the Brethren. But she couldn't tell this man she barely even knew. Bishop or not, he was still a man with a mouth and a church full of parishioners who would, no doubt, ridicule Zenovia if she ever came back to the church.

"So don't tell me about what happened on Sunday. I understand your reservation. Would you like to talk about your old church? Why did you leave there?"

Zenovia didn't appreciate feeling interrogated, but she knew that Corrine was behind it. "I committed some very grave sins against God; I was punished by the church leaders and that sums it up."

"You were punished by the church leaders? How so?"

Zenovia willingly shared the details of her chastening. It was easy to do so, because deep down she believed that she deserved the punishment, even if she'd had a hard time enduring it.

"And who then chastened that so-called Council of Elders for their sins?" Bishop Wilcox asked after listening to the story.

"I don't know what you mean. I was the fornicator."

"Perhaps so, but the Bible says that all have sinned and fallen short of the glory of God. So I ask, who chastened these men?"

Zenovia shrugged. "I don't know, Bishop. They were the ones in power, and I don't really know who they answered to."

Bishop Wilcox shook his head sadly. Then he opened his Bible and flipped through the pages. "Here Zenovia. Read out loud, John Eight, Verses One to Eleven."

Zenovia took the Bible from Bishop Wilcox and began to read.

Jesus went unto the mount of Olives. And early in the morning he came again into the temple, and all the people came unto him; and he sat down, and taught them. And the scribes and Pharisees brought unto him a woman taken in adultery; and when they had set her in the midst, They say unto him, Master, this woman was taken in adultery, in the very act. Now Moses in the law commanded us, that such should be stoned: but what sayest thou? This they said, tempting him, that they might have to accuse him. But Jesus stooped down, and with his finger wrote on the ground, as though he heard them not. So when they continued asking him, he lifted up himself, and said unto them, He that is without sin among you, let him first cast a stone at her. And again he stooped down, and wrote on the ground. And they which heard it, being convicted by their own conscience, went out one by one, beginning at the eldest, even unto the last: and Jesus was left alone, and the woman standing in the midst. When Jesus had lifted up himself, and saw none but the woman, he said unto her, Woman, where are those thine accusers? hath no man condemned thee? She said, No man, Lord. And Jesus said unto her, Neither do I condemn thee: go, and sin no more.

The passage left Zenovia speechless. What Jesus said to that woman was what she'd needed to hear from the Council of Elders. She hadn't even planned to continue in her sin. She'd just wanted to feel something other than condemnation.

"Zenovia, I asked you to read that passage so that you can understand that those men had no right to punish you. Their job as shepherds was to guide and protect you and to help you to see the error of your ways."

"But sometimes people don't want to stop their sinning. Then what?"

"Another job of the shepherd is to protect the sheep from wolves. But not everyone who sins is a wolf. Were you a wolf? Were you a danger to your congregation?"

Zenovia took pause, and tried to justify the punishment in her own mind. She knew that she'd never be at peace unless she debated both sides of the argument.

But she could come up with no rationalization at all. She had sinned against God and had finally been ready to receive guidance and to turn away from her sins. But she was not a wolf. She was not a threat to anyone. Not Tristan or any of the other Brethren.

"I was not a wolf," Zenovia said.

"No, you weren't. And God has forgiven you for your sins. This I know for certain."

Zenovia narrowed her eyes skeptically. "How do you know that?"

"I know because the Bible says that God is faithful and just to forgive us our sins when we ask for His forgiveness. But I also know because He's still using you and blessing you with a tremendous gift."

Zenovia was overwhelmed by Bishop Wilcox's compassion. Somehow, he had acknowledged her sins without making her feel like a harlot. He'd reassured her of God's love without saddling her with more guilt than she'd already been carrying.

"Bishop Wilcox...I want to tell you exactly what happened on Sunday. And I hope you can explain it all to me, because I really need some answers."

Chapter Thirty-two

Zenovia beamed with joy as she looked at her final in Systems Analysis. It was the last test that she had to take to fulfill her graduation requirements to earn her Bachelor of Science in Computer Science. She got an A on her final, which meant that she would indeed graduate summa cum laude.

"Well, let me see it!" Corrine exclaimed. She may have been even more excited about receiving the test score than Zenovia.

Corrine shrieked as she looked at the test paper. "Your mother is going to be so proud of you! Have you invited her to graduation?"

"I haven't talked to her, Corrine. She may not even know that it's time for me to graduate."

Zenovia plopped down on her secondhand sofa, and wiped unexpected tears from her face. She thought that she was far from still being emotional over Audrey's illness and their lack of communication. But it was the important times in her life when it was apparent that Audrey was missing in action as a mother.

"Do you want me to call her?" Corrine asked.

"No, Corrine. Don't do that. If Audrey hasn't called me, she's either too sick to think of me, or she's going along with the Brethren and purposely not dealing with me. Either way, she's not going to be at my graduation."

"That Brethren of the Sacrifice ain't nothing but a cult! Someone should call Oprah or something."

Zenovia shook her head and chuckled. "What would Oprah do, Corrine?"

"Girl, she'd blow the roof right off that thing. Oprah loves to tackle social injustice. That's her thing."

"Well, right now I can't worry about what Ms. Winfrey might think about the Brethren. I'm getting ready to graduate from college!"

"I will be sitting front and center, and no matter what you say, I'm screaming when you cross the stage," Corrine said proudly. "Are you inviting your man?"

By *your man* she meant Justin, of course. "Justin is not my man, Corrine. He's just my friend."

"Okay, whatever. Are you inviting *your friend?*"

"Yes, I am inviting my friend, Justin." Zenovia was completely unsuccessful in hiding her smile.

She and Justin had gone on several "dates," although Zenovia didn't know if she could actually define their outings as dates, because there was none of the typical date activity. They spent most of their time comparing notes on the Brethren over takeout food.

After speaking with Bishop Wilcox, Zenovia was determined to free herself of the guilt that had plagued her since she left the Brethren. Justin was on the journey with her because he too carried similar feelings of guilt and unworthiness.

"That Lynora sure wants to beat you down," Corrine said. "You stole her man."

Zenovia had been visiting Reaching the Masses for four weeks in a row since her meeting with Bishop Wilcox. Justin visited, too, and sat with Corrine and Zenovia each time. Lynora was not the least bit happy about this, and her facial expression let everyone in the congregation know. But Justin was always the gentleman and he greeted Lynora each Sunday with a hug.

"Oh well. I don't think they were anything more than friends, even though she seemed to believe that they were. Justin is not the kind of guy you can really claim."

"If he was the kind of guy you could claim, would you be trying to claim him?"

Zenovia put one finger up into the air. "Uh-uh, Corrine. You are not going to do this. Justin is my friend and I enjoy his company. That's as far as it's going right now."

"Well, I guess that's better than nothing. I thought you were going to become a nun or something."

"Are you coming to my graduation?" Zenovia asked Justin as they devoured a box of pepperoni pizza.

"Are you inviting me?"

"Only if you're coming."

Justin laughed out loud. "Yes, Zee, I'm coming to your graduation."

"Will you be able to get off work?"

"Yes. I've got some personal time stored up. It shouldn't be a problem."

Zenovia smiled. "Good, because you and Corrine will be my entire cheering section. I sure appreciate you."

"I wish I was graduating too. If it wasn't for the Brethren..."

Zenovia placed one hand over Justin's. She wanted to stop him before he went down his recurring road of anger that turned into a personal pity party. She'd heard it all over the past four weeks, and while she was patient with her friend, he was beginning to sound like a broken record.

"If it wasn't for the Brethren we wouldn't be friends, right?"

"All right, Zee, I'll give you that. But I still wish I'd gotten some scholarships when I was in high school. It's gonna break the bank for me to go now."

"You should still go, though. You'll just have to work your way through."

Justin nodded and pulled an envelope out of his pocket. He tossed it across the table to Zenovia. "What is this?" she asked.

"Open it."

Zenovia opened the pretty ivory envelope and realized that it was an invitation. A wedding invitation.

To Tristan and Mia's wedding.

The lettering on the invitation was done beautifully in an elaborate script. It made the invitation look more expensive than it probably was. That was typical of Mia.

But it was not typical of Tristan. Neither the invitation nor the bride was typical of the levelheaded, reasonable Tristan that she'd once called her friend. What had happened in his life to make Mia the bride of choice? It didn't make any sense.

She slid the envelope back to Justin. "Why did you show me that? I don't care about them. I thought Alyssa was the one who was engaged."

"She is, but that looks like it's going to be a long engagement. Mom doesn't approve and her guy is broke."

Zenovia couldn't really describe what she felt when she read the names on the invitation. As much as she'd tried to deny it, she'd always known that this was the inevitable end for Tristan and Mia. Why couldn't she have had a vision about Tristan and Mia getting married? It would've saved her a lot of hurt feelings, wasted energy, and teenage angst.

Zenovia asked, "Are you going?"

"If you'll be my date."

"Are you serious?"

"I'm dead serious."

Zenovia considered the request for a moment. "Won't it be weird? People won't talk to us, right?"

"Maybe they'll talk to you, because you haven't officially been cast out. But they won't talk to me. I'm not even really invited. Alyssa sent me this invitation as a joke."

"You're not even officially invited to your only brother's wedding," Zenovia said, slowly digesting the words. "If it's a joke, it's a cruel one."

Justin's smile didn't hide his sadness. "Zee, I'm going to see my brother get married, even if it's to that airhead Mia. I want you to come with me."

"Just to make everyone talk?" Zenovia asked.

"No. I want you with me because I don't know if I'll be able to endure it alone," Justin said sincerely. "You are the only one who would understand."

"How is Tristan getting married, anyway? Doesn't he still volunteer at the Brethren headquarters? That's not a real job! How is he gonna take care of a wife?"

Justin replied, "Oh, he'll just take Mia back up to headquarters with him. They'll live happily ever after unless she gets pregnant."

"What do you mean unless she gets pregnant? Isn't that part of the happily ever after? You know first comes love, then comes marriage...."

"It's different if you're serving at the Brethren headquarters. They don't even like the men to get married, but they let them. If they didn't, there'd be all kinds of immorality going on there."

Zenovia was curious. She asked, "What happens if she gets pregnant?"

"They get the boot. There are no children at the Brethren headquarters."

Zenovia's mouth dropped open, "So let me get this straight: if they get pregnant, they'll have to go home? And do what? How will they live?"

"Off of family members until Tristan can find a job. Doesn't it sound great?"

Zenovia laughed. "Just like a fairy tale."

"So are you going to go with me or not?"

"Okay, Justin. I'll do it. We'll be two outcasts sitting up there looking crazy, but I'll do it."

"We'll be two very attractive-looking outcasts."

Chapter Thirty-three

Corrine was dead set against Zenovia going to Tristan's wedding. And she had no problem letting Zenovia know about her feelings.

"It just sounds messy," Corrine declared as she stuck a bobby pin into the side of Zenovia's graduation cap.

"How is it messy?" Zenovia asked. "Justin wants to see his brother get married, and I'm going as his date."

"It's messy because his family hasn't invited him," Corrine explained. "Neither of you will be welcome. I can't see anything good coming from this."

"I haven't been home in four years anyway, Corrine. I need to visit my mother. I was going to go and see her after graduation."

"Well, didn't you say you dated this Tristan person? Why do you want to see him get married?"

"No, I never dated Tristan. I had a very serious crush on him when I was in high school, but nothing ever came of it."

"Well, you better call me immediately if something messy happens. I'm an hour plane ride away."

Zenovia laughed. "Thanks, Corrine, but I don't really think there's going to be a problem."

Zenovia had to admit that she was curious about what would happen at Tristan's wedding. She and Justin had gone shopping over the weekend to pick out their outfits. Zenovia was shocked that he wanted to color coordinate, but since it was his idea she went along with it. She was wearing a stunning peach and gray form-fitting dress and he was wearing a gray suit. They were going to look fabulous.

Zenovia couldn't shake the feeling that Justin was trying to prove something to his Brethren family members. But she didn't have anything to prove to anyone and had moved on with her Brethren-free life.

"Is someone knocking on your door?" Corrine asked.

"Yes, can you get that please? It's Justin. He's going to drive us to the graduation ceremony. Is that all right with you?"

Corrine grinned. "I'll drive myself. You two can ride together."

"You are relentless, Corrine. I keep telling you we're only friends."

Corrine waved her hand as she walked out of Zenovia's bedroom. "Whatever! I know what I see. Something tells me that you and Justin are going to be the next ones walking down an aisle."

"No ma'am. Absolutely not! I've got a career to launch. No time for all of that."

"Mmm-hmm..."

Zenovia chuckled as Corrine left the room. She looked at her reflection in the mirror and hoped that no one could tell that her eyes were just a little red and puffy. She'd spent the night tossing, turning and crying about Audrey not attending her graduation. Part of her regretted not reaching out to Audrey to let her know about her special day, but another part of her believed it was for the best.

Justin peeked in her bedroom door. "Congratulations, graduate! I brought these, but I didn't know if I should give them to you now or later. But if I wait until later they might wilt in this heat."

Zenovia took a huge bouquet of white and yellow roses from Justin. "Thank you, Justin."

"Are you almost ready to go?" Justin asked. "I don't want us to get caught in traffic."

"We've got a couple of hours yet. Don't worry, we'll make it on time."

Corrine popped into the bedroom and took the flowers. "These are lovely. I'm going to put them in water. How *friendly* of you Justin!"

When Corrine was out of earshot, Zenovia released a flurry of giggles. Justin asked, "What was *that* about?"

"She's trying to hook us up. I keep telling her we're only friends."

Justin cleared his throat and said, "That's your choice, Zee."

"What's my choice?"

"I didn't say anything about only being friends. You've made that decision without me. I'd like to be more than friends."

Zenovia scratched the side of her neck nervously. She didn't know if she wanted to think of Justin in more than friendly terms. First of all, it felt weird because she had tried to give her heart to Tristan first, even if he hadn't wanted her. There had to be some rule about that. And second, Justin was way too tempting to have as a boyfriend. She'd been celibate since Emil and planned on keeping it that way, but every touch from Justin was filled with electricity.

"I don't know if that's a good idea," Zenovia finally responded.

"Why? Because you used to be in love with my brother? That was years ago, and it's not like you were a couple."

Zenovia rolled her eyes and sucked her teeth, demonstrating her frustration. "I wasn't in love with your brother. Get it straight. But it still feels weird."

Justin shrugged. "It doesn't feel strange to me, and he's my brother. Plus he's getting married."

"Tristan is not really my biggest concern, Justin."

"Well then, what?"

Zenovia sat down next to Justin and replied, "I can't sleep with you. I'm celibate."

Justin took a very long pause. Too long for Zenovia's tastes. "Now I'm offended," he said.

"What? Why?"

"Zee, I would never try to sleep with you if you weren't my wife. I'm saving myself for marriage."

"What do you mean, you're saving yourself?"

"Well, contrary to what you may think of me, I'm a virgin."

Zenovia gasped. "Get the heck outta here! You are? Wow! I never would've thought...."

"That was one thing good about our Brethren upbringing. I think that's something special and I only want to make love to my wife."

Zenovia swallowed hard. "You do know that I'm not a virgin, right?"

"I didn't know for sure, but I heard rumors about you and Emil."

"Is that going to be a problem?"

Justin's eyes lit up. "Are you saying that you want us to be together?"

"Ugh! I hate when you answer my question with a question."

"Sorry," Justin said. "No. It won't be a problem. What you've done in the past doesn't matter to me. It's the future that matters."

Zenovia took a deep, mind-clearing breath. She certainly couldn't answer him then and there. This was going to take some thought, deliberation, prayer, and faith. If only she'd had a vision about them, then she'd feel more comfortable. But lately her visions had only been coming at church, as if God was trying to send her a message about how to use her gift.

And then what about the visions? She'd never been close enough to anyone to share her deepest secret. She couldn't imagine having an adult relationship and keeping that from Justin.

"Can I get back to you on this, Justin? It is a lot to think about."

"Think long…think wrong," Justin said.

"Are you kidding me? That was absolutely not an acceptable response."

Justin chuckled lightheartedly. "You're right, that was unacceptable. We'll revisit this another time. But I'm definitely not leaving it alone."

The way Justin stared deeply into Zenovia's eyes and

held her hand for dear life made her believe him. He wouldn't leave it alone, that was a certainty. But Zenovia couldn't understand why.

Trusting Justin with her heart was going to take a leap of faith, and she didn't know if her legs were strong enough.

Chapter Thirty-four

Zenovia watched the luggage ramp spit out every suitcase, box, and overnight bag from her and Justin's flight. And her bag—her black suitcase with the purple ribbon—was nowhere to be seen.

That could not be a good sign.

She and Justin had scored some discount plane tickets to Cleveland from Washington D.C., so they'd decided to fly instead of drive for six hours. As more bags slowly rolled past Zenovia, she started to think that maybe it was a bad idea.

"Your bag didn't come around yet?" Justin asked.

Zenovia held both her hands out in front of her. "Do you see me holding the suitcase, Justin?"

"Don't get snippy with me. I'm just trying to help."

Zenovia sighed, revealing her exasperation. "I'm sorry, Justin. Can you help me watch for it?"

"Of course."

Dread built in Zenovia's stomach as almost every bag was taken from the rotating belt. It was a full flight, so the crowd surrounding the baggage claim area started off large. As people retrieved their bags, the crowd thinned out, finally leaving Justin and Zenovia alone.

"How in the world can your luggage get lost on a direct flight from D.C. to Cleveland? We were barely in the air for an hour."

"Thank you, Justin," Zenovia snapped. "This is really helping."

"I'm just venting. I'm going to see if anyone can help us. Don't worry, we'll figure this out."

Zenovia smiled weakly as Justin marched toward the information booth. She watched the muscles in his back stretch as he strode away. Quickly, Zenovia adjusted her vision back to the luggage belt. She couldn't keep noticing all of Justin's manliness when she was trying to resist him.

He'd spent the entire flight giving Zenovia all of the reasons why she should go ahead and say yes to him. He'd told her that he was faithful, that he understood her, and that he'd always have her back and never leave her alone.

His reasons were pretty convincing, and she believed every word that he said. But Zenovia also knew all of the reasons that she couldn't say yes.

Justin was a virgin. He'd done all of the right things, and kept himself pure before God. How could she deserve him? He needed someone who'd been as patient as he had.

A teenage girl walked up to Zenovia pulling a black suitcase behind her. Zenovia's eyes lit up when she saw the purple ribbon.

"Is this yours?" the teenager asked. "I think I took it by accident."

"Thank you!" Zenovia gushed. "I thought it was lost."

Justin had witnessed the scene and rejoined Zenovia. "You've got your bag! Great. I knew everything would work out fine."

Justin placed an innocent kiss on Zenovia's forehead, and a shiver ripped through her body. His touch still carried currents of electricity, and Zenovia felt just like a copper penny—the perfect conductor.

Justin seemed completely oblivious to Zenovia's reaction. "Let's go. We've got a rental car waiting."

They picked up the rental car, a silver Honda Accord, and Zenovia got into the passenger seat while Justin packed in their bags. She tilted her head back, and inhaled. The exhale was slow and measured, as Zenovia tried to calm her nerves.

"Are you all right?" Justin asked as he pulled out of the parking spot.

Zenovia glanced over at Justin and examined his profile. His nose was the same as Tristan's, a clear indicator of their American Indian ancestors. But his features were softer than Tristan's sharp angles. Zenovia decided that she preferred Justin's face.

"I'm fine. I just haven't been home in four years. I don't know if I'm looking forward to being here."

"I definitely feel the same way," Justin concurred. "So let's talk about something that has nothing to do with the Brethren, our families, or Tristan and Mia's wedding."

"Like what?"

"Like us. When are you going to say yes to me?"

Zenovia replied, "When did you start begging? I don't ever remember you being so desperate."

"Desperate?" Justin laughed out loud. "Wow, you telling me that I'm desperate because I know what I want?"

"No. You're desperate because you keep hounding me for an answer, and I'm not ready to give it."

"I'm not hounding you. Pretty soon, I'll just stop asking altogether, because I'm absolutely not desperate."

Zenovia countered, "It's almost like you're trying to make me your girlfriend before we get to Tristan's wedding, like you want to throw it in his face. Isn't it enough that we'll be there together?"

"Are you serious? You think me wanting you is some kind of sibling rivalry thing that I have with my brother?"

Zenovia nodded. "You've tried to steal me from Tristan from the very first time we met. But it shouldn't matter now, because Tristan doesn't want me, and I don't want him. He's marrying Mia."

"You're right. Nothing about Tristan should matter to you anymore. I'm not even sure why we're talking about him."

"Tristan does not matter," Zenovia said.

Justin frowned deeply, his displeasure shadowing his handsome features. "Zenovia, I don't want to argue with you, because I really need you to have my back this weekend. I also need you to know that the only reason I didn't pursue you more when we were teenagers was to protect my brother's feelings."

"What?" Zenovia asked.

"I thought that my brother was attracted to you, and I could see that you *thought* you were attracted to him. I love my brother, and I'd never try to hurt him. But now, there's nothing keeping me from pursuing you, Zee."

Zenovia stared at her lap. There had definitely been chemistry between she and Justin from their first meeting. If she hadn't been so enchanted by Tristan's idealism and goodness, things would've been different.

It was almost as if she'd chosen Tristan because he was the one she was supposed to pick. There were very few sparks between them even though they'd become good friends. Justin, up until now, was all spark and no substance. She was excited to see that he was more than a walking pheromone, but she was still not ready to make a final decision.

"I don't want to argue with you either, Justin. I'm so sorry. I think this entire visit is stressing me out."

"I forgive you, Zee."

"I just have one request."

"Okay..."

"Please, let's talk about us when we get back to D.C."

Justin nodded in agreement. "I agree. Let's just get through the weekend."

Chapter Thirty-five

When Zenovia and Justin pulled into the parking lot of the Northeast Devotion Center it felt like the past four years had been erased. They were early, the first ones there. All of the courage and audacity Zenovia thought she felt evaporated at the thought of walking through the doors of that building.

Memories of her Elder tribunal flooded Zenovia's mind. "I don't know if I can do this, Justin."

Justin took her hand in his and held it. "You don't have to. We can leave if you want."

Zenovia squeezed Justin's hand. "We'll go in. Just give me a minute okay. I have to get my nerve up."

"Take as long as you want."

Audrey stares at herself in the mirror. There is a blank expression on her face as she pulls out a tube of lipstick.

"Audrey, you already put on your makeup. We're going to be late for the wedding."

"Who gettin' married?" Audrey's voice is low and gravelly.

"Tristan and Mia."

"Humph. He used to like Zee."

Phillip frowns. "You know we don't talk about her in our house."

Audrey's blank expression turns dark. "I can talk about whatever the hell I want. You don't tell me what to do."

"Audrey, we don't have time for this today. C'mon let's go."

"As soon as I finish putting on my makeup."

"Zee, you're shaking. Do you want to leave?"

Why had her visions chosen now to start popping up? The scene played before her mind's eye troubled Zenovia as well. In the vision, Audrey was frighteningly pale, and the fire-engine red lipstick had looked like blood on her lips.

A tear trickled down Zenovia's face. "Justin... it's my mother."

Justin scanned the parking lot. "Yes, there they are. Audrey looks good."

Zenovia watched her mother stumble across the parking lot. Phillip tried to hold her arm, but she pulled away.

"Justin, she does *not* look good," Zenovia said.

Zenovia had barely spoken above a whisper, but Audrey's head snapped in her direction as if she'd heard. Then she started marching toward Justin's rental car. She seemed determined, on some type of mission.

"She's coming over here," Justin said stating the obvious.

"Zee, is that you?" Audrey yelled before she reached the car.

Zenovia got out of the car and stood there waiting for Audrey's appraisal. "Girl, what is up with your hair?"

"Do you like it?"

Audrey cocked her head to one side, "Yeah, you look like one of those island women. I been telling you to go natural for years, so them little baldy-locks could grow on out. Now look at you, looking just like Pam Grier or somebody!"

Zenovia covered her mouth to contain her laugh. Somehow it didn't seem appropriate to break into spontaneous laughter when she hadn't seen her mother in four years, especially when her vision just told her that Audrey's mental health was worse. It seemed like there should be tears, but not laughter.

Audrey continued, "You coulda told somebody you graduated. I woulda came."

"Phillip wouldn't have let you come, Mom. You know that," Zenovia explained. "How'd you know about my graduation anyway?"

Audrey put a hand on her hip and rolled her eyes. "You think I can't count? You been gone four years, Zee. That means graduation. *And* that sapsucker don't tell me what to do."

Zenovia wanted to mention how Phillip had told her to stop taking her medication and she had. But she let it ride. She knew Audrey was perched right on the edge of an episode. The extra helping of lipstick smeared on Audrey's lips and teeth told her as much.

Audrey peered into the car. "Justin Batiste. What y'all two doing together?"

"She's my girlfriend," Justin said from the car.

A huge smile spread across Audrey's face. "Hey! I *knew* y'all was gone end up together. I saw that a long time ago."

"I'm not his girlfriend...."

"I don't know why not!" Audrey said while winking at Justin. "He is fine, girl. Nice and chocolate!"

Justin was so tickled that he had tears in his eyes, but Zenovia was beyond mortified. Audrey always found a way to embarrass her, even when she wasn't doing it on purpose.

Phillip refused to cross the parking lot, but he didn't have any problem yelling. "Audrey, come on here."

Audrey lifted one of her eyebrows, and to Zenovia, almost looked like her old self. "Y'all coming in?"

Zenovia nodded and Justin joined them. They walked across the parking lot as a trio, because Phillip jetted into the Devotion Center when he saw the three of them walking together.

Justin whispered to Zenovia, "Sounds like everybody thinks we should be together except you."

"Maybe all of y'all need some medication," Zenovia whispered back, but she did not pull away when Justin linked his arm through hers.

Chapter Thirty-six

Audrey separated from Justin and Zenovia before they walked through the doors of the Devotion Center. She may have been in need of antipsychotic medication, but Audrey obeyed rules—especially rules about God. Audrey took God rules more seriously than most, which was one of the reasons Zenovia didn't even think about inviting her to the graduation.

And the Brethren's rules said that Justin was cast out and Zenovia was an apostate. They were like Brethren outlaws.

"Are you ready?" Zenovia whispered to Justin who was squeezing the life out of her hand.

He nodded. "I am. It's just that I was almost a celebrity here, and now..."

"Don't think about it. Let's just do this and get it over with. Then you can take me somewhere fun tomorrow."

Zenovia threw her shoulders back proudly and glided through the doors of the Devotion Center. Maybe it was her friendly conversation with Audrey that had given her hope, or perhaps she really only cared about reconciling with her mother. Either way, she felt ready to dodge any stones the Brethren of the Sacrifice wanted to hurl in her direction.

At the door was a young lady serving as a hostess. Her face wasn't familiar, so Zenovia greeted her with a big smile.

The young lady asked, "Are you guests of the bride or groom?"

Justin spoke up. "The groom is my brother."

"He is? Wow! I didn't know Tristan had a brother. You must be proud of him, serving at headquarters and all."

Zenovia flinched at the words. If she knew Tristan well enough to be a hostess at his wedding then how in the world did she not know that Tristan had a brother? Had the Batistes tried to erase Justin from existence?

Justin smiled and Zenovia watched the girl partially melt. "Follow me. I'll seat you with the family."

"You are crushing my little hand," Zenovia whispered to Justin.

Zenovia gave Justin a reassuring squeeze. She tried to ignore the obvious hush that fell over the congregation as they made their way to the front. Fortunately, none of the immediate Batiste family was seated in the sanctuary. Zenovia assumed that their father was somewhere with Tristan. Sister Batiste and Alyssa were probably with Mia in the women's dressing room, no doubt helping her put the finishing touches on her wedding-day look.

After the initial silence from the congregation, the whispering began. Loud, rude whispering that would never be tolerated by cultured or couth adults. But the crowd assembled was neither cultured nor couth—they were the self-righteous Brethren of the Sacrifice. Zenovia felt a surge of boldness, as if the whispers had themselves empowered her.

She did a half turn and sent a beaming smile in the direction of several groups of onlookers. The expressions she got in return were mostly shock, but some were full of scorn. She remembered how friendly each face was on the day she and Audrey first walked through the doors of the Devotion Center. She'd thought that they were some of the most loving people on the planet. But clearly, the love came with conditions.

Justin and Zenovia sat in the second row from the front. Zenovia was so happy they'd decided to color co-ordinate. It added more to the illusion that they were together as a couple. And as perfectly matched as they were it was all just an illusion, because Zenovia's mind was not made up about her future with Justin.

Soft music played, alerting everyone to get into their seats for the start of the ceremony. The groups of whisperers reluctantly dispersed. Zenovia concentrated on looking forward and not making eye contact with anyone except Justin.

Zenovia jumped when she felt a tap on her shoulder. She looked up to see Bryce Goodman. She shivered involuntarily. Of all the people she wanted to avoid eye contact with, Bryce had to be number one on the list.

Her eyes formed the question, *What do you want?* She was not sure she could speak a word to Bryce and it not be profanity.

"Zenovia, you and . . . Justin can't sit here. The Council of Elders has asked that you all take a seat in the rear if you want to stay."

Justin replied, "We are sitting in the family section, Bryce. I'm Tristan's only brother."

Bryce ignored Justin and spoke again to Zenovia. "By fellowshipping with someone who is cast out, you accept their treatment."

"Um, yeah…not really caring about that right now," Zenovia replied. "By the way, we're not moving."

"We don't want to remove you from the building," Bryce warned.

"You just try it!" Justin said in a menacing voice.

Zenovia stroked Justin's arm. "You can try to remove me if you want, Bryce. But then, I'll make sure to have a conversation with your wife before I leave town. She looks mighty pretty today in that yellow dress."

Bryce fumed. "You two better not make a scene or by God, I'll remove you myself."

Zenovia smiled wickedly. "I'm terrified, Bryce. I really am."

Bryce stormed away angry and defeated.

"What do you have on him, Zee?" Justin asked.

"If and when I officially become your girlfriend, I'll spill it."

"That's not an if, Zenovia. It's definitely a when."

Zenovia grinned. She was glad that Justin was so confident that they would be together. It made it easier for her to imagine it to be true as well.

Tristan and Brother Batiste entered the sanctuary and walked down the center aisle to oohs and aahs from the same crowd that was just sending vile expressions to Zenovia and Justin. Zenovia kept her eyes to the floor. She didn't want to make eye contact with her ex-friend.

Finally, she did steal a glance in Tristan's direction and was confused by what she saw. He did not have the look of joy that should come standard on a man about to be married. He was still devastatingly handsome, but there was a tremendous melancholy draped over his entire countenance. It made the beginning of the ceremony seem like a solemn occasion.

Tristan stopped at the altar, and turned to face the crowd. He made eye contact with Justin and finally a smile appeared on his face. It was the same smile that had captivated Zenovia in Charlotte Batiste's van so many years ago.

Zenovia watched Tristan's eyes take her in. She could tell that he didn't recognize her at first, because there was interest in his expression, but nothing else. Then, he squinted and leaned forward a few inches, and Zenovia wiggled her pinky in a small hello gesture. He mouthed "Zee" and she nodded.

Time stopped for Zenovia.

She waited to see how her heart would feel. She expected a gaping hole to open up and make a chasm in her chest. She placed a hand over her heart in case she had to hold herself together. But it didn't happen.

"Am I going to have to beat my brother up at his own wedding?" Justin whispered.

Justin took Zenovia's hand in his and entwined their fingers. The message should've been obvious to Tristan, and Zenovia believed that it had been. Tristan looked away from them with an expression that Zenovia didn't know how to take. But for some reason, she thought it was more about their status as former Brethren members than their relationship.

Zenovia recalled Tristan's warning about Justin. He'd told her that Justin wasn't the one. But maybe his judgment was off, because unless someone had given Mia a personality transplant, Zenovia couldn't see how she could be the one for Tristan.

The bridesmaids walked down the aisle one at a time, and they were mostly girls that Zenovia didn't know, so she paid them no attention. She was, however, excited to see Alyssa, who was the maid of honor, according to the program.

"Here comes Lyssa," Justin said.

Unlike Tristan, Alyssa immediately spotted Justin and Zenovia. She shocked them both, and everyone else in the room, by walking out of her place in line to give them hugs. One of the bridal party members hissed for her to get back in line, because Mia was about to start the bride's march.

Mia was a gorgeous bride. Her skin and makeup were flawless, and her hair was pinned to one side with curls cascading over her shoulder. The flowers in her hair were a beautiful ivory color that matched the color of her dress.

Zenovia looked again at Tristan, who for the first time that day, looked truly happy. He smiled lovingly at Mia and even had tears in his eyes as she approached. His emotional display touched Zenovia, and his tears were contagious; she struggled not to shed a few of her own.

But Tristan's tears made Zenovia feel at peace with his decision. In her heart of hearts she had wondered if Tristan had carried a torch for her all of those years. His joy at seeing Mia proved that he had not.

Zenovia was free to love Justin.

She squeezed Justin's hand and then gently kissed his cheek. Zenovia couldn't decipher the strange expression on his face. She made a mental note to ask him about it later.

Besides Bryce Goodman's ill-advised attempt at strong-arming, Charlotte Batiste's behavior was the only ugly spot on the ceremony. She spent the entire time glaring at Justin and Zenovia instead of watching her youngest son share marriage vows with Mia.

When the ceremony was over, Justin whispered to Zenovia, "Let's get out of here. We'll call Tristan later. He can't talk to me now, anyway, not with the Brethren hovering."

Zenovia and Justin hurried toward the rear of the sanctuary and almost made a clean escape. They both stopped suddenly when they heard Charlotte's voice.

"Why did you come here? Why did you want to ruin your brother's day?" Charlotte asked, apparently not caring who heard her.

Zenovia touched Justin's back, to calm him and to let him know that he had her support.

Justin turned around slowly. "I'm happy to see you too, Mother. It's been too long."

"Don't play games with me Justin. I hope you don't plan on turning up at the reception with this tramp. Neither of you are welcome and no one wants to break bread with you."

Tramp? Zenovia flinched as if the word was a blow to the head. She needed someone to rub her back and calm her down.

"Did you just call my daughter a tramp?" Audrey had appeared in the foyer of the Devotion Center just as Charlotte began her tirade.

"I call them like I see them, Audrey. She was determined to have one of my sons. She started on Tristan, but couldn't get her hooks in him. I guess she settled on Justin. He's clearly the weaker of the two."

Audrey's pale face turned an alarming shade of red. "You need to take that back right now, Charlotte. I ain't tryin' to act a fool up in here, but I swear if you don't take that back, you're gonna be pulling my high-heeled sandal out of your extra-large behind."

Charlotte rolled her eyes. "Lord knows you're certainly capable of acting a fool, but I will not apologize to this sinful heifer."

Fortunately for Charlotte, Phillip had been right on Audrey's heels. He grabbed her by the arm, too roughly for Zenovia's liking, and pulled her toward the door.

"I apologize, Sister Charlotte. Tell your husband and Tristan congratulations for me."

Zenovia shook her head angrily. Phillip was such a punk. He never had a problem trying to flex his authority to Zenovia, but when dealing with higher-ranking Brethren members, he was a totally different person.

Alyssa burst into the foyer and took Charlotte's arm. "Mom, come on. We have to greet the guests and Mia wants you to be in the pictures."

"I'm just making sure your brother and his trash don't disrupt this day any further."

Alyssa gave them an apologetic glance. "Come on, Mom, before Tristan gets upset."

Justin's eyes were wet with tears that he refused to let fall. He took Zenovia by the arm and they walked out of the building. No one but Zenovia could tell that he was leaning on her as they made their way to the car.

Justin seemed to start breathing again when the car doors were safely closed. "We survived."

"Yeah, we did," Zenovia replied. "But I'm not walking through those doors again unless somebody dies."

"I feel the same way," Justin concurred.

He pulled out of the parking lot as dozens of eyes followed them.

"Do they really have to stare like that? It's like some kind of horror movie, or something," Zenovia replied.

"They were staring because they wanted us to feel uncomfortable."

"Well, it worked. Even though it was nice seeing Audrey, Tristan, and Alyssa again, I'm glad we're done with that."

"Hmmm…"

"What?" Zenovia asked, "What are you hmmming about?"

Justin asked, "I was wondering why I finally got a kiss from you. I know it was only on the cheek, but what was that about? Were you trying to make Tristan jealous?"

"No, but I don't know how to explain…."

Justin drummed his fingers on the steering wheel. "I really wish you'd try."

"It's like, I knew I didn't still have any feelings for Tristan, but I didn't know how he felt about me."

"And…"

"Let me finish. If he *did* still have feelings for me, then I wouldn't be able to date you, Justin, no matter how much I want it."

"How much do you want it?" Justin asked. Apparently, he was unable to resist a double entendre, no matter the circumstances.

"Justin!"

"Okay, I'll stop. Please continue."

"But seeing him there with Mia, and truly happy with Mia... that was all I needed to see. Because, if he's in love with her, then he could've never loved me."

Justin tilted his head to one side. "Tristan ending up with Mia is odd. He's never cared for her personality. He always said she wasn't very intelligent. I don't get why all of a sudden she's the love of his life."

"Does it matter why? It's true, and that's all I need to know."

Justin asked, "So you kissed me because now, after seeing Tristan, you can date me guilt-free."

"Yes."

"I don't know how I feel about our relationship being contingent on Tristan's feelings."

They drove for a few minutes in silence. Zenovia was grateful for the break in their conversation. She didn't want to talk about Tristan's feelings for the rest of the evening.

"Do you think your mother really would've done something to my mother with that high-heeled shoe?" Justin asked, breaking the spell of silence.

Zenovia laughed. "Your mother was about five seconds away from an Audrey beat down."

"And is that worse than a regular beat down?"

"You think I'm joking. Next time you see your mother you better hope she's in one piece, because I guarantee, it ain't over with Audrey."

Nothing was ever over with Audrey. There was something about her schizophrenia that made her memory sharper than the average person. She could repeat conversations word for word that she'd had years before. It was like she played them over and over in her head, each time reliving the hurtful words that had been said. This uncanny ability made it easy for Audrey to hold grudges.

"Audrey is carrying around about eighteen million three hundred thousand grudges, give or take a few hundred thousand," Zenovia shared.

"Sounds painful."

"You don't know the half."

Zenovia had insisted on separate hotel rooms, even though Justin had assured her that it was perfectly safe for them to slumber in the same room. Virgin or not, Zenovia wasn't buying it. The closest Justin was getting to her sleeping body was that locked metal door that joined their rooms.

In spite of all the day's events, she'd slept soundly and felt a sense of peace as the daylight caused her to open her eyes. The feeling of discomfort came when she thought of Audrey and her medication-free antics.

She already knew the state laws on forcing medication on the mentally ill. It all came down to them doing harm to someone else or to themselves. Zenovia had argued the case that Audrey was destroying her mind by refusing her medication, but that was not the state's definition of harm. They needed some tangible, quantifiable measure of harm that Audrey had not yet accomplished.

Maybe she should have egged her on in a fight with Charlotte. That would've been amusing to watch and maybe a reason to have some antipsychotic medication forced on Audrey.

The phone in her room rang. "Hello?" she asked.

"Hey, sleepyhead," Justin said. "Are you dressed? We've got company."

"I just woke up. Who is it?"

"Tristan."

Zenovia banged her head lightly on the headboard. "Why is he here? Shouldn't he be on his honeymoon? What does he want?"

"He just wants to see us, I think. He hasn't said much of anything yet. But he said he wants to talk to both of us, together."

"All right. Give me a couple minutes. Can you order some coffee or something?"

"Already done."

Zenovia smiled at his thoughtfulness. "Okay. I'll be over in a second."

Quickly, she brushed her teeth, washed her face, fluffed her afro, and put on the gym suit she'd traveled in. The thought crossed her mind to put on lip gloss, but she erased it immediately. It was only Tristan, and he was married. No need to get pretty for him.

When she was ready she knocked on the door dividing their rooms. Justin opened it and stood aside for her to walk through. She stood on her tiptoes and kissed his cheek, then took a seat on the edge of his bed.

She locked eyes with Tristan who was sitting at the room's tiny desk. "Hi, Tristan. Congratulations on your wedding. My invitation must've gotten lost in the mail, but luckily Justin had his, so I was able to see you exchange vows with Mia, of all people."

"I would've invited you, Zee, if I'd known where to find you," Tristan explained.

Zenovia chuckled. "My mother always had my address, Tristan. You didn't try too hard."

"Would you have come if it weren't for Justin?" Tristan asked.

"Hmmm...probably not."

"I thought you wanted to talk to both of us? It sounds like you only want to talk to Zee," Justin said with a twinge of sadness in his voice.

"Justin, I don't even know where to begin with you. You *left* headquarters! I got interrogated because of your doubts. I thought they were going to send me away."

"I didn't leave because of my doubts. I left with facts, Tristan. It's wrong the way the High Council decides what the rank-and-file Brethren believe!"

Tristan roared, "You have no right to question the High Council! They are ordained by God and anointed by His Spirit!"

"They vote on the doctrine, Tristan, did you know that? I walked in on one of their meetings. Brother Jennings needed his medication and I had to bring it to him."

"I'm not listening to this," Tristan objected.

"You need to hear it, Tristan!" Justin exclaimed. "If you're going to continue as one of the Brethren, at least make it an informed decision."

"What you have is created by the apostasy in your heart," Tristan declared.

Justin continued in spite of Tristan's protests. "The vote was on the issue of alcohol abuse. It was on whether someone should be cast out for being an alcoholic."

Tristan was now interested. "And what was the outcome?"

"The vote was seven to five in favor of *not* casting out a Brethren member who is an alcoholic."

Tristan looked confused. "There must be an explanation."

"If each of these men is ordained by God and anointed by His Spirit, how then is there a difference of opinion?"

Tristan objected, "Paul and Barnabas had a difference of opinion!"

"But Paul and Barnabas were not deliberating on doctrine that could destroy families and lives."

"Someone being an alcoholic...that's an addiction," Tristan explained. "I can see how that was a tough decision to make."

"But they can cast someone out for fornication?" Zenovia asked in a quiet voice.

"Well, of course! The Bible is clear on that," Tristan said dismissively.

Justin cleared his throat. "First Corinthians Six Verses Nine and Ten. It says 'Know ye not that the unrighteous shall not inherit the Kingdom of God? Be not deceived: neither fornicators, nor idolaters, nor adulterers, nor effeminate, nor abusers of themselves with mankind...'"

"'Nor thieves, nor covetous, nor drunkards, nor revilers, nor extortioners, shall inherit the kingdom of God,'" Tristan finished the passage.

"So...tell me, Tristan...is there any distinction here between a drunk and a fornicator?"

Tristan shook his head, but he didn't open his mouth.

Justin continued, "So if the Bible doesn't make a distinction, why should there even be the need for a vote?"

"I don't know," Tristan replied.

"I'll tell you why. Because half of the Brethren Elders would be cast out for being drunks! The High Council is obsessed with sexual sins to the point where nothing else matters to them. I cannot and *will not* be a part of that!"

Zenovia listened intently to the reason for Justin's flight from the Brethren. She walked over to him as he shook with anger, and stroked his back, trying to calm him down.

"So that's it?" Tristan asked. "That one little thing is going to pull you away from the religion we've practiced our whole lives? From our family? You were supposed to be my best man!"

"I didn't choose to separate myself from the family. You all made that choice."

Zenovia said, "Tristan, we understand and respect your reasons for being one of the Brethren. Do you think maybe you can respect your brother's reasons for choosing not to be one?"

"I can't respect them, because I want my brother to be saved. He will not have salvation outside of the Brethren. Neither will you."

Zenovia was surprised that the words had no effect on her. There was a time when they would've caused her months of sleepless nights, because she'd believed what he said to be true. But she no longer believed that the Brethren had the true revelation of God's will.

His words were only words.

"I'm so happy that God is more merciful than the Brethren," Zenovia said with a slight smile.

Tristan replied, "We'll see on Judgment Day. All of

you churchgoers will be just like those people in Sodom and Gomorrah."

Zenovia refused to engage Tristan further, so he stood to his feet and walked to the door.

"Is this how you're going to leave, Tristan? Aren't you going to say goodbye to your brother?" Zenovia asked.

Without turning to look back, Tristan replied, "I don't have a brother."

Tristan walked out of the hotel room and let the door close behind him. Justin's shoulders slumped sadly as the tears started to pour down his cheeks. Zenovia did her best to encircle him in her arms as he wept.

Chapter Thirty-seven

Is this a date?" Justin asked.

Zenovia and Justin strolled hand in hand through the courtyard of her apartment complex. He had picked her up from her ministers-in-training class at Reaching the Masses and had taken her for Chinese food afterward.

"I don't think it's a date, Justin. You just gave me a ride home," Zenovia replied.

"And I gave you a free dinner. Anytime a guy picks you up, springs for dinner, and then takes you on an evening stroll, it's a date."

Zenovia grinned. "Well, you didn't ask me out on a date. You asked if I needed a ride home from my minister class."

"How is your class going? You don't talk much about it."

"It's going..."

Justin was right, Zenovia didn't talk much about the class. She wasn't sure how she could share all of her excitement about ministry without revealing her secret.

She and Justin had grown closer in the two months they'd spent together after Tristan's wedding, but she still hadn't shared anything about her visions.

"If you don't want to tell me about it, that's fine," Justin replied.

"It's not that I don't want you to know about the class. It's really good. There are just some things about me that I'm not ready to share yet."

Justin asked, "Does it have anything to do with what you've been doing in church every Sunday? People are calling you a prophetess?"

"Yes. It does have something to do with that."

"Are you going to elaborate?"

"No."

Justin sighed and dropped Zenovia's hand. "Every time I think we're getting close to having a relationship, you pull back."

"I don't want to pull back, Justin. I want to tell you everything. And I'm doing good. I've told you all about Audrey."

Justin inhaled deeply and raised his eyes to the clear night sky. "Yes, you've told me more than I've ever wanted to know about Audrey's mental illness. But I'm not falling in love with Audrey...."

Zenovia swallowed hard. Justin kept hinting at the fact that he was falling for her, but the word "love" was never mentioned. The last time a man professed his love for her it was Emil, and she'd believed him with every shred of her being.

And that had gone absolutely nowhere.

"You're not falling in love with me, Justin. You're only saying that because we've got the Brethren in common."

"No, that is not the reason. I want to be with you because you are smart, hilarious, sweet, and original, not to mention beautiful. I've never known anyone like you, Zee."

"That's just your hormones talking," Zenovia replied dismissively.

"Why are you trying to talk me out of feeling this way? Don't you think you deserve to be loved?"

Zenovia hugged herself and bit her bottom lip. "Okay, Justin. I'm going to tell you and watch you run for the hills."

"I won't go anywhere."

"I see things, Justin. They're visions really. Future and past events. I see them whenever God feels like showing them to me."

Justin's jaw dropped. "Have you had any visions about me?"

"No, I haven't. God is surprisingly quiet about you."

When Zenovia started the minister's class, Bishop Wilcox told her to pray to God about revealing the fullness of her gift. He told her to seek direction in her prayers and to ask God to show her visions that would reveal her destiny.

Since she'd started praying, Zenovia received visions every Sunday at church, and Bishop Wilcox would allow her to share with the individual she'd seen. Most often, the conversation was followed by the altar workers praying with that person. Sometimes she saw sin that a person was engaged in, but most of the time it was a vision of what God had planned for that person's future.

Zenovia prayed fervently about her own future. She had to know for sure if Justin was a part of her destiny.

He seemed to be everything that she needed. He understood her past with the Brethren, and he didn't pressure her for sex.

Justin said, "Maybe God wants you to have faith for some things."

Zenovia nodded. "I think that you're right about that."

"So do it. Have faith about us. Marry me and get it over with."

Zenovia choked on the breath of air she'd been inhaling. "Are you crazy? I can't marry you. We haven't even been on a date."

"According to your definition, that is true. But I've been going on dates with you since we met up at Reaching the Masses."

Zenovia could tell by the look of sincerity on Justin's face that he was serious about his request. She could, without question, spend the rest of her life with him, especially after his reaction to her secret. He had not cringed or run away from her. He was still standing there, professing his love.

"Okay, Justin. I will consider marrying you, but you have to court me properly. These sneak dates are really not doing it for me."

Justin laughed loudly. "Of course I'll court you properly. Now that I have your permission. Do you know how happy Corrine is going to be?"

Zenovia rolled her eyes. "I forgot about her. Do we have to tell Corrine?"

"You can tell her after I buy your ring."

Again, Justin caught Zenovia off guard and wrapped her in an intimate embrace. He'd never been as forward, but since his feelings were out in the open, there was really no reason for restraint.

When their lips met, Zenovia was taken back in time to their first kiss. The one he'd stolen on the day he was leaving for the Brethren headquarters. Their second kiss was full of passion that was missing from the first time.

"I can't wait to make you my wife," Justin said when the kiss was through.

It was rare for Zenovia to be rendered speechless, but Justin had done just that.

Chapter Thirty-eight

Zenovia sat across the table from Corrine at their weekly brunch date. They did it every Saturday morning at a little soul food spot that made ox tails and rice that tasted like Audrey's. Zenovia loved the place because it always reminded her of her mother.

Zenovia held her hands under the table and fiddled with the ring she was wearing on her finger. Justin had made good on his "proper courtship," and she had finally said yes to his proposal. The small, inexpensive ring on her finger made it all real.

Telling Corrine would make it surreal.

But Zenovia was finally ready to share her news. She just wished she was sharing it with Audrey.

She'd called her mother several times, but Phillip was the only one who ever answered the phone. As soon as he heard Zenovia's voice he would hang up the phone.

It worried Zenovia that she hadn't heard her mother's voice since Tristan's wedding four months before. To make it worse, Alyssa had passed on news to Justin that Audrey had been absent from services at the Devotion Center. Zenovia suspected that her mother's mental state was beyond what even her medication was able to repair.

"I'm going to Cleveland to see my mother," Zenovia said to Corrine as she sipped her sweet tea.

"You should. I don't trust that Phillip."

Zenovia shook her head. "Me, either. He's unstable himself, I believe."

"What is that on your finger?" Corrine asked finally noticing the ring.

"What does it look like?"

"Don't get smart with me girl! Did Justin propose?"

Zenovia nodded. "He did. We're getting married in Bishop's office in two weeks."

"No, you are not getting married in Bishop's office!" Corrine objected. "Your mother would have my head if she knew I didn't put on a wedding for her only child."

"Justin and I think it's best, since we won't have any of our family here."

"You'll have your church family. Everyone at Reaching the Masses will come."

Zenovia shook her head. "I'm not walking down the aisle if my mother's not going to be there."

"Well, go see about her, and tell her about your wedding."

"That is the plan."

Corrine asked, "Are you going to take your fiancé with you to Cleveland?"

"No. This is something that I need to do without him, I think. This is about Audrey, so you know, it's private."

"Private! You can't have anything private from your husband. You might need him."

"He's not my husband yet, and until he is, Audrey is my issue."

"You are so stubborn, but you get it honest. No one could tell your mother anything, either."

Zenovia smiled. "How do you know how Audrey was? You must've been little when she left home."

"I was ten. I remember the day vividly because it was my tenth birthday. I was having a party and Audrey ruined it."

"She did?"

"Yes. Everyone was in an uproar because Grandfather had put her out of the house. I mean, why did she have to tell everyone she was pregnant on my birthday?"

"That was pretty bad. Did you have your party anyway?"

"If you want to call it that. Grandmother threw something together, but I didn't even have any balloons. It was supposed to be a tea party."

Zenovia was a little amused by her cousin's anger. "Seriously, Corrine, it sounds like you have some unresolved issues. Maybe you need to leave that on the altar and let God handle it."

"Whatever! Audrey owes me a tea party."

"Okay, maybe she does, but why was Grandmother throwing you a party? Where were your parents?"

Corrine sighed. "I keep forgetting that you don't know anything about the family history."

"Well, I just kind of assumed that your parents weren't around."

"My mother was around, but if you had met her, you'd think Audrey was the most normal woman on the planet."

Zenovia's eyes widened. "What was wrong with her?"

"Well, she had that gift too, you know."

"You know about the gift?" Zenovia asked, thinking it had been a secret between herself and Audrey.

"Of course I know about it. That's why Grandfather was so angry with Audrey for getting pregnant. He wanted her to preach right alongside him, but she wasn't even thinking about that."

"So your mother had the gift too?"

Corrine nodded. "Yes. Her name was Persephone, and she went crazy behind those visions. She started cutting and scratching herself when she was a little girl."

"What happened to her?"

"She hung herself when she was nineteen. I was only seven."

Zenovia's mouth dropped open. "She was twelve when she had you?"

"Yes."

"Who was your daddy?"

Corrine cleared her throat. "No one knows. She took that one to her grave."

Zenovia shook her head sadly. Was she destined for insanity because she also shared the gift? Was going mad a part of the package?

"Do you have the gift too, Corrine?"

"I thank God every day that I don't. I can't imagine what it must be like."

"You don't have to do this alone."

Zenovia took Justin's face in her hands and kissed him lightly on the lips. Then she placed another folded pair of jeans into her suitcase. She had no idea how to make him understand that she needed to see Audrey alone. That she needed to make peace with the decision to move her life forward.

"I know that, but I need to do this alone. I need to see what my mother is going through, and having you there will only be a distraction."

"What if Phillip tries something?" Justin asked. His face was scrunched into a maze of concerned lines.

"Like what?"

"I don't know. Anything! Who knows what he's capable of doing?"

Zenovia replied, "I'm not afraid of him. Phillip is the least of my worries."

"What is your biggest worry, then, Zenovia? You've got to stop shutting me out."

Zenovia sighed with frustration. "I'm not shutting you out. I just need to see about my mother. That's not really your concern."

"How is the welfare of my future mother-in-law not my concern?"

Zenovia zipped her suitcase shut. "Justin, I know that you love me. You don't have anything to prove."

"Did you ever think of the fact that you might not be able to handle how Audrey is living right now? I saw your face at Tristan's wedding, before Audrey walked up to the car. Something wasn't right."

He was right. Zenovia had seen a vision of Audrey that day, and it had been disturbing.

"All right, then, Justin. Come. I didn't want to burden you with this, but since you insist on being burdened, you might as well know what you're marrying into."

Justin stood from his seat on Zenovia's bed and encircled her with his arms. "I don't care what I'm marrying into. I'm marrying you, the woman that I love. Please stop trying to talk me out of it."

"What?" Zenovia asked while pushing Justin away gently. "I've never tried to talk you out of marrying me."

"Every time you do one of your big revelations, it's like you expect me to run away. You told me that Audrey is schizophrenic...I'm still here. You told me about the visions, and guess what? Still here."

Zenovia gazed into Justin's eyes, knowing in her heart that he was sincere, but finding herself looking for dishonesty in his expression.

"What do you see?" Justin asked. "Are you waiting to have a vision about me?"

Zenovia smiled at Justin's discernment and her own transparency. She was somewhat irritated that she had still not seen Justin in any of her visions.

The previous Sunday, she'd waited on God to show up and finally give her a sign of the direction that she should take in her own life. God did show up, but He'd given her a word of encouragement to a woman who'd been searching for a job for six months. Zenovia had been instructed to whisper to her a familiar scripture, "I have not seen the righteous forsaken, nor his seed begging bread."

The woman had gone running down the center aisle of the church, leaving Zenovia standing in amazement. Sometimes, what God gave her to give to people was something they would know themselves if they studied the Bible. Zenovia was sure that woman had heard that verse before, but it was what she'd needed to hear at that moment.

Zenovia had talked to Bishop Wilcox about her uncertainty about Justin and her lack of direction from God on the matter. Bishop had repeated Justin's sentiments, and told her that her decision to marry Justin would involve her stepping out on faith. But Bishop had also told her to seek God in prayer, and that perhaps the Lord would give her a sign.

She'd prayed and even fasted. The latter was difficult; fasting was not her strong suit. She lacked the self-discipline needed to deny herself pasta and sweet tea. But she'd struggled through it, waiting on a prophetic manifestation.

She was still waiting.

Zenovia kissed Justin's cheek. "I don't need a vision to know that I love you."

"It's good to hear that, Zee. You don't say it enough."

Saying "I love you" didn't come naturally to Zenovia. She had to force the words from her mouth. The feelings of love were alive and well, but she never felt the need to say them. She'd grown up with Audrey and her nonverbal ways of communicating love. Saying the words was a totally new thing.

"I love you, I love you, I love you. That ought to last for a while, right?" Zenovia teased.

"Right, Zee," Justin chuckled. "It will last for a while."

Chapter Thirty-nine

A sense of dread filled Zenovia as she and Justin pulled into Audrey and Phillip's driveway. There was nothing supernatural about the feeling; anyone would've felt the same on viewing the scene.

The front yard was a complete mess. The grass was so long that it had to have been months since its last trim; there were weeds where Audrey used to have chrysanthemums, and there was a couch sitting in the middle of the lawn. The upholstery on the couch was discolored with bleach splotches.

"This place looks like a disaster area," Justin said, giving voice to Zenovia's thoughts.

"Phillip's car isn't here."

Justin took a deep breath. "Well, let's go see if your mother is home."

"Wait. I need to say a prayer."

Justin took her hand and prayed, "Dear heavenly Father, please give us the strength to deal with whatever we're about to face in this home. Give us the wisdom to deal with the situation according to your will, and then we ask that you give us peace after we've made the decision. In the name of Jesus we pray, Amen."

Zenovia was grateful to Justin for praying for her. It amused her to hear him pray out loud, because he sounded like one of the Brethren. They always started their prayers "dear heavenly Father." He would probably never get that out of his system.

"You ready?" Justin asked.

"No, but let's go in before I lose my nerve."

The fact that Audrey might not open the door occurred to Zenovia as they stood on the porch preparing to knock. That fact made her pause. Justin, she supposed, misread her pause as nervousness and took it upon himself to knock.

"We should've had a plan," Zenovia whispered.

"This is your mother, you don't need a plan."

But before their discussion went any further, Audrey flung the door open. "Well, why didn't y'all call and say you was coming? I would've made y'all a peach cobbler. You know that's Zenovia's favorite, right, Justin?"

Justin tried to smile. "No ma'am, I didn't know that."

"Well, how in the world are you marrying my daughter and you don't even know her favorite dessert?"

Zenovia could do nothing but gasp as she took in her mother's appearance. She was emaciated, pale, and wearing a ratty-looking wig. Even in her insanity, Audrey had always taken extra care in her appearance, mostly due to the fact that she was trying to catch a man.

"Y'all gone have to sit at the table, because I had to throw that couch out. Come on in."

The familiar scent of bleach burned the hairs in Zenovia's nostrils. She was used to the smell, but Justin looked like he was about to be overcome by the fumes.

"Baby, why don't you see if there's a lawn mower in the garage," Zenovia suggested. "Maybe you can do something to the yard."

Justin looked relieved and immediately fled the house. Audrey laughed. "He can't take a little bleach? Well, I don't know how he gone live with you, cause that's what we clean with. Right?"

"Right," Zenovia agreed. "Ma, why are you wearing that wig?"

"Girl, you ain't gone believe this."

She snatched the wig from her head, and Zenovia had to look away. Audrey's hair had been butchered, partially cut, partially shaven. The beautiful red hair that had been Audrey's pride and joy was gone.

"What happened to your hair?" Zenovia asked, trying to keep the quiver out of her tone.

"Girl, my head got to itching one day. Itching like crazy. I think I had some of them head lice, got them from that demon-infested couch."

"There is shampoo for lice, Mom, you could've gotten rid of it."

Audrey cackled. "Who was gone give me some money for that shampoo, huh?"

"Phillip? Your husband?"

"That sapsucker didn't even believe me when I said I had it. He said he didn't see nothing. I told him them bugs is pretty much invisible, but I felt 'em. They was crawling all over my head."

"Mom, lice are not invisible, and if they were crawling all over your head then Phillip would've at least seen one."

Audrey rolled her eyes. "Anyway! I got that sucker good. He wouldn't give me the money for that shampoo, so I just cut my hair off. That got rid of the bugs, thank the Lord."

Zenovia looked around the kitchen. There were piles of potato peels on the counter.

"Were you making mashed potatoes?" Zenovia asked, trying to get Audrey's mind off of the imaginary lice, because she'd started scratching her head.

"Naw. I was trying to make some potato salad to go with some chicken that Phillip says he's bringing home."

"Well, do you need my help?" Zenovia asked.

"Since when do I need your help cooking anything? You can't cook no way."

Zenovia laughed. "I can cook, Ma. You've never eaten my cooking."

"Well, I sure hope you can do something other than comb that nappy hair of yours! Your man gone have to eat something when y'all get married."

Zenovia covered her mouth with her hand. She knew that Audrey was not intending to be funny, but she was anyway.

"Mom, I need to use the bathroom. I'll be right back."

Zenovia did not miss the look of alarm on Audrey's face. She started toward the hallway, and she could hear Audrey whispering a prayer.

As she walked down the hallway, Zenovia could see that there were little crosses painted on the walls. Some of them were done with what looked like nail polish, and then some were done with marker and others done with ink pen. But the entire wall from ceiling to floor was covered with crosses.

Zenovia cringed when she opened the bathroom door. She could barely see the floor, because it was covered with wet rags and towels. There was also dirty underwear strewn through the mess, and there was a sour, mildewed smell coming from the entire pile.

Suddenly, Zenovia no longer felt the urge to urinate.

When she rejoined Audrey in the kitchen, Audrey was singing a Gospel hymn and peeling the skins from boiled eggs. The sulphur smell of the eggs mixed with the intense bleach fumes was especially unappealing. Zenovia wished that she'd escaped outside with Justin.

The entire scene was bad, but not as bad as Zenovia had expected. Audrey was still partially functioning, although it was clear that her delusions were slowly taking over. The imaginary lice and the crosses on the wall were both signs that she felt demons were in the house.

Zenovia asked, "How are your friends at the Devotion Center? Have you seen Charlotte lately?"

"Charlotte ain't none of my friend! How she gone be my friend and she don't even like you? You my daughter. She can go pound salt."

Zenovia had hoped that Charlotte had gotten over her disdain for her and Justin's relationship and reconciled with Audrey. Although she was sure that Charlotte wasn't a bit understanding of Audrey's mental state, she was Audrey's only real friend. She was the one who'd introduced Audrey to the Brethren; the least she could do was care about the well-being of her convert.

"How is Phillip?"

"Humph. He betta be glad I had a vision about being married to his black behind. One of these mornings, he gone be wearing a hot grits facial. Let him keep putting his hands on me."

Zenovia's anger flared. "He hits you?"

"Naw. He keeps trying to have sex with me. I told him he ain't gone touch me till he let me check him for them lice. I think I got them from him."

"I thought you said it was the couch."

"Coulda been the couch, coulda been his nasty black behind. You know he don't even wash his behind?"

Zenovia sighed wearily. She walked over to the living room window and glanced outside to see Justin's progress. He had managed to get the lawn mower on, but he was only about a third of the way through the tangled mess. He'd used a weed whacker to shorten the length, but it was still a mess.

As she stood at the window, she had the urge to use the bathroom again, but knew that she wouldn't be able to use it in her mother's house.

"Ma, I'm gonna have Justin take me to get us something to eat. What do you want? Boston Chicken?"

"Ooh, yeah! Bring me some of those cinnamon apples. You know I love those."

Zenovia smiled. Some things never changed. "Okay. I'll be right back."

Zenovia dashed out of the house and into the driveway. "Come on!" she called to Justin. "I've got to pee!"

Justin jumped into the car next to Zenovia, who had already started the ignition. "Why didn't you use it in there?"

"It's not usable, Justin. She and Phillip have made a mess of that house."

"Seriously? I wonder why the missionaries haven't checked on them, especially since Audrey hasn't been to the Devotion Center."

Zenovia had her suspicions. She and Audrey had been members of many churches, and the missionaries at none of those churches had ever thought to check on her and Audrey. Zenovia thought it was because black folk were unnerved by mental illness, like it was contagious. She suspected the Brethren of the Sacrifice weren't any different.

"Well, if anyone had tried to check on Audrey, she probably wouldn't let them," Zenovia replied truthfully.

"What's up with that wig your mom is wearing? Her own hair is so pretty."

Zenovia told Justin about the almost-invisible lice. He seemed uncertain of how to respond. Zenovia was glad that he hadn't yet said anything careless and stupid. He also hadn't laughed at any of Audrey's actions.

"We've got to get her some Boston Chicken. She loves that place," Zenovia announced.

"First, let's make another stop."

Before she could ask where, Justin made a right turn into the Cleveland Heights police station. At that moment, Zenovia couldn't think of fussing at him, because she just needed to find a bathroom.

After about a half an hour, they were finally able to speak with an officer. Although Zenovia didn't think it was necessary, Justin insisted on going into the small office with her.

"What seems to be your concern?" the officer asked.

"It's my mother," Zenovia said, "She's schizophrenic, and she hasn't taken her medication in about six years. She's deteriorating, and her house is a shambles."

"Does she live alone?"

"No, she is married. She lives with her husband."

The officer asked, "Is he your father?"

"No. Just her husband. He's the reason she stopped taking her medication. It was his decision."

"Has she done harm to anyone? To herself?"

"She hasn't done any outward harm to anyone, but she's destroying her mind by not taking her medicine," Zenovia's tone became frantic. "Her delusions are getting worse."

"Calm down, ma'am. I'm just trying to get the facts here. So she hasn't tried to assault anyone or tried to take her own life?"

Zenovia shook her head. "No, I don't think so. But if she did, I'm sure Phillip wouldn't tell me."

"Ma'am, unfortunately there's not really much we can do here."

"What do you mean there's nothing you can do?" Justin asked.

The officer explained. "Until your mother is a physical threat to another person or to herself, we can't do anything."

"You can't pick her up and take her to the mental hospital?" Justin asked. He seemed desperate to find a solution.

"No. Even if she is ill, she has rights. And if she's done nothing to harm anyone, we can't pick her up. Even if we could take her into the hospital, they wouldn't be able to administer any drugs against her will."

Zenovia sighed. "So that's it. My mother has to deteriorate to the point of violence before anyone will do anything."

"You could try to talk her into giving you power of attorney. Then you could have her committed," the officer said with a tone of finality.

Taking the hint, Zenovia and Justin stood to their feet. Zenovia knew it was pointless to try to get power of attorney for Audrey. She was way too cautious of everyone to put Zenovia in charge of her affairs. Plus she knew that Zenovia wanted to medicate her.

Audrey had schizophrenia, but she was nowhere near stupid.

Zenovia and Justin made good on their word and brought Audrey her chicken dinner, but when they approached the house, Phillip's car was in the driveway.

"Phillip is home," Zenovia said, stating the obvious.

"He shouldn't have a problem with you visiting your mother, right?"

Zenovia shrugged. "I don't know. He has a problem with me calling her, because he never gives her the phone."

"Well, let's take your mom her food anyway and see what happens. It may be different with you here in the flesh."

Phillip stepped out on the rickety porch before Justin and Zenovia had a chance to approach the house.

"Y'all can go on back to Washington, D.C. We don't need any help from ex-Brethren," Phillip called from his post.

Zenovia replied, "I'm here to see my mother, not you."

"You were here earlier. You saw her. Now get going before I call the police."

Justin said, "We brought food for Audrey. It doesn't look like she's been eating."

"We're eating just fine, thank you very much."

"You don't look so good, Phillip. Maybe you could use some medication," Zenovia said.

She wasn't being facetious in her appraisal of Phillip's appearance. He looked as if he hadn't shaved or had a haircut in weeks and his clothes had stains on them. She wondered how he kept a job.

Audrey stepped out on the porch. "Thanks anyway for the food, Zee. You and Justin can go on home now and let us be. Nobody in this house will be taking no pills."

"But, Mom..."

Audrey placed one hand in the air. "Just go ahead and get married. Why don't y'all have me some grandbabies, too. I'd like to have a grandbaby before I die."

"Before you die? Mom, you are too young to be talking about dying."

Audrey frowned. "I don't feel young. I feel tired."

"That's because you're not taking your meds. They make you feel better," Zenovia offered.

"No. Those pills keep me from knowing anything. Like, I wouldn't have even known about those demons that live between the ceiling tiles in the hallway if I was taking pills."

Zenovia's frustration was evident on her face. "Ma, why don't you come stay with me for a while?"

"Naw. I've got to stay right here with my stuff. I can't expect him to watch my stuff," Audrey pointed at Phillip.

"When we go back to D.C. we're going to be checking

on you often, Audrey. If Phillip doesn't let Zee speak with you, we're going to assume that something has happened and we will send the police over."

"Why wouldn't Phillip let you speak to me?" Audrey asked.

"Ask him!" Zenovia replied.

"Zee's been calling me?" Audrey asked Phillip.

"Yes, but she is an apostate, and I don't have to take calls from her in my home. It's against the Brethren rules. If you want to talk to her you can call her yourself."

"I don't care about them rules. They stupid anyway."

Phillip shook his head angrily. "Well, you're gonna be sorry at the end times. You all will be."

Phillip stormed inside the house and Audrey stomped behind him, childishly making a *pffft* sound at the back of his head.

"Now what?" Justin asked.

"Now we go home. She's good for now, but I'm still worried."

"Do you think she'll come to the wedding?"

Zenovia shook her head. "No. I don't think Phillip will let her. But she really didn't seem concerned with attending at all."

Justin had prayed before they'd seen Audrey, but Zenovia felt no peace in her spirit. Even though not taking medication had been Audrey's choice, Zenovia wondered if she could've done anything to counteract Phillip's influence.

"We can move back here if you want," Justin said.

Zenovia quickly shook her head. "No. Our life is in D.C. Our careers, our church...they've made their choices, now I've got to make mine."

"Okay, but if you ever change your mind on that, just say the word."

Zenovia couldn't keep from getting misty-eyed at Justin's unwavering support. "See, look what you made me do. Why didn't I know you when I was a teenager?"

"You did know me."

"No, I didn't know you. I thought you were some panty-raiding freak who just liked having girlfriends for the sake of having girlfriends."

Justin laughed. "Wow! But yeah, that was pretty much it back then. I always knew you were different, though. I hated that my brother saw you first."

"Tristan never saw me, Justin."

"Too bad for him! You're it for me, Zee. Sometimes I get so mad about all of the years I spent being a slave for the Brethren. But then, I think about how I would never have known you if it wasn't for the Brethren."

Zenovia smiled. "So you should be thanking them, right?"

Justin didn't reply, but he scooped Zenovia up in his arms. She couldn't breathe, but thought that if she'd never take another breath it would be okay with her. Even with Audrey's issues, she'd never been happier than in that very moment.

Justin was *it* for her too.

Chapter Forty

Zenovia placed the framed photograph on her and Justin's brand-new mantelpiece. It was from their wedding day. In spite of all Corrine's very loud protests, they had exchanged their vows in Bishop Wilcox's office. It was simple and glorious, and now they were official.

"Baby, that looks good," Justin remarked as he walked into the room.

"You think so? I think it looks lonely."

Justin slipped his arms around Zenovia's waist. "Well, soon we can fill it up with pictures of all our children."

"How many children are we talking?"

"Five or six sounds about right," Justin teased.

"You've got me messed up."

"All right, Zee. I can live with two."

"That's more like it! What are you cooking in there? It smells really good."

"Oh, that is Charlotte Batiste's secret family gumbo recipe. Her grandmother in New Orleans perfected it and passed it on down to the women in the family."

Zenovia giggled. "Then why do you have the recipe? Shouldn't Alyssa be the one whipping up batches of gumbo?"

"Yes, you would be correct, but since Alyssa can't even boil hot dogs, Charlotte entrusted the recipe to me."

Zenovia could hear the hint of melancholy in her husband's voice as he talked about his mother. She knew that they hadn't spoken since Tristan's wedding, but Justin was mostly silent about his hurt feelings.

"I wonder how Charlotte is doing. Have you talked to Alyssa lately?"

Justin nodded. "I talked to Alyssa earlier today. She wants you to know that she's not speaking to either of us, because she wasn't invited to the wedding."

"We should've thought to ask her."

"I think it was perfect the way it was."

Zenovia agreed. "Still, it would've been nice to have some representation from the Batiste family."

"Maybe in ten years we'll have a huge anniversary party, and they'll all be there."

"That would be wonderful."

Zenovia moved the photograph a little to the right and smiled. Even though she teased Justin, she was excited about the prospect of having little Batiste children with him. But before she settled into the mommy role, she felt God had something else planned for her.

She said, "Bishop asked me to do a five-minute sermon on Sunday morning."

"Wow, baby! That's awesome. What are you going to speak about?"

"I don't know. I'm used to God giving me a message during service. Do you think I should plan something?"

Justin shrugged. "Maybe, but that's up to you, I guess."

Zenovia took a seat on the couch. "I don't think I will. I haven't done that before and God's shown up every time. I'm just going to trust Him on this."

Making the decision to marry Justin was the biggest leap of faith Zenovia had ever taken. But it felt right, and she was at peace with her choice. She knew that he felt the same way.

"I was thinking we'd drive to the coast next weekend. Stay in a cheap hotel, walk on the beach at night, and have some fresh crab cakes. What do you think?" Justin asked.

"It sounds good—especially good—since we didn't have a honeymoon!"

"Cool. I'll book the hotel, then."

Zenovia walks down the center aisle of a small room where a plain pine casket awaits. She's in a funeral parlor, and Justin is holding her hand. There is no one else in the room, but Zenovia feels as if she's being watched. She approaches the casket slowly, but when she looks down, she cannot see the face.

"Zee, you're white, like you've just seen a ghost. Did you just have a vision?"

She nodded slowly. "How long was I like that?"

"A few seconds. You just kind of zoned out a little. Did it scare you? You're shaking."

"Somebody's going die, I think. Or somebody died. But I think it's in the future, because I was in the vision and I don't remember that happening. You were there too. You were holding my hand."

"You don't know who?"

"No, but I feel in my spirit that it's Audrey." Zenovia choked. "I think it's my mother. Who else would it be?"

"Well, it could be far in the future, Zee. Everybody dies at some point."

Zenovia took a deep breath and slowly released it. Justin was right. The visions never came with an expiration date. Audrey had found her husband seventeen years after she'd had a vision of him. The only thing that concerned her was that she and Justin hadn't aged in the vision. They had looked exactly the same.

Zenovia felt that the Lord was preparing her for something that was sooner rather than later.

She spent the entire day waiting for the phone to ring. When it didn't ring, she called her mother's number, only to be greeted by Phillip.

"What do you want?" Phillip had asked.

"I want to know how my mother is doing."

"She's doing the same way she was when you saw her. Fine," he'd said sarcastically. "Why do you keep bothering us with your apostasy?"

Zenovia had slammed the phone down, no longer being able to stomach hearing Phillip's voice.

On Saturday night, the night before her sermon, Zenovia paced back and forth in their bedroom. For a while, Justin watched her silently.

"Do you want to fly to Cleveland? You can go tonight if you want," Justin said.

"No. I prayed about it, Justin. And if God can't help my mother, then how can I?"

"God can do anything, sweetie. But if you prayed about it, then why are you pacing the floor?"

"I don't know. I can't stay put. I don't feel any peace."

"Come here," Justin said with outstretched arms.

Zenovia joined Justin in their queen-size bed and nestled into his arms. He stroked her hair as he whispered a prayer in her ear. It had a calming effect, even if it didn't take away all of her dread.

"Thank you, Justin. I sure appreciate you."

After a little while had passed, Zenovia fell into a deep and fitful sleep. She dreamed sporadically, about nothing in particular. She didn't realize it, but she tossed and turned in her sleep and spoke out loud.

One scene played over and over in her dream:

A man dressed as in Bible times is on a dirt floor with his face to the ground. He's crying out and throwing dirt into the air. Another man walks in, and says, "The child has died."

The man then rises from the floor and wipes his tears. He changes his clothing, eats a meal, and goes into the sanctuary to worship.

The second man asks, "I do not understand. You wept for the child while it was alive, and now that it's dead, you eat and worship the Lord."

The first man replies, "I wept while the child was alive, because I prayed for God's mercy. What good will weeping do now that the child is dead? Can I bring him back again? I can go to him, but he cannot come back to me."

And the first man continues to worship with singing.

Zenovia's eyes flew open, but she didn't move. She knew immediately what the scene in her dream was. It was King David after his illegitimate child with Bathsheba had died.

The dream left an uneasy feeling in the pit of her stomach, but she thought she knew the meaning.

Then the telephone rang.

Chapter Forty-one

Zenovia stood in the pulpit before the congregation at Reaching the Masses. Her heart felt heavy, like a giant boulder nestled in the center of her chest. Only Justin knew about the news she'd received in the wee hours of the morning. She had convinced him not to tell Bishop or Corrine until after service.

Her mother was dead.

Audrey had committed suicide, but Phillip said differently. Phillip claimed it was a horrible accident and that she'd fallen down the basement stairs while trying to clean. The vision that Zenovia had seen right before his call told a different story.

But Zenovia had also spent the night dreaming of King David and how he worshipped God in the midst of his grief. His son died and he went into the sanctuary to worship God, even though he'd prayed fervently for the child's life to be saved.

Zenovia had prayed about Audrey. She'd prayed for Audrey to be healed since she was a little girl. She'd prayed for her once she moved on with her adult life.

But God had not healed her.

He had, however, given Audrey peace, which was something she probably never had. Zenovia almost smiled when she thought of her mother—changed. In heaven with her heavenly body that was not plagued with schizophrenia.

She finally spoke into the microphone. "Good morning, everybody. I believe the Lord has given me a message for the congregation. He came to me in my dreams last night to minister about King David. At this time, David was at his lowest. He had sinned against God by carrying on an adulterous relationship with Bathsheba and then killing her husband to cover it up."

Corrine jumped up from her seat and said, "You betta preach it like you know it!"

"Then, the child of their sin came into the world," Zenovia continued. "And the child died. Could you imagine yourself worshipping God in the midst of all that? In the midst of the guilt, shame, and sorrow that David felt, he worshipped God?"

"But he did! And I believe that is what God's message is today for the body. He wants our worship and dedication, even in the midst of our storms. When we trust Him in trials, He'll reward us with peace."

Zenovia opened her Bible. "I'm going to leave you with one of my favorite Gospel passages. It's in Mark Chapter Four starting at Verse Thirty-seven. This is how it reads:

'And there arose a great storm of wind, and the waves beat into the ship, so that it was now full. And he was in the hinder part of the ship, asleep on a pillow: and they awake him, and say unto him, Master, carest thou not that we perish? And he arose, and rebuked the wind, and said unto the sea, Peace, be still. And the wind ceased, and there was a great calm.'"

As the scripture verse drove home Zenovia's message, the congregation began to stand on their feet. Zenovia knew that her message was simple and that everyone in the church had probably heard something like it before, but she was grateful that they had listened to her.

Zenovia said her closing and left the pulpit. When she got down to the sanctuary, the reality of the early morning events enveloped her. She could barely feel her feet touch the floor as she quietly walked back to the pew where Justin was waiting for her. Nearly in a trance, the grief rolled over her in waves.

Justin stood to his feet and rushed to Zenovia; caught her just before she fell to her knees. He held her tightly and guided her back to the pew.

She whispered to him as they sat, "She's gone, Justin. I can't believe she's gone."

"But you're still here, and you're going to be all right."

Zenovia gazed up at Justin. "I need to go to Cleveland."

"Of course we do. I already bought the tickets."

Corrine rushed over to Justin and Zenovia. "What's wrong, Zee?"

"It's Audrey...."

"She's dead, isn't she?"

"She is."

Corrine dropped her head as the tears started to flow. Zenovia felt her heart go out to her cousin but didn't shed any tears of her own.

Zenovia surveyed the entire congregation with awe. Bishop Wilcox had not preached a word, but encouraged the congregation to come up for prayer off of the power of her message. She watched as people streamed down the aisle and brought their prayer requests to the altar.

For the first time in her life, she felt like she belonged. She belonged with Justin at Reaching the Masses and she belonged in ministry. It felt like it was meant to be; something fated.

Actually, it felt like her destiny.

Discussion Questions

1. What did you think of Audrey and Zenovia's first encounter with the Brethren of the Sacrifice?

2. Do you know anyone who is a member of a church like the Brethren? Would you try to get them out or do you think it's just another form of Christianity?

3. Do you think Zenovia's care of Audrey affected her view of the world? The Brethren? How so?

4. Zenovia's visions were haphazard, but they always seemed accurate. Do you believe they were a gift from God or a trick of the enemy?

5. Tristan and Zenovia have an interesting conversation about fate and destiny. Do you believe there's a difference? Do you agree with Tristan's view?

6. Was Emil a logical choice of boyfriend for Zenovia?

7. The Brethren have an unconventional view of mental illness. Is there any merit to their point of view?

8. Were the Brethren's views on grace, mercy and chastening in line with Biblical views? Why or why not?

9. Was Zenovia's meeting with the Brethren council the same as mental rape?

10. When did it become obvious whom Zenovia would choose? Did it take you by surprise?

11. Was Audrey's outcome inevitable? Was there something Zenovia could've done to prevent it?

12. Did the story ultimately have a happy ending? Why or why not?